THE
SINFUL
KING

NEW YORK TIMES BESTSELLING AUTHOR
CLAIRE CONTRERAS

The Sinful King
Claire Contreras
© 2020 Claire Contreras
Cover design By Hang Le
Edited by Erica Russikoff
Proofread by Janice Owen
Formatted by Champagne Book Design

THE
SINFUL
KING

PROLOGUE

Past

"**Y**OU PROBABLY SHOULDN'T BE HERE."

I jumped slightly at the gruff voice behind me and turned to watch the man walk over until he was standing beside me on the balcony, overlooking the beach before us. Not that we could see anything in the dark, but the sound of the waves was enough. I tried to make out his face before I answered him, but couldn't with the mask he had on. If I had to judge it based on what I could see, I'd say he was classically good-looking, with a strong jaw, straight nose, pouty lips, and thick dark hair that was brushed back.

"It's the princes' party." I cleared my throat. "Everyone's here."

"Everyone's inside, partaking in the debauchery. You're out here, drinking water." His lips twisted as he took in the glass water bottle in my hand.

"Why are you out here?"

"I got bored."

"Bored of the debauchery?"

"Bored of all of it. The party, the people, the pretending, the masks."

"So take off your mask." I shrugged a shoulder. "I don't think they'll kick you out for that. Or you can just leave."

"Are you leaving?"

"I'm here with a friend." I sighed heavily and looked over my shoulder and spotted Etienne dancing with some woman. They looked like they were doing more than just dancing, so I looked away quickly. "We practice the whole *no man left behind* thing, so I have to wait until he's finished."

"He?"

"My friend, Etienne."

"Etienne." The man beside me nodded once. "I believe I met him."

"He loves a party."

"Where are you from?"

"That's a complicated answer." I looked up at him again. It was difficult to see what color his eyes were. They were definitely dark though.

"I like complicated."

"Okay. I was born here in Marbella. It's my mother's hometown. My father is French. They met in university. I grew up in the States—in Connecticut, where I went to school and stayed with my aunt and uncle—while my parents traveled back and forth between there, here, and France. My grandmother is dying, so my mother spends most of her time here, and my father works in Paris, so he's over there." I bit my lip when I finished talking, unsure if he'd been able to keep up with all of that or even cared to. I wasn't even sure why I'd actually explained all of it at all. I guess because he asked and I was as bored as he said he was.

2

"Where do you live now?"

"I've been living here for the last two months, but I go back to the States tomorrow."

"What for?"

"School. I was accepted into the University of North Carolina, so I'll be there for four years, and then . . . I don't know. I'm thinking I'll settle in London."

"What's your ultimate goal?"

"I want to start an event-planning company. It's my mother's dream, and I really think we can do something great together. We'll see though." I smiled as I thought about it. "I'm studying Hospitality Management and landed a part-time position in event planning at a hotel near the school, so I'm hoping to learn as much as I can."

"I didn't realize you needed a degree to plan events."

"You don't."

"So, why bother?"

"My parents." I shrugged. "They both went to college. It feels weird for me not to go after they spent all that money on boarding school."

"It seems weird for you to spend more of their money going if you already know what you want to do and don't need a degree to do it."

"Starting up a business requires money, and time, and a lot of dedication, which I'd gladly give, except I have no money for it, and time and dedication are great, but you have to have money to back it up." I shook my head. "What do you do?"

"I work for the government."

"Ew. Like the cabinet?"

He chuckled. "What's wrong with the cabinet?"

"I don't know." I shrugged. "I've heard mixed things."

"Like what?"

"Well, I'll admit the things I've heard are biased, being that my father works for a newspaper that's extremely critical of the Crown and the way they built the cabinet. I mean, the king handpicks his subjects. It's a bit . . . communistic."

"Ah, your father is one of those." His lips formed a small smile. "I bet he has a lot of strong opinions about the way things should be run."

"He does. I mean, I guess everyone does, right?"

"It seems like the critics have more opinions than those in office. You'd think if they want something to change, really change, they'd run."

"Is that why you ran?"

"Partly."

"Well, then, I'm sure you're doing a good job."

He chuckled. He had a nice chuckle. Our eyes met again, and this time, I found myself standing a little closer to him. His smile turned serious after a moment of looking at me, and I felt my own expression mirror his. Suddenly, I was hyperaware of him—his height, his large hands resting beside mine, seemingly inching closer, the way he smelled, like delicious cologne and something else—and when he parted his lips slightly, the hint of tequila on his breath.

"Where do you live?" he asked quietly.

"Right over there." I pointed at the villa beside the one we were in.

His eyes widened slightly. "You're joking."

"Not joking." I laughed. "Why would I be joking?"

"I've never seen you around here before."

"Do you come around here often?" I asked.

He must know the princes. I'd never been home to

4

experience these parties, but I'd heard enough rumors about them. The princes were a staple here every summer. It was their escape from the paparazzi and whatever else they were supposed to be doing. Etienne knew one of them. It was the reason we'd been invited to attend. The parties were notorious for being invite-only. Cellphones were taken at the door. Costumes were provided. Masks were always in place. Even though I'd spent little time inside, the debauchery the man beside me mentioned earlier wasn't exaggerated. In the hour I'd been inside, I'd seen drugs passed around and taken, drinks constantly being poured and refilled, and a lot more than just dancing going on. Plus, the DJ was famous and outside of here we would have had to pay top dollar to see him spin. It wasn't my crowd. I'd partied through high school and it had been fun until it wasn't, so now I measured myself whenever I went places. I drank more water than alcohol and said no to every pill passed my way. I'd learned a hard lesson a year ago and wasn't willing to go through that again.

"Often enough," he said, ripping me from my thoughts. "Etienne does as well. He's friends with Prince Aramis."

"Me too." He grinned. "He's great. Big on parties."

"I've heard Prince Elias is even bigger on parties."

"Really? I'm quite certain it's the opposite."

"Who knows?" I shrugged. "Where do you stay when you're in town?"

"Who says I'm not from here?"

"No one is from here." I laughed. "I mean, I am, and even I'm hesitant to claim that after being away so long. Besides, your French accent is too thick for you to be from here."

"I live in Paris," he said, smiling. "But, like you, my mother is from Spain. Barcelona to be exact."

"And your father is French?"

"Yes."

"Funny coincidence."

"I'm not sure I believe in coincidences. We seem to have a lot in common."

"Like being bored at the biggest party of the summer?"

"Maybe you should offer your party-planning services to the princes. They'd pay you well and if you think you can throw a better party . . . "

"Not likely." I looked back inside. "This is the 'it' DJ right now, and honestly, it is a great party. I'm just not feeling like myself tonight I guess."

"And you have a flight tomorrow."

"And that."

"Spend the night with me." He set a hand over mine.

My heart slammed into my chest. No one had ever asked me to have sex with them like that. Or like anything, for that matter. In my group of friends, I was the only eighteen-year-old going off to college who was still a virgin. I had no reason for it either. It just hadn't happened for me.

"I understand if you don't want to," he said, taking his hand back.

I looked into his eyes again, the eyes I could barely see, from underneath a mask I was grateful for right now. I'd never thought about who I'd lose my virginity to. I was vehemently against having a serious boyfriend during college, so at this point, I kind of figured it would be some frat boy in North Carolina and I was okay with that option. Looking at this man right now, whom I didn't even know the name of, I knew deep in my core I wanted it to be him.

"I want to." I slid my hand over his and squeezed.

He took my hand in his and led me down the stairs on the side of the house, and then down another set. The villa was three stories, with windows that faced the view of the ocean behind. My father and his brother had built these villas with the full intention of renting them out to tourists. Instead, their renters had been royals, actors, models, and celebrities from all around the world. Our own house had never been rented out. When my parents weren't there, they had it locked, regardless of how much money was offered for it. I was familiar with the layout and I knew he was leading me to the first floor, where there was a bedroom—the only bedroom away from the chaos upstairs. The only bedroom in which we'd have ultimate privacy. My pulse quickened as we reached the back door and he pulled out a key to open the room from the outside.

"I stay here when I'm in town," he explained. "Most of us do, unless you sign up too late and you're forced to stay in one of the other villas."

"I think it's cute that they travel with their friends."

"I think it says a lot about their state of loneliness," he said.

"I guess I've never thought about that."

He closed the door behind us. The room was dark, and when he walked over to the other door and pushed the button to black out the windows, it was darker still and I found myself blinking rapidly to adjust to it. He pressed another button and a light came on, but even that was extremely dim, just enough for us not to bump into anything, but not enough to actually see clearly. I was grateful for it. He walked over to me, his shoes tapping against the hardwood as he did, and I braced myself for . . . something. Instead, he stood right in front of me and brought a hand up to my face, cupping my jaw as he looked at me.

"You're nervous."

"I am." I swallowed. "I don't normally do this."

"That's okay." His lips formed a slow smile. "We'll take it slow."

"Should . . . should I take my mask off?" I whispered.

"Do you want to?"

"Are you going to take yours off?"

"Do you want me to?"

"Yes." I let out a shuddering breath. "I think we should."

He didn't hesitate. His mask came off immediately, and even though I couldn't fully see him, I could fully appreciate his gorgeousness. He must have been a model. Or an actor. Or something. My rapid thought process reminded me of something.

"I don't even know your name."

"I don't know yours."

"That doesn't bother you?" I felt my eyebrows pull in.

"You're leaving to another country tomorrow. Does it make a difference? Will it stop you from doing this?"

"No." I pulled the mask over my head and tossed it aside.

"You're beautiful." The tips of his fingers caressed my cheek, my lips.

"You can barely see me."

"And yet, I know you're beautiful." He brought his lips to mine then and kissed me.

My breath hitched. I brought my hands up to his face and kissed him back, parting my lips to make way for his tongue to dance with mine as my entire body came alive. His kiss was electric, his touch an awakening as his hands made their way down my body, unzipping my dress and letting it pool at our feet. He touched my naked breasts and explored my hips, stopping at the elastic of my panties. I undid his bow tie and unbuttoned the white dress shirt he had on, my fingers fumbling on a few. When I reached his belt and undid it, I paused, breathing heavily as he broke the kiss.

"You okay?" The tip of his nose touched mine.

"Better than okay."

"We can stop any time you'd like."

"I don't want to stop." I continued working on his pants until they met the same fate as my dress, and then we stood there, chest to chest, in the middle of a darkened room, with only our underwear on. "Do you want to stop?"

"Never."

Our lips met again. This time, with more ardor. My hands quickly pulled down his boxer briefs and began exploring the large, hard instrument in front of me. He was slower, more methodical, as he deepened the kiss and slid his hand into my panties, exploring, quickly finding the root of my incessant throbbing. I cried out against his mouth, and cried out again shortly after when he brought me to climax again. He growled his acceptance and pushed me gently onto the bed. His lips became more frantic as he kissed his way down my body, licking and tugging my nipples into his mouth before moving further south. He yanked my panties down and replaced his hand with his lips. It was a sensation unlike anything I'd felt before. With each lick, I felt like I might die. Like my heart might give out on me at any moment. It was too much, yet not enough. When I stated that, he smiled against my skin and took it as ammunition to keep going until my hips buckled and I shouted out jumbled words that didn't even make sense into the void of the room.

I heard the rip of a condom as I was coming to, but still

breathing heavily, and then he was pushing himself inside of me, ever so slowly. He gasped as he filled me completely and planted his hands on either side of my head.

"So tight." He wheezed out the words as he moved out slowly. "So fucking tight."

I bit hard on my lip to not yell. It didn't feel as good as his tongue, but I didn't dare say that. I'd read enough articles and heard enough stories from friends to know that your first time wasn't magical, no matter how gorgeous the guy or how incredible his body was. My nails dug into his sides, and then his back as he found a steady rhythm. He squeezed his eyes shut as if he was the one in physical pain, and his forehead settled on mine.

"What's your name?" he panted.

"I thought . . . it didn't . . . matter." I lifted my hips to meet his thrusts, finding my own rhythm in this.

"I want to know."

"Adeline."

"Adeline. Adeline. Adeline." He used it as a chant with each thrust, as if he needed to remember who it was he was fucking, and when he flipped us over so I was on top, I made sure to make it so he'd remember this chant tomorrow when I was far away from this place and he was attending another one of these parties.

He brought his hands up to my breasts and squeezed my nipples, making my back arch on its own accord. My orgasm took me by surprise, the sensation crawling through me all at once until it felt like I would explode from the inside. I felt when he found his own ecstasy, his well-formed abs clenching beneath my fingertips as he pumped inside me and growled my name once more. I never once said his. I didn't know what to say if I wanted to. It was better that way. I knew I'd remain completely unattached if I had no face to his name and no name to every other part of him. We lay beside each other, breathing hard, covered in sweat, and I wondered if I should get dressed and leave now. Etienne was probably still upstairs. I'd left my phone at home, knowing they'd take it away from me if I brought it, so it wasn't like he had any way to reach me.

My answer came when the man beside me began to snore lightly. I pushed the sheets away and went to the bathroom. That was when I noticed tiny trickles of blood. I didn't think he'd broken my hymen. I was pretty sure gymnastics and horseback riding had done that, but now I wasn't so sure. My thoughts raced. Were the sheets bloodied? No. This was too little blood to begin with. I flushed, washed my hands, and dressed quickly, placing the mask back on my face before making my way to the door. I glanced at him one last time. The sheet was covering just the right parts, as if it had purposely been draped over him for a photograph. I sighed as I opened the door and closed it quietly behind me. A part of me felt the loss the moment I stepped out of that room. I'd never given my virginity much importance until that moment when I no longer had it.

By the time I got to the floor that the party was taking place, I was smiling again. It hadn't been a fairy-tale experience with rose petals and candles, but it had been perfect nonetheless. I found Etienne, standing near the back door with his hands on his hips, and I knew he was looking for me. When I reached him, he shook his head.

"I've been looking everywhere. I even walked to your house thinking you were home."

"No man left behind, remember?" I arched an eyebrow.

"Where were you?"

"Around." I shrugged. "Didn't you tell me to have fun?"

"How much fun did you have?" He eyed me closely, a smile tugging on his lips.

"More than I've ever had."

"Adeline Sofia Isabella Bouchard!"

"Etienne Pierre Bellerose," I said in a mocking tone.

"We are leaving this party right now." He grabbed my arm and led me outside with a laugh. "Your father will murder me if he finds out this happened under my watch."

"Oh please. As if he doesn't know your reputation."

"Still." He yanked his mask over his head as we walked over to my parents' villa. "Who was he?"

"I don't know." I pulled my mask off as we reached the door.

"What do you mean you don't know?"

"I don't. He was . . . dreamy. Gorgeous. So, so hot." I sighed. "But I didn't get his name. It doesn't matter anyway. I'm leaving tomorrow."

"Today," he said, glancing at the big-faced watch on his wrist. "Your flight is in four hours. You need to finish packing and we need to go."

"Shit." I practically ran inside the house.

I showered, changed, and finished packing quickly as Etienne sat in the living room, telling me about the woman he was talking to at the party. My parents were gone for the weekend, which was why Etienne was staying with me. He'd been my best friend since I was born. Our mothers were best friends and their wish was that we'd end up together. Unfortunately for them, we weren't each other's types. Etienne was an artist and his type was model-thin, with more issues than *Vogue*. The kind of woman he could try to fix and take care of. My type was . . . well, probably the man I'd just lost my virginity to and would never see again. We talked quickly and about everything as he drove me to the airport. He spent an hour trying to figure out every single man at the party and who it could have been that I slept with. I let him because I was curious and also because watching Etienne decipher anything was a comedy in itself.

At the airport, I bought a magazine to entertain myself with. As I flipped the pages, I landed on a familiar face. My heart stopped. Prince Elias. That was the . . . surely it couldn't be . . . except, it was. I knew it without a shadow of a doubt. I'd just lost my virginity to the future king of France.

CHAPTER ONE

Five Years Later

BEING BACK IN MARBELLA SUCKED. MY MOTHER REFERRED TO this as home, and expected me to as well, but after living in so many places and finally settling in London, I didn't consider this home at all. The last time I'd been here was two years ago; we celebrated Christmas here instead of Paris. Ever since I started my own event-planning business, I focused solely on work. That was, until a sex scandal rocked my entire world. It had been a few weeks, but after watching everything I worked so hard for going down the drain, along with the tears I had left to cry, I decided maybe going on a bit of a break like my mother suggested wasn't such a bad idea.

It was confusing and hurtful to have people who claimed to be friends suddenly turn on me. For a few days, I was mostly just angry at my ex-boyfriend for letting the video leak, but it wasn't his fault that his devices were hacked into and the world was skewed and unfair against women in these situations. It wasn't like he'd asked for me to leave town and spend my summer in Marbella. It wasn't like anyone asked me to leave the events I had planned in the capable hands of my mother and assistant while I helped my uncle run the bookstore that he was completely ruining by only stocking biographies and political books, and it wasn't like anyone told me I'd be getting a huge slice of humble pie when he asked me to take over delivering baskets to the princes, who were back this summer, renting their usual four villas on our property. Nope. No one asked me to do any of this, yet here I was, angry and alone and completely hating every single decision I'd made in the last year of my life.

"My father said he could make the tabloid stories go away," Etienne said, from the floor, where he was helping me stock new books I'd ordered for the store to liven the place up.

"It's not your father's job to erase my mistakes." I walked over with another stack and placed them on the floor. "It's my job to stay out of the tabloids. I should have known better." I sighed. "God, it's so embarrassing that your father even knows about them."

"He's a celebrity lawyer, Addie. He knows about everything," Etienne said. "In all fairness, you were dating a banking heir. Staying out of the tabloids would have been impossible."

"Yeah, but filming a sex tape was plain dumb." I sighed heavily. "I'm an idiot. End of story."

"Thomas is an idiot. He should have never let it leak and I'm sorry but I don't believe he had no part in it."

"Why would you think he had anything to do with that? Because he looked like a fucking god in the tape and I looked like absolute shit?"

"You didn't look like shit."

"You watched it?" I aimed a book at him, ready to throw it.

"No," he said quickly. "I saw the stills on the tabloids though. Everyone did."

"I hate myself." I lowered the book and closed my eyes.

"You shouldn't."

"I should've worn a wig or something."

"You shouldn't have recorded it at all."

"I was having fun with my boyfriend! I didn't realize the entire world would have access to it."

"Well, look at the bright side, some families have become billionaires because of sex-tape fame."

"That is not how they became billionaires, but I see where you're going with this and trust me, I don't want my company to get any fame over my nudity." I covered my face with the book in my hand and thumped it against my forehead. "I just want to fast-forward the next couple of months until a new scandal arises and I'm forgotten."

"I'm sure it'll happen soon," he said. "The prince is in town, after all."

My heart raced. I lowered the book. "Which one?"

"Didn't your uncle ask you to take baskets to the villa every night? He didn't say?"

"No."

"It's the summertime, Addie. It's always the princes' time here."

"I really thought they'd be bored with this by now."

"You thought wrong. It's the only place they can escape to without the tabloids getting to them." He chuckled. "I spoke to Aramis the other day and he said he wasn't coming this time. It's only Elias."

"Which one is that one?" I asked, even though his face was seared in my brain. His face and other parts of him, which I wouldn't discuss with my best friend, no matter how close we were.

"The one you may or may not have had sex with."

I threw the book at him. He laughed and swatted it away as it reached him. I turned around and busied myself with things behind the register as Etienne kept talking. I completely tuned him out. My mind was too busy racing. Would Prince Elias recognize me? No. He wouldn't. Right? I was supposed to deliver a basket to his door every night at seven thirty sharp. Those were my uncle's orders. It was a simple task, one my uncle had left perfect instructions for. Five large wicker baskets were already stacked up in the guest room in my villa, along with the contents of what went in each of them. I hadn't really paid much attention to any of it, but I would tonight. My stomach coiled. I'd see him tonight. Maybe not. I'd seen security outside of the villa I assumed was his, the same one we'd . . . my face flamed. Oh my God. I couldn't do this.

"Adeline?" Etienne walked over to me and stood on the other side of the counter. "What's going on?"

"Nothing." I blinked up at him. He looked concerned. I sighed. "I don't want to deliver the baskets."

"If you want, I'll take it tonight," he said. "But I'll be gone tomorrow."

"Why do you have to leave?" I groaned.

"Because my girlfriend is waiting for me in London."

"Can't you tell Mira to come here?" I rested my elbows on the counter with an exhale.

"No." He laughed. "Don't be ridiculous. Elias won't bite you, and even if he is the guy who took your virginity, he . . . I don't know how to say it in a way that doesn't sound awful, Addie, but he's slept with a lot of women."

"He didn't take my virginity. I gave it to him. There's a difference." I met his gaze. "He didn't even know I was a virgin."

"I don't think I would know either, to be honest." He pursed his lips to think. "Unless a woman starts bleeding." He shrugged. "And even then I may just assume she's on her menstrual."

That made me laugh out loud. Men were so clueless about women's bodies. Maybe Etienne was right. Prince Elias had absolutely no reason to remember me. Even though I remembered the night I had with him, I was just a notch on his bedpost.

"Why don't you prepare the basket and go with me to deliver it? That way he'll know that you have a mutual friend."

"Okay."

"Good. Let's finish up here, please. I'm starving and feel like I'm going to die under a pile of romance novels."

"Hey, there are worse ways to go." I raised an eyebrow. "You could die under a pile of autobiographies."

The look he gave me told me he wasn't impressed by my joke, so I went back to work, trying to ignore the fact that I may or may not be seeing the prince tonight.

CHAPTER TWO

"**S**TOP FIDGETING," ETIENNE WHISPER-SHOUTED.

I stopped. We were standing outside the door, waiting for someone to answer. When it opened, I held my breath, then let it out when I saw one of the security detail standing on the other side.

"Monsieur Bouchard told us he'd be sending his niece to bring the baskets," the man said, eyeing Etienne with curiosity.

"I'm a friend of his niece and the princes'. You must be new," Etienne responded.

"What is your name?"

"Etienne Bellerose IV."

"Oh. Monsieur Bellerose," the man said, bowing ever so slightly. "My apologies."

Etienne wasn't a prince, but as the great-grandson of a duke, he had his own pull on society's strings. The Bellerose name carried prestige and honor and unlike my own name, which had been on the decline in some circles for reasons that had nothing to do with me or my leaked sex tape, Etienne's was respected on all grounds. The man before us opened the door wider and stepped aside, allowing us to walk inside the villa. Etienne offered me his arm, which I gladly took, and I stepped inside with him. He was holding the basket in his other hand and I was unsure of what to do with my free hand, so I brought it up to hold his arm with both of mine. It was either that or I'd start fidgeting again and I didn't want to seem like a silly young girl with heart eyes for a prince I hadn't even seen in five years.

"I'll tell His Royal Highness that you're here." The man shut the door behind us and disappeared into one of the halls. I let out a breath.

"Am I supposed to curtsy?" I whispered. "I don't even know how to do that. Do you bow when you say hi to him?"

"He's not the king," Etienne whispered back.

"Yet."

"Yet," he agreed gravely.

"So I can just shake his hand like normal?"

"If he tries to shake yours, then yes." He eyed me curiously, then added, "Don't take offense if he doesn't."

My brows shot up. I tried to picture what Prince Elias would look like now. Unlike his brother, Aramis, who was always in the spotlight, Elias hadn't been seen in years. If the rumors were true, he was too busy preparing for his future role as king to attend any of the usual events. It wasn't that he wasn't doing things, more so that the things he was doing weren't being documented and reported on. Once in a while, you could catch a grainy photo of him arriving or leaving an event or more likely, a halfway house he spent a lot of time helping. Of course, that deed too, came with rumors of its own.

Somehow, as I stood there, I felt some of my tension slip

away. That was, until I heard footsteps approaching and I was right back to a tense ball. The man in the black suit came into sight first, followed by Prince Elias, who was far more gorgeous than any grainy photo could ever encompass, and definitely far more man than I could remember from that night so many years ago. For a moment, I second-guessed myself. Maybe this wasn't the man I'd lost my virginity to after all, but then he spoke and my heart took a life of its own, galloping from my chest to my ears.

"Etienne," he said, "I wasn't expecting you."

"I'm not really here for a visit," Etienne responded. "I'm helping out a friend with this basket."

Prince Elias, who had definitely already seen me standing here, but had made it a point not to look at me, now turned his attention toward me. Despite my galloping heart, I tried my best to paste a nonchalant smile on my face.

"Hello." My voice was so weak and low and pathetic. I licked my lips.

"Hello," he said, not taking his eyes off mine. They were dark and I still couldn't see their color from where he was standing, but I knew they weren't brown like mine. "You're the niece bringing my basket?"

"Yes, sir."

"It's her first time in charge of it, so if she got anything wrong, take pity on her. She's not much of a rule follower." Etienne chuckled lightly.

"I followed all of the instructions perfectly." My face whipped in Etienne's direction momentarily before I looked at Prince Elias again. He walked closer to us, finally closing the gap between us, and effectively making my insides haywire again. "I . . . I think the basket is perfect."

"I'm sure it's fine." He reached for it and took it from Etienne's hands, his attention now on its contents. "Looks right to me."

"It's a lot of champagne," I said, then swallowed. There were two bottles of Dom Perignon in the basket, which I thought was entirely too extra for anyone, but I definitely shouldn't have pointed it out.

"Do you want to stay a while?" Prince Elias asked Etienne, ignoring my statement.

"I would, but I can't. Mira is waiting for me in London. I have a flight to catch and Addie is driving me to the airport." He slung an arm around me and pulled me closer.

"Right. My brother mentioned he was meeting with you over there," Prince Elias said, his gaze sliding over to me. He lifted the basket. "Thank you for bringing the basket on time."

"You're welcome. Same time tomorrow." I smiled and pinched Etienne in the back so he could speed this up.

"Will you be here all summer?" Etienne asked.

"I'll be here a while. Traveling in and out, but I plan on getting a lot of rest while I'm here."

"Right. You should get as much of that as you can." Etienne lowered his voice. "My thoughts are with all of you."

I bit my lip. I knew they were talking about the king's declining health and I really had nothing to add in this scenario. I was the daughter of a man who was completely opposed to all things in the monarchy, especially the way the king and his family ran things. They were traditionalists in every sense of the word. Had it not been for the pushback that happened when my father was growing up, a movement he had a lot to do with, from which the cabinet was born, the king would still be the sole leader of France. So, I had no room to speak when it came to this. Instead, I focused on looking at him while he was speaking to Etienne. He really was so incredibly good-looking. And tall. And fit. He was wearing khaki pants and a white short-sleeve button-down that framed his toned physique perfectly. He had a swimmer's body. A surfer's. With broad shoulders and muscled arms that weren't bulging, but just right. My assistant, Joss, was all about body-building-type bodies. I preferred Prince Elias's body though. And his lips. On mine. Making their way down my body. Between my legs. I forced myself to look away to fight the blush I felt creeping. I needed to get out of here.

"Addie?"

"Huh? What?" I blinked and looked at Etienne, who was staring at me with a raised eyebrow. "Sorry. I zoned out."

"I was telling Elias that if he needs anything you're right next door."

"Oh. Yeah. Right next door." I jutted my thumb in the direction of my villa.

"Your family owns that villa?" he asked.

"Yep." I watched him to see if he gave away any kind of hint that he might remember. He didn't.

He'd asked me the exact same question the night we hooked up and I'd gotten no reaction out of him just now. Was I that unforgettable? I took a breath. I wanted to be unforgettable. I wanted to be invisible. I didn't want him to remember me at all. Wasn't that what I wanted? It didn't matter. That was the reality.

"So, I guess I'll be seeing you around," he said.

"I guess so." I smiled again. "Actually, I'm only available after five on weekdays."

"But if you need anything, she can pause what she's doing," Etienne said.

"My uncle asked me to fix up the bookstore," I responded as way of explanation.

"That isn't your . . . " Etienne exhaled heavily, shaking his head.

I already knew exactly what he was going to say. It was the same thing he'd been saying to me since he arrived four days ago. The bookstore wasn't my job. If I was going to take time away from my actual career planning events, the least I could do was actually decompress and relax. Blah, blah, blah. But I had already promised my uncle I would help out and I was going to make good on that promise. He was alone out here all of the time. He hadn't taken a vacation in over ten years before I came along, so yes, I would help.

"I won't bother you before five," Prince Elias, or Eli, as Etienne referred to him, said.

"It's not a bother," I said quickly. "I mean, the cellphones don't work anyway so I'm not sure how you'd get ahold of me."

"Landlines," Etienne suggested. He was speaking to me like I was five. I glared at him, hoping he understood I'd slap him if he continued. He seemed to understand it, because his attention shifted back to the prince. "So, any big parties I need to come back for?"

"If I decide to host one, you'll be on the invite list."

"Right. Well, I guess I'll see you around then." Etienne bumped his fist against the prince's and I gave a little weak wave, unwilling to touch him even with my fist out of fear of what I might feel.

When we got outside and the door was shut behind us by the security guy, I punched Etienne in the shoulder.

"Ow. What the hell, Addie?"

"What the hell you! What was that in there?"

"You were fidgeting and talking too much and then zoning out in the middle of conversations. Telling the prince you wouldn't be at his beck and call. You needed to get your shit together."

"I won't be at his beck and call. My job is to make and deliver him baskets and help my uncle with his bookstore. That's it."

"Well, you looked like an idiot back there," he said, and then started laughing.

"You're an idiot." I unlocked the door and let us in. "Go pack your bag for your stupid trip."

"I'll be done quickly." He shook his head as he walked down the hall and disappeared into the guest room. "You really need to get a grip before you take that next basket."

I walked toward the guest room he was in. Even though my parents hadn't been here in a while and never rented it out, they set it up ready for rent. The only thing they left that was ours were some family photographs on the wall by the entrance, and I was sure my uncle would take those down if they ever decided to rent this out to anyone. Everything else was new. Absolutely no memory of my childhood or adolescence was left in here aside from whatever was stored in my brain.

"Why does he need so many baskets anyway?" I asked. "And so much champagne?"

"Maybe he's having guests over."

"Maybe."

"So I guess it is true what they say about your first time."

"I knew you were going to say that." I groaned, covering my face with my hands. "I was over there acting like an idiot and he doesn't even remember me."

"Oh, he definitely remembers you."

"What? No he doesn't." I sat on the bed as he continued packing the suitcase. "He didn't act like he did."

"Trust me, he remembers."

"I really don't think so." I bit my lip. "I mean, maybe it's best that he doesn't."

"It won't erase the fact that it happened." Etienne looked up from the suitcase he was packing. "But I know him. Eli has the memory of an elephant."

"I guess he couldn't very well say *'Oh, hey, you're that girl I fucked once'* in front of you." I crossed my arms, fighting a shiver. "God, I just want the earth to swallow me whole and spit me back out in a few months."

"You can just leave." Etienne zipped up his suitcase and placed it on the floor. "You can go back home. I'm sure it's blown over by now."

"I'm not ready to do that. I'd rather deal with this embarrassment than that one."

"You built a company, Addie. You're missing out on all the events you dreamed of putting together because you're scared of a little gossip."

"It's not a little gossip when everyone's seen your vagina, Etienne."

"So? Everyone saw Thomas's penis."

"Yeah, and celebrated its size. My vagina, unfortunately, wasn't even talked about. The only thing people have said is what a whore I am." I sighed. "I know I have to go back and deal with it, but I'm not ready."

"Well, don't hide out too long." He started walking out of the room, rolling the suitcase along with him. I stood and followed. "Has Thomas been in touch?"

"Yeah. He feels bad."

"You need to move past it." He stopped walking and put a hand on my shoulder. "I know it's easier said than done, but I've known you since you were born and I've never seen anything get you down like this. Not even those high school photos of you smoking out of that bong."

"Oh, God." I laughed weakly. "That's because I was fully clothed."

"Well, for what it's worth, all of my friends think you look great naked."

"Etienne!" I pushed him away as he laughed and shrugged before walking past me, to the front door.

"This too shall pass, Addie. This too shall pass."

I said those words to myself as I drove back from the airport after dropping him off. *This too shall pass.* Maybe if I said it enough, I'd believe it. It wasn't only the tabloids and having my business out there that bothered me. It was also the fact that I couldn't look my father in the face after the fact. It was that every single man he knew had probably watched the sex tape and also judged him for it, even though he had nothing to do with his daughter's poor decisions. My father was a proud man.

He'd moved mountains and went from anchor in the nightly news to part of the king's cabinet. And then my ex-boyfriend and I became the news and I ran away from the problem, but where was he supposed to hide? If I was being honest with myself, my father was the reason I decided to take a break until everything blew over. I figured creating distance between us might help him move on from it and allow people to forget all about it.

Out of everything the scandal had done, the way it affected my loved ones was what bothered me most. Etienne hid his anger under humor because he wanted me to feel better, but I knew he'd lost his cool in front of his friends more than a few times. My assistant, Joss, who had become one of my closest friends, hated what the tabloids had printed about me. I'd been called a gold digger and prostitute more times than I could count at this point and just when another headline took over and ours was buried, Thomas went out for a night on the town and brought the naked photos of us back to the surface. It was just a matter of time and either this too would pass or I'd have to trample over it and take my life back, but right now I was perfectly content working at my uncle's bookstore and providing baskets to the guests for the time being.

CHAPTER THREE

I'D SPENT MY MORNING ON THE PHONE WITH A BOOK DISTRIBUTOR, making sure they got the boxes I sent back to them. My uncle had entirely too many boring books in the store. Books that had been here for over ten years and not sold, but he'd been hesitant to send back. He said it was because he didn't want them to destroy them. I told him he was destroying himself by keeping them here. It was no wonder in the week I'd been here only two people had walked in. I glanced over to the front door. I needed to do something about the storefront as well. I'd called a couple that flipped houses here to see if they could help me with this and they were due here any minute. I didn't have a ton of money to spend on my uncle's behalf, but I had enough saved up to hopefully make a difference around here. When the door opened, I stood and set the books in my hand down, passing my hands over my sundress to make sure it fell into place. The house-flipping couple came into view and I moved forward to greet them.

"Hi. I'm Adeline. Thank you so much for coming." I smiled, shaking each of their hands.

"I'm Lenora, this is Pedro."

"So nice to meet you both." I took my hand back and waved it around the store. "Well, this is the place. As you can see, it's not very big, but it looks much smaller than it is. I've been trying to somewhat fix the clutter."

"It's cute," Lenora said, looking around.

"The outside has potential," Pedro added. "I know you said you wanted to stay within a very small budget."

"Yes." I gave them a small smile. "I want to help, but I don't have a ton of money to put into it."

"Let me see what we can do," Pedro said, taking his tape measurer out and heading outside.

Lenora walked around, her eyes on everything. "Like Pedro said, it has a lot of potential. The inside just needs to be reduced. There are books everywhere." She glanced to the second floor. "What's up there?"

"Nothing," I said. "He uses it for storage. He can totally turn it into a small café."

"That's a brilliant idea." She smiled at me. "How long do we have?"

"He comes back in a month. He's traveling all over Europe with his wife right now. On what she's calling their second honeymoon. They don't get out much."

"One month." Her brows hiked up. "He must have some kind of money."

"He does. My family owned a lot of the land here. They used to farm cattle and sell milk to everyone within a twenty-five-mile radius, but that dried up, quite literally, and they sold the land. Most of it anyway. We still own the beachside and most of the villas around here."

"Ah, you're a Bouchard! I've never seen you around." She studied me closer. "I went to school with a cousin of yours."

"Sylvia?"

"Yes! How is she?"

"She's doing well. We're not close, but I hear about her whereabouts from my mother and aunt. She's living in Barcelona with her husband and two children."

"That's so nice. Is she still painting?"

"She is. It's going very well for her." I smiled.

"So great." She smiled back. "She was a very good friend to me in school. I'll have to give you a friends and family discount." She winked.

"I appreciate it. My uncle isn't paying for any of this. He loves this store and refuses to sell it, but he's in over his head and he doesn't understand change. I'm kind of doing this as a surprise."

"Oh. Well, he'll be surprised." Lenora laughed. "We'll do everything to make sure the store can stay open while we work. Aside from that spot upstairs, I don't think we'd have to do much construction in here. I may send a guy or two to come help you move some of these heavy bookshelves."

"That would be so helpful," I breathed. "And you really think we can stay under budget? I know I'm not really willing to spend much."

"It should be fine. It doesn't need much, but let's wait to see what Pedro says."

As if on cue, Pedro walked in. "We should be able to knock this out in a weekend."

"A weekend?"

"We have enough people and it's really not much. It needs paint and new landscaping. It's small enough that it'll be a quick job."

"Wow. A weekend would be incredible." I smiled wide.

"Let me know what you need from me and when you can get started."

We agreed on the upcoming weekend, since things were slow for them right now, which meant that if everything went well, they'd be finished by Monday and I would have time to figure out how to set up a coffee shop upstairs. As soon as Lenora and Pedro left, the phone rang, and the caller ID said it was my mother. I answered quickly and updated her on what was happening with the bookstore. She listened quietly, which was never a good thing when it came to my mother. When she liked an idea, she was either speaking over you or pitching in every five seconds. When she hated an idea, she was as quiet as a mouse.

"Mum?"

"I'm here, Adeline. Just trying to figure out where all of this fits into your already hectic schedule," she said. "I know you're taking a break from London society, but we just got hired to do the biggest party of the summer and I don't want you to drop the ball on behalf of your uncle's dwindling bookstore."

"What party?" I sat up quickly.

"The royal family is having a masquerade ball in Versailles in honor of the prince's impending engagement."

"Oh." I blinked. "Versailles? Which prince?"

"The only one who's required to be married, silly. Prince Elias."

"Oh." I sat down, placing an elbow on the table, to counteract the sinking feeling in my belly. "And they hired us? How did they hear about us?"

"Evidentially, Joss is friends with Princess Pilar and she attended the wedding you planned for the Princess of Spain last summer and told her mother, the queen, about it, and here we are." She was quiet for a second, waiting for me to react; when I didn't, she continued, "This is the event of your dreams, Addie. You get to go above and beyond and wow them. Who knows, maybe they'll even hire you for his wedding."

"For his wedding," I said blandly. "Yeah, that would be nice."

"Adeline! What is the matter with you? I thought you'd be jumping and shouting over this. Don't tell me this has to do with Thomas Evans."

"No. No, why would it have anything to do with Thomas?"

"I don't like how distracted you sound. This is the event you've been waiting for your entire career," she said. "Please don't tell me you're going to pass up being there on account of the leaked video."

"I'll be there, Mother." I shut my eyes and took a deep breath.

"Good. Can you meet Joss and me in Versailles this upcoming weekend?"

"Sure."

"Splendid," she said and I could tell she was smiling wide. "I'm so incredibly excited about this and you should be too. Your hard work has paid off and that nonsensical video didn't deter them from hiring you."

"They probably didn't hear about it."

"Trust me, the Crown hears about everything."

My stomach coiled. Did that mean Prince Elias had heard about it? And if so, why did I care? He didn't even remember me. I finished talking to my mother and tried to sound as enthusiastic as I could about the entire thing, but part of me really didn't want to have any part in an event like that. What did impending engagement even mean? Would he propose at the party? If so, to whom? And again, why did I care?

CHAPTER FOUR

I PAUSED, EXHALING HEAVILY AS I LEANED OVER TO SET THE BASKET down and catch my breath. I wasn't used to carrying heavy things and this wicker basket filled with everything from fresh white towels to bath salts and champagne was definitely amongst the heaviest I'd carried. I opened and closed my hands to stretch out my red fingers. My grandmother, who lived her entire life in the service of families, carrying things, washing clothes, and cleaning houses, would have been disappointed in me. Taking a deep breath, I closed my eyes and took in the soothing scent and sound of the beach, and opened my eyes as I crouched and lifted the basket once more to continue my trek. The golf cart I normally used was being replaced and therefore, I had no choice but to walk across the lawn and deliver the basket by hand.

When I arrived here, I knew I'd be serving penance for my sins, and I was ready to do whatever my uncle assigned to me as a job. As far as jobs went, delivering this basket should have been the easiest thing I had to do, but ever since yesterday's experience I'd been trying to figure out a way to hand the job to someone else. My uncle only asked me for two things: a few hours at the bookstore each week and help with the rental villas on the property. He was very specific on one rule—I could not speak to the prince. *Too late,* but I couldn't tell my uncle that. I'd planned to make good on that promise from here on out though. The last thing I wanted was to drag the prince into an unnecessary scandal, and if we were seen talking to each other, people could easily make up rumors.

It wouldn't look good if we were caught appearing friendly. Not with who my father was and how he was notorious to speak out about the injustices of the Crown. His way of thought was the reason people started to question the monarchy and the purpose it served. The fact that the king no longer killed those who spoke up against him was huge and something everyone had come to respect, but some people felt the monarchy was antiquated. Those people thought Prince Elias should not acquire The Crown once his father passed away.

I was on the fence about the whole thing. Probably because unlike a lot of those people, I had not been directly impacted by the economy. As the old saying goes, the poor stay poor and the rich keep getting richer. That didn't mean I didn't want to see people thrive though. I just wasn't vocal about things like that. I was raised in the States most of my life and later, moved to a neighboring country with another set of royals, so it wasn't my place to speak out on things. I left that to my parents. I finally got near the villa and slowed down at the sight of the security guards around the premises. They were dressed in all black, from the hats on their heads with brims that covered their eyes, to the boots on their feet. The one near the door, a tall, GI Joe figure-looking one, with a fit physique and rigid stance, nodded at me in approval to approach.

"There's a lot more security today," I said to the one standing beside the door. Because of the hat and the darkness, I couldn't see much of his face, but his fingers were long and his hands seemed strong as he lifted the basket out of my hands, so I focused on those.

"There's always more security when we have an important visitor." His voice was slightly clipped.

"Oh." I opened and closed my hands to stretch them again as I looked around, not that there was anything to see.

"You're Monsieur Bouchard's niece?"

"Yes."

"Your father is in the king's cabinet," he said and I couldn't tell whether or not he meant that as a good thing.

"Yes." I bit my tongue. Normally, I was proud of my father, but standing outside the villa where the prince my father was constantly questioning resided felt shameful.

"Don't worry. You won't be beheaded for having your own thoughts." The guard chuckled quietly. "Not anymore anyway."

"Thank God for progress." I smiled.

"So you will be dropping these off every night?"

"I guess so. It's part of my penance."

"Penance for what?"

"It's a long story, but trust me, I deserve worse than delivering heavy baskets to the future king." I glanced up at him.

"I'd like to hear that story." He smiled wide. It was a boyish smile, one that made me smile instantly.

"Maybe I'll share it with you."

"Over a pint?"

"Sure." I shrugged a shoulder, feeling grateful that despite everything I could still sort of flirt. "When are you free?"

"When do you want me to be free?"

"Is that how this job works?" I laughed. "If so, sign me up."

"I have two days off, but my line sounded better than saying that."

I laughed again. Suddenly, the door beside us burst open and we both froze as if caught doing something wrong. I'd only ever seen Prince Elias smiling that charming, panty-dropping grin he liked to flash at photographers just as they snapped his photo, the one I'd seen yesterday when Etienne was with me, so the fact that he was standing before me, glaring, threw me for a loop. I blinked away from his eyes and it was then that I noticed he wasn't wearing a shirt. My eyes widened on his torso. There was no question that the prince worked out.

"Do you need something?" he snapped.

"Um. No." I blinked rapidly at his tone, wondering why in the world it was directed toward me. "I was just dropping off a few things."

"Do we have everything we need, Pierre?" His gaze swung to the guard.

"Yes, sir."

"Please bring it inside." He spoke to him in a direct yet polite tone. It was me he was saving the disdain for and that was perfectly clear when he looked at me again. "Thank you for bringing it. That will be all. I'll be needing my things much earlier tomorrow."

In response, I could only nod and blink. I couldn't even say another word. Pierre followed the prince inside and the door was shut in my face. It was definitely not what I'd been expecting and not something I wanted to experience again.

CHAPTER FIVE

"**I** NEVER WANT TO GO BACK THERE AGAIN," I said.

"He's notorious for his mood swings," Etienne said.

"I felt so . . . small."

"I'm sorry, Addie. That's just him." He sighed heavily into the phone line. "Just steer clear."

"Oh, I am. I'm going to drop off his basket at five o'clock today and make sure I don't call attention to myself at all. I can't wait for this weekend to arrive already so I can leave."

"So you are doing the Versailles event."

"How do you know about it?"

"Mira told me."

"How does Mira know about it?"

"I don't know. How does Mira know anything? Gossip," he said.

"Still. I would love to know who she heard it from."

"Hold on." Etienne sighed. "Mira, who'd you hear that Pirouette Events was doing Versailles from?" He was quiet for a moment. I could hear Mira talking in the background before Etienne said, "She heard it from Sarah who heard it from Rita who heard it from Francis who heard it from Princess Pilar."

"Oh. I always forget how many connections Mira has."

"She's been a good ally for you right now, I'll tell you that. The only people judging you for your mishap are the older ones who forgot what it was like to be young and make mistakes."

"Well, thank her for that." I could only imagine what Mira was saying to defend me. Out of all of Etienne's girlfriends, she was definitely my favorite.

"I'm sorry Eli gave you a shitty time," Etienne said, lowering his voice. "He's known to be an asshole sometimes, but it doesn't make it okay."

"Thanks. I just wasn't sure what I did to deserve that."

"Nothing, Addie. You did nothing. Go about your day, go plan the hell out of the Versailles event, and forget all about him."

"I will." I nodded once in determination and smiled.

At five o'clock, I was walking toward Prince Elias's villa delivering his basket. This time, I'd completely pushed aside any thoughts of the prince and the concept of him I had in my head from the first time we'd met. In doing so, I prepared for disappointment and I was okay with that. Better to be prepared for the bad than expect the good and have a harder time accepting the reality. The same security, Pierre, was at the front door.

"I'm off tomorrow evening," he said upon seeing me.

"Beers, then?" I asked as I walked up the three steps and set the basket down in front of the door.

"Sure. Which villa do you stay in?"

I stared at him for a long moment, wondering if I should tell him. He probably already knew though. I pointed next door.

"Oh." He laughed. "You know you could walk here."

"I could, but the basket would make my fingers fall off, so I'd rather drive the little golf cart over."

"They are pretty heavy." He lifted it.

Now that he was standing in front of me, I realized he was much taller than I was, but then, most men were. I was five foot five and usually wearing flats. He was also standing much too close to me. Close enough that I could make out that his eyes were pale blue and his face needed a shave.

"You're really pretty," he said.

"Thank you." I smiled. "I don't think I even told you my name last night."

"What is it?"

"Adeline."

He smiled. "I'm Pierre."

"Nice to meet you, Pierre."

"May I pick you up at seven tomorrow?"

"I . . . can you make it seven thirty?"

"Seven thirty it is." He smiled wide. When he did that, his eyes twinkled.

The door opened beside us and he took a giant step back, leaving me exposed to the person on the other side of the door. Prince Elias. Again. This time, he was wearing a white button-down shirt, his dark hair in disarray. He had the perfect bedroom hair. And bedroom eyes. And they were staring right at me. My heart pounded in my ears. Again, I couldn't seem to move. It was as if he'd cast me under a spell and there was no escaping it.

"Miss Adeline brought your things, sir," Pierre announced, his back toward me now.

"Set them inside, please," Prince Elias said, his eyes still on mine, his voice a command no one would dare to contend. Pierre disappeared inside.

"I . . . " I licked my lips, clasping my hands together. "I hope you find everything well. If you need anything else, please don't hesitate to tell me. Good night."

I turned around, my skirt whooshing with my movement as I did so. I needed to get out of here before I made a fool of myself. Why was I even talking to him? He hadn't said one word to me. Why was he even opening the door every time I got here? It was annoying and unnerving and I hated the way he made me feel. Thankfully, my feet worked quickly and I was off the porch and back in front of the cart in no time.

"Adeline."

My heart ceased at the sound of my name coming from his lips. I stopped walking. Stopped moving. Stopped breathing. Somehow, I managed to turn around and face him. Prince Elias was just walking down the last step when my gaze met his.

"I'm having a party tomorrow night."

"Oh." I perked up. *He was inviting me to one of his famous parties?*

"I'd love you to serve drinks for us."

"Serve drinks?" I blinked. "I . . . um . . . I don't think I'm qualified to do that."

I wasn't a bartender. Besides, I didn't do this. I didn't serve people or make them baskets or work parties I wasn't being paid to plan. I hired people for that. *How in the world had I found myself in this position?* I didn't expect Prince Elias to know that but surely he knew I was wearing designer and wasn't meant to be his houseworker? Then again, his nannies and house employees probably wore designer too. The point was, I was usually invited to parties like these, not working them.

"It doesn't matter. I would appreciate your help and you being there anyway."

"I really can't. I can hire someone to do it though." I smiled politely.

"I'd prefer it if you did it yourself."

"I can't. I . . . " I paused, trying to decide how much I wanted to explain. Finally, I simply smiled again and said, "I have a date."

"A date," he repeated, his eyes assessing me closer now, as if he was trying to figure out who would ask me on a date. It was the moment I realized I could definitely grow to hate Prince Elias. *How had I ever slept with this man? How could I have given him my virginity?* I was disgusted with myself.

"Yes, a date."

"So you won't be available at seven?"

"No," I said too quickly, then added, "I will bring your basket and whatever else you need at seven, but after that, I'm indisposed."

"What about nine o'clock?"

"I'll still be on my date."

"Eleven?"

"What are you getting at here? I'm not a bartender, Prince Elias. I can hire you one from the bar down the street if you'd like, though I'm sure your staff probably has a list of capable bartenders who can go to your party." I was losing my patience and trying really hard not to. "I won't be available tomorrow night and you should be grateful for that. I make shit drinks.

All of my friends say I do. I put too much alcohol and too little mixer and everyone ends up getting drunk way too quickly and feeling sick at some point or nursing massive hangovers. I'm not available tomorrow night nor am I here for your entertainment. I'm sure it's a concept you're not familiar with, but some of us have actual lives and actual jobs that don't revolve around the Crown."

When I finished my rant, I slapped a hand over my mouth, wishing I'd done so before I started talking. *Oh my God.* Had I just . . . *why, why, why* had I opened my mouth to respond? Prince Elias was no longer watching me with interest. He was shooting daggers at me. I lowered my hand from my mouth.

"I'm so sorry. That was . . . That was not what I intended. I just—"

"I believe you've said enough, Miss Adeline. I will not be needing your services tomorrow evening." He turned around, but looked over his shoulder one last time to add, "Have fun on your date."

He said the word *date* with such disdain, I was sure he absolutely hated me. I just couldn't figure out why I cared so much.

CHAPTER SIX

A T SEVEN O'CLOCK THE FOLLOWING EVENING, I WALKED UP TO the prince's villa and sat the wicker basket down in front of the door. Unlike yesterday, Pierre wasn't standing beside it. Tonight, there was security everywhere, though. I'd overheard two of them saying they were expecting a lot of people at the party tonight. A lot of ruckus and nudity the other added. I'd just placed the basket down, when, like clockwork, the front door opened. Prince Elias was standing on the other side of it, with a short glass in his hand. His white shirt was unbuttoned up top and his sleeves were rolled up as if he'd just gotten home from work, but I knew better. The man didn't work. I hadn't seen him leave the premises the entire week.

"Are you ready for your date?" he asked, disapproval dripping from his voice.

"I am. Are you ready for your party?"

"I am." He took a large gulp, draining the glass of alcohol. His dark, mysterious eyes never left mine. "Do you drink, Miss Adeline?"

"Occasionally."

"Come in. Share a drink with me."

"I can't."

"Because of your uncle?" His head tilted slightly as he looked at me. "I heard he doesn't want any of his female employees talking to me."

"I'm not his employee," I said, though my uncle had warned me to stay away from the prince. "I have a date and I don't want to be late."

"You're nervous," he said. "Do I make you nervous?"

"A little." There was no point in lying to him.

"That's interesting." He let go of the door and took a step toward me. "I'm sure your date can wait a few minutes."

I stared at his chest, at the button that was undone and the golden skin that peeked from underneath. I couldn't bring myself to look at his face directly. Not when he was standing dangerously close to me. Not when the scent of his cologne made it nearly impossible not to feel as though he was completely taking control of my body.

"Come on, Adeline," he said, his voice low, sexy. "One drink."

The way he said my name made me instantly transport back to our night together and the way he chanted my name as he came. It took everything in me to clear that thought away and shake my head no.

"I can't."

"Are you afraid you'll enjoy my company?"

"No." I met his gaze. "I know I wouldn't."

He chuckled darkly. "You know, not once since I've been here have you curtsied to me."

"Am I supposed to curtsy to you?"

"Am I not your future king?"

"You're not king yet." I matched his cold stare. "Besides, I live in London. Your Crown doesn't extend that far."

"It extends this far though."

"Well, then, it's a good thing I'm just a passerby."

His eyes narrowed and after a few seconds of a staring contest I wasn't prepared to engage in, I turned and walked away, heart beating frantically. As I reached the last step, I glanced over my shoulder to see that he was still standing in the same spot I'd left him, staring after me. "Have fun at your party."

"You seem preoccupied," Pierre said across from me.

We were at a pub in town having fish and chips and beer and so far, everything was going well. It was all easy conversation and not much flirting at all, which oddly, I appreciated.

"I was just thinking about what an asshole the prince is."

Pierre coughed, patting his chest as he set his beer down. "He's going through a lot."

"Right." I rolled my eyes, lifting my own beer to my lips. "He doesn't even leave his villa. It's not like he's working."

"He's a good man."

"Well." I set my beer down. "It's all the same to me. I still don't like him."

"A lot of people have issues with the royal family. Your father is always criticizing them publicly."

"My father works with them. He only criticizes certain aspects of what they're doing that he doesn't agree with."

"Do you agree with him on the matter?"

"I don't have to. I no longer live here. I bow to the Queen of England."

"That's a cop-out."

"What, bowing to another queen?"

"Not giving your opinion because you feel like it doesn't apply to you. It's a cop-out."

"Do you think the king should have as much power as he does?"

"Yes."

"Yes? No hesitation?" I felt my lip turn up. "You say that because you work for them."

"For centuries they had all the power. Now they have a little less power and it's still running smoothly. Why change something that's not broken?"

"You don't think the economy is broken in its current state?" I asked. "There are doctors and lawyers getting paid wages way below the average. And that's only a few who have suffered in the recent years since the king's health has been on the decline. This is what started the French Revolution. They were lucky the Crown was saved all of those years ago. I don't think they'll get lucky again. He should've stepped down years ago, or let the cabinet have more power. Let the people have more power."

"You have a lot of opinions for someone who doesn't even care to address her prince with courtesy." The voice was Prince Elias's and it came from behind me.

I thought I'd already been sitting up straight, but I was wrong. At the sound of his voice, my back arched and my shoulders pushed back as my heart dropped into the pit of my stomach. How long had he been standing behind me? How long had Pierre let me speak without telling me to stop? From the look on his face, he seemed like he had tried to warn me but I wouldn't quit speaking. It was a flaw of mine. When I was passionate about something, I couldn't stop talking about it. Slowly, I glanced over my shoulder to find Prince Elias standing in the center of the pub. Everyone around us seemed to have completely stopped what they were doing to stare at him. Some women were still curtsying. Some men still bowing. Everyone's mouth was agape. And then there was me, whose face was aflame and wanted to die of mortification.

"You weren't supposed to hear any of that," I whispered.

I thought he'd glare some more, but his eyes lit, as if he was thoroughly enjoying my discomfort. He closed the distance between us and stood right beside me, setting a hand on the table, right next to my arm. We were sitting at one of the tall tables by the bar, with high barstools that, had he been a tad shorter, maybe would have given me an advantage, but even still I had to crane my neck to look at him. Not that I had any intention of looking him in the eyes right now. I mulled over what I'd been saying and was filled with horror. My father would kill me. If this got back to him, he'd kill me.

"This is your date?" He glanced at Pierre. "I thought you said you were going out with a friend."

"I . . . am, sir."

"So, it's not a date," Prince Elias stated, still looking at Pierre, who looked at me.

"It's a date if she says it is, sir." Pierre turned a deep shade of red as he looked over at me. "I'd like for it to be a date."

"It is a date." I met Prince Elias's gaze. He was much too close to me. Way closer than Pierre. And the way he looked at me made my blood roar in my ears. "What happened to your party? Couldn't find someone to pour drinks for you?"

"I have a full staff. Of course I found someone." His jaw twitched. "But I got bored."

"Bored?" I blinked. "So you left your own party?"

"I needed fresh air and someone told me Pierre was here, so I thought I'd come hang out for a bit with my old friend and meet his local friend." His gaze slid to Pierre. "I hadn't realized this was a date, otherwise, I would not have imposed."

"Please. Feel free to join." Pierre stood and rearranged the table so we had another stool.

He looked over my shoulder and pulled up another stool, and then another. I closed my eyes briefly. We'd officially been invaded by the prince and his posse. I wondered if I should stand up and excuse myself now. It seemed like a good time to do that. I'd wait though. For Pierre, because he seemed at a loss and I didn't want to do that to him.

"So, you're old friends," I said, once Prince Elias and the two men he was with sat around the table.

Pierre and I were still across from each other. Prince Elias was beside me on one side, one of the men who hadn't yet introduced himself, but looked like he was a friend, not security was on my other side, and another wearing all black was beside Pierre.

"We are," Prince Elias said. "Pierre's older brother and I served together."

"Oh." I raised my eyebrows. I may have my reservations about the Crown, but I had enormous respect for the military. I looked at Pierre. "Are you close to your brother?"

"I am. He's retired now. Lives a quiet life not too far from here." He smiled. "Lots of nieces and nephews."

"Define lots." I matched his smile.

"Four girls, two boys."

"Holy . . . wow. Lots, indeed." I laughed, taking a sip of my beer.

"How did you two meet?" The man beside me asked. "I'm Charles, by the way."

"Adeline." I smiled. "We met—"

"She's part of the local staff. She brings my baskets every night," Prince Elias said.

Part of the local staff. I didn't agree with it, but I wasn't going to argue with him about it in front of everyone. I raised my beer to that explanation instead and hoped he understood I meant it as a big fuck you.

"She's . . . " Pierre started, then stopped. We shared a look and I knew what he was going to say and I was eternally grateful that he hadn't. I didn't want anyone at this table to know who my father was. The next wave of shame hit me and felt like a whip on my hand. "She's the prettiest girl in town," Pierre said, smiling.

"She is, indeed," Prince Elias agreed.

I felt my chest expand with his words, but controlled the emotion on my face. I wouldn't let myself be controlled by the handsome soon-to-be king. I wouldn't let myself go down the same road so many of the women in this town had gone down before. I was already a notch in his bedpost. I didn't want to add another.

"You should come back to the villa. Have some drinks with us," Charles said beside me. "Let your guard down. Let your inhibitions run wild."

"I can't afford to let my guard down." I drank the rest of my beer and set it down on the table as I pushed my seat back and hopped off the stool. I walked around the table and stood beside Pierre, leaning in so only he could hear me. "Thank you for the lovely evening. We should do this again sometime. In private."

"I'm sorry." He sighed. "Would you like me to go with you?"

"That's okay. I'm just going up the road anyway." I leaned up, pressed a kiss to his cheek. "I really did have a good time with you."

"Can I . . . I would say call, but the cellphone reception is shit." He laughed quietly.

"Just pass by my villa. Any time." I flashed him one last smile before turning to address the rest of the table. My breath caught when I found Prince Elias watching me closely. "Good night, gentlemen."

With that, I grabbed my things and left. I'd parked the golf cart up the street and when I looked over to where it was, I noticed two similar golf carts beside it. *Property of the Crown.* I wondered if Prince Elias had spotted it and decided to go inside. I assumed so. He probably thought it was Pierre's and not mine.

"Adeline."

My head whipped toward the sound of my name and I saw Pierre walking toward me. I smiled at him.

"Did you get bored?"

"No." He smiled. "I figured I should join you on the drive up the hill though." He paused. "And the prince needs a few things for his party."

"You mean the party he's not even attending?" I rolled my eyes.

"I know he comes off as . . . arrogant, but he is a good man." Pierre signaled for us to start walking across the street.

"You said that already." I shrugged. "I'm sure he's a lovely human."

"He is." Pierre laughed.

"It doesn't matter. It genuinely makes no difference to me."

"He's taken an interest in you."

His statement gave me pause. I started the golf cart and sat there for a second, waiting for Pierre to sit in the passenger seat.

"Interest how?"

"I'm sure you can imagine how many people are constantly throwing themselves at him. Everyone wants to be the one to make the most eligible bachelor, notorious playboy, next king, settle." He glanced over at me. "You don't do that. Therefore, you're interesting."

"I'm not interested in the monarchy."

"I'm not either, but you'd be surprised at how many are. You'd be surprised at the lengths they'd go through for even one night with Eli."

"You call him Eli." I stopped at the crossway and looked at him. "Why does he have you work outside his house? Securing the door?"

"I chose that job. He keeps offering me to be his private secretary, so I'll move into that role eventually. He didn't want to bring too many of the personnel, so I guard the door sometimes." Pierre flashed me a sad smile. "It didn't end very well for the last guy."

"What happened to the last guy?"

"He tried to kill the prince, and well . . . " Pierre shrugged. "It ended badly for him."

"I heard about that," I whispered. "The man was killed shortly afterward."

I started driving again. When we reached the prince's villa, I could see colorful lights and hear loud music coming from inside. It looked like an actual nightclub from out here. Pierre signaled me to stop beside it.

"He wasn't. The prince intervened and the guard was sentenced to life in prison."

"Why not death?" I asked. If someone had tried to kill me, I'd probably want them dead.

"Eli is not a vengeful man. He doesn't believe in an eye for an eye."

My brows rose. "His father does."

"His father does." Pierre nodded. "His father ultimately had the guard killed."

"I'm not surprised."

"I know you don't agree with the way the king does things, but you can't hold the entire family accountable for the actions of one man." He set his hand over mine. "Think about what that would mean for you if people held you accountable for your father's actions or him for yours."

"They already do," I said sadly. "Besides, I'm not holding him accountable for those things, I'm holding him accountable for his poor attitude."

Pierre got out of the car. "Maybe we can do this again sometime."

"I'd like that."

"By the way, the prince wants you to attend the party."

"I thought he got someone to serve drinks."

"He'd like you there as a guest."

I glanced inside. "That's not my scene."

"It's a masquerade," he said. "Great Gatsby attire."

"Definitely not my scene. I don't have anything to wear to that and masks lead to poor decisions."

"I think that's what he's hoping for." He smiled. "I'll be there. You can always come for ten minutes, say you did it, and leave."

"I guess I can do that." I glanced at the house, my eyes on the strobing lights. "It's not like I have anything better to do."

CHAPTER SEVEN

I'D BEEN HOME FOR ALL OF TEN MINUTES WHEN THE DOORBELL RANG. I walked to the door slowly, confused, and opened it to find Pierre standing outside holding a garment bag. He looked handsome in a tuxedo and stepped forward to hand me the garment bag.

"This is for the party."

"Are you serious?" I took it in my hands and unzipped it to find a short black flapper dress full of frills, the kind that dance with each movement you make.

"I told you it was a Gatsby theme."

"With masks," I said, taking out the beautiful, black feather mask inside the garment bag. There was a short brunette wig behind it. "And wigs."

"It'll be fun."

"This is dumb."

"Now you can say you've been to one of the princes' famous parties."

"Yeah." I laughed weakly. Except, I had been to one of his famous parties and I'd slept with him last time, which in retrospect was probably a mistake on my part.

"Ten minutes," he said again, as if reminding me I didn't have to be there long.

"Ten minutes." I laughed, for real this time. "You actually expect me to wear this get-up for ten minutes?"

"I don't expect you to. The prince does."

"He wasn't wearing a tuxedo at the pub."

"He hadn't changed yet," Pierre said. "Which . . . there's another thing I need to . . . ask you?"

"You sound confused about the asking."

"He needs somewhere to change before he goes back in there to make his grand entrance and I thought maybe it would be a good idea for him to come here."

"Here?"

"Well, he would have gone to one of our quarters to do so, but yours is the closest house to his, so it would make more sense. Thinking of it from a security standpoint."

"A security standpoint. Right." I took a deep breath. "I guess he can come here. I have two spare bedrooms with bathrooms."

"Would you, um . . . " Pierre licked his lips. "Would you mind giving me a key so he can let himself in? In case you're busy."

I glanced away and looked out the window, toward the party that was definitely happening. From here, I could make out someone in the garden, and she was wearing a similar dress to the one in my hand, so I knew this was real. I exhaled, walking over to the kitchen, grabbing the spare key, and handing it to Pierre.

"He gives it back tonight."

"You have my word."

With that, he left and I went to my room and locked the

door. If Prince Elias was going to be in my house, my room would be off-limits. We called them villas, but they were more like miniature mansions in the guise of cute beach villas. The rooms were bigger than my one-bedroom apartment in North Carolina had been, with large sitting areas and large windows that gave view to the beach on the other side of the cliff. There were five in total. This one, which was the house I'd spent my teenage years living in, when I was home. My uncle's, and the three he rented out, which essentially belonged to the royal family every summer.

I thought about what Pierre had said about Prince Elias and then about Prince Elias's own words at the pub. He'd deduced me to a nobody without a second thought. I glanced at the party in the next villa and wondered if attending was a mistake. Surely, the people over there were all aristocrats of some sort. Despite my accomplishments, to them, I was just the lowly girl who took them alcohol and provided fresh towels. It didn't matter that my father was powerful or that I had a degree from a prestigious university under my belt. It didn't matter that I was living in London, or that I'd built a well-respected event-planning company. None of it mattered because ultimately, to Prince Elias, I would always be a peasant.

CHAPTER EIGHT

I TOOK MY TIME UNDRESSING AND RE-DRESSING AND THEN CURSED ALL of it when I realized I needed help zipping up my dress. It would have been fine, had it not been for the fact that cellphone reception was nonexistent out here and I wouldn't be able to get ahold of Pierre unless I walked over to the party. Overall, the dress looked good on me though. The fabric hugged my curves and the bust was cut low up top. Once it was zipped up, it would definitely give the illusion of my breasts being larger than they were. I still wasn't sure if I was going to wear the wig or not. My natural dark brown hair was down to my waist and I wasn't sure how I'd pile it all under a short bob wig.

The sound of the front door slamming made me jump in place. Since he didn't arrive earlier, I figured Prince Elias had changed his mind and wouldn't be coming. I looked at my exposed back again. Maybe one of the guards could help me with this. When I opened my door, I saw Prince Elias standing in the entrance, a garment bag hanging over his right arm as he looked at the photographs of my family on the wall. We hadn't been here as a family in years, but the memories remained. I took a second to look at him as he admired the photographs. If I was being honest with myself, had it not been for the fact that he'd been a complete jerk to me, I would have probably been drooling over him the entire time. He was the kind of man that was exactly everyone's type. Tall, broad shoulders, dark hair that he seemed to just let do its own thing, and its own thing was a perpetual state of sex hair. His lips were full, his teeth were blindingly white and straight, and his eyes were the darkest shade of green. His jaw was square and gave him an appearance of a man that was always serious. He was absolutely every bit of the prince I'd always dreamed would whisk me away.

Except, in reality, he was everything I'd always told myself I would never fall for, because in spite of all of his good looks, he was downright mean. And if there was one thing I didn't like, it was mean people. I didn't care that Pierre had a different experience with him. I didn't care that the very first time I met him, he was completely dreamy and kind and treated me like I was special in his bed.

"Don't you have a party to get to?" I asked and bit my bottom lip as he turned to face me, those dark eyes drinking me in slowly.

"It looks good on you."

"Thanks." It wasn't like I'd been expecting him to give me a great compliment, but *it looks good on you* in that tone was the equivalent to *you should change.*

"It looks like you had a nice upbringing," he said.

"I can't complain."

"The prime minister's daughter." He said it casually, but I could tell he was ticked by it from the way his expression was set.

"That's me."

"You don't sound as thrilled as I imagined someone in your position to be."

"That's funny coming from you."

"What does that mean?" He tilted his face to study me.

"I thought endless jewels and the respect of everyone in most nations would mean you'd be happy."

"I don't have the respect of everyone in my nation, let alone others." He shot me a pointed look.

"You're mistaking my father's beliefs for mine. Besides, I don't think we should have this conversation." I walked over to him. His eyes widened a fraction as I stood in front of him and turned, glancing up at him over my shoulder. "Can you zip me up?"

His eyes met mine and held as he tossed the garment bag onto the nearest couch and brought his hands to my lower back, where the zipper was. I wanted to turn away, especially when I felt his fingers on my back, but I couldn't bring myself to break the spell he seemed to be casting. He tugged on the zipper and slowly brought it up. I gasped as he reached the top and ran a finger over my back, then held my breath as his expression darkened. He was finished zipping me, but hadn't lowered his hands. There was a loud knock on the front door, followed by the door opening quickly. I stepped away, forcing Prince Elias's hands to drop between us; his gaze was still sharp on mine.

"Sir, the Princess of Austria is in attendance and asked to see you," Pierre said, clearing his throat as he stood there.

I turned away completely and walked back to my room, my galloping heart chasing after me. I closed the door and shut it behind me, slamming my back into it and letting out a breath. *What the hell had just happened?*

I waited until I heard doors slamming and the sound of Prince Elias's shouting had dissipated before I opened the door and made my way to the party. Pierre was standing outside with today's guard as I shut the front door and locked it.

"Men don't wear masks?" I asked.

"We do." He took a mask out of his pocket and put it over his eyes for me to see.

"You look good."

"Thanks. So do you." He eyed me up and down. "I see you decided to wear the wig."

"It's a bit uncomfortable." I patted the top of my head. "But I think it'll stay. Are you ready to go or do you have to wait for him?"

"We can go ahead. I'm off duty, remember?" He smiled, offering me his arm.

I gladly linked my arm through it, grateful that I had someone to keep me from falling. I didn't wear heels often and even though these were comfortable, I wasn't used to walking on small pebbles with them.

"Do they just have outfits for every theme readily available?" I asked as we walked.

"Pretty much. There's this one. There's a seventeen-hundreds theme where everyone looks like King Louis and Marie Antoinette. That's my personal favorite." He paused, pursing his lips. "I'm sure there are more."

I filed away the seventeen-hundreds theme. It would be a good one for the Versailles event.

"Any excuse to have a party," I said.

"Or any excuse to liven the party up," Pierre responded. "He gets bored with all of this."

"So why do it?"

"That's a question you'd have to ask him. If you dare."

"I dare, but I don't care. It won't make a difference in my life."

We arrived at the villa and stood on the porch for a couple of minutes as we set our masks in place.

"Can you tell it's me?"

"Not at all," he said. "Can you tell it's me?"

"Not really." I looked at the man that walked outside as we stood there and noticed he was wearing the exact same outfit as Pierre. A woman walked out and she was wearing the exact same dress and mask as I was. "Are we all supposed to be wearing the same thing?"

"Everyone wears the same exact outfit. It makes things more interesting." He offered me his arm again. "Let's go get some drinks."

CHAPTER NINE

I DIDN'T DRINK MUCH. NOT BECAUSE THERE WASN'T PLENTY TO drink, and then some, but because people-watching was much more fun when you did it sober. When I was dating Thomas, I'd rubbed shoulders with world leaders and even some members of the royal family in London, but that didn't make me any less intimidated to be at this party. I had no idea who was who beneath the masks and even though that was the beauty of it—we were all equal in here—it was still extremely jarring to think about.

"That right there is Benjamin Drake," Pierre whispered beside me.

"What? Where?" I followed his finger to one of the men dancing on the dance floor. "How do you know?"

"I saw him without his mask earlier," he said.

"You're a real fan, eh?"

"Aren't we all?" He grinned. "I've met him a few times. Nice bloke."

"Well, that's good to know. I would really hate to toss his jersey."

Pierre laughed. "Hey, I'm going to get another drink. Want one?"

"No, thanks. I'm going to look for the toilets." I hesitated. "Well, I know where everything is, so, yeah."

He laughed again. The villa was the same layout as mine, so finding one wouldn't be difficult. It was finding one that didn't have people standing outside of it waiting that would prove to be a challenge. I glanced around the room. The longer the party went on, the more risqué people seemed to become. Apparently, inhibitions really did run wild when people had something to hide behind. I decided that going into one of the rooms may be the best option, so I tried the first one and found a couple making out on the bed. I shut it quickly. I moved on to the next room and found a group of men having a conversation. I shut that quickly as well. There was only one room left and it was the master downstairs. That level had a guest bathroom outside of the bedroom, so I could use it without going into his room. I headed toward the stairs and walked down there.

I felt uneasy. It was completely dark down here and I felt like I was trespassing. I had to pass his bedroom to reach the bathroom at the end of the hall, and my steps slowed as I walked past. I heard movement inside, the sounds of a conversation between a man and a woman. Was it the Princess of Austria? She'd been looking for him earlier. Was she the one he was to be engaged to? She was beautiful and royal and fit the bill. One thing I'd learned in boarding school was that all of those royals and billion-dollar heirs had flings with each other at one point or another. It was a cesspool of future monarchs and the outside world couldn't begin to understand them, so it made sense. Still, for some reason, the thought didn't sit well with me.

I went into the guest bathroom and locked the door. I stayed in there a little longer than necessary and re-did my wig and fixed my mask before walking out. The door to the bedroom opened as I stepped out of the guest bathroom and a woman walked out. She was fixing her dress and running a finger underneath her lip to fix her lipstick. She didn't even glance my way as she walked down the hall and up the stairs. I didn't even realize that I was frozen in place until he walked out of the room shortly afterward. He was wearing the exact same thing as everyone in the party, but there was absolutely no doubt that it was him. Unlike his companion, his head whipped in my direction and his eyes found mine.

Something about it propelled me to move forward. My heart pounded hard as I walked past him, and just when I thought I was going to leave him behind, he grabbed my arm and pulled me toward him. I stopped breathing. My heart was suddenly pumping in my ears, throbbing as relentlessly as the spot between my legs, because despite me thinking he was mean, there was no denying that I wanted him. My body wanted him. I pressed myself against him, taunting, tempting, and when he lowered his face to mine and bit my lower lip, I gasped into his mouth and threw my arms around him, deepening the kiss. It was unlike anything I'd ever experienced. The way my body moved into his hands as they explored my body was purely erotic. Purely carnal. The music stopped as it switched into another song, that started off low, and the sound of heavy footsteps rang out in the hall. It was then that I snapped out of it and pushed away from him, my chest heaving as I struggled to catch my breath. His hand held mine for a second, as if he didn't want to let me go, but I tugged and walked away.

I walked by a man going the opposite direction, my face burning beneath my mask. I wondered if he'd seen anything and if so, how much. When I got upstairs, I idled around, watching the people on the dance floor having fun dancing while others started hooking up around them. I took that as my cue to leave. I made an effort to find Pierre to say goodbye, but it was no use. Everyone looked the same in there and the darkness wasn't helping. I made my way to the door.

Once the door was shut behind me, I let out a long, deep breath. Normally, I liked parties because I felt like I could get lost in them. At a party, I could drink and dance and be wild without judgment. After the whole thing happened with Thomas, I was hesitant to let others see me like that. I didn't want to be known as the wild child of London, despite the papers and their headlines. I chanced another glance inside, where the strobe lights were whirling and the people were whooping and laughing. Maybe I'd had my fill of parties after all. I started walking toward my villa, but upon hearing the waves crashing the rocks below, I decided to take the stairs between the villas and go down there. I hadn't visited the water since I'd arrived and the ocean felt like it was calling me now.

I slipped off the mask on my face, and the wig, as well as my shoes as I reached the bottom of the stairs and walked on the lukewarm sand. It had been hot today, the sun blazing and seeping into the sand beneath me. I knew from experience that if I'd walked out here during the day, my feet would've burned. Now, with the cooler temperature, the warmth the sun left behind was a mere memory. I sat down and inhaled the calming scent of the ocean, closing my eyes as the first wave crashed. How many times had I sat out here and pretended I was a mermaid and my prince was going to come save me? This town had been entirely too small for me when we lived here. It had been my father's way of ensuring I stayed humble during my teenage years, despite the boarding schools and trips around the world.

"Did my party bore you?"

My heart stopped beating as my eyes popped open. I turned my face and looked up. Prince Elias seemed impossibly tall from this angle, like a giant who could touch the sky. Maybe he could. He sat down beside me, slipping the mask from his face and tossing it on the sand. Glancing over my shoulder, I could see his security detail standing by the steps. Near, yet far enough to give him privacy. I wondered if he'd bring up what just happened inside. I wondered if I would. No. Forget about it. It was a mistake. A one-time thing that happened at a sexy party. Nothing else.

"Did it bore you?" I asked after a beat.

"I'm here, aren't I?"

"You make it sound like this may not be that much better." My lip tilted at that. "You really are an asshole, you know that?"

"So you've said."

"I'm sure I'm not the only one who's brought that to your attention." I glanced at him. He had his long arms set on his knees, his hands dangling as he looked out into the ocean.

"Outside of my siblings and maybe a few cousins, you are the only one who's said it to me." He met my gaze after a moment. "To my face, anyway."

"Interesting."

"It is interesting." He inched closer. "Do you know why they won't say it to my face?"

"They're afraid of the consequences?"

"I guess so. I could end them. Easily."

"Perks of being the future king."

"There aren't many perks to that job." He made a sound that sounded between a snort and a scoff as he looked away from me. I stared at his profile. He had pretty features. Rugged yet pretty.

"There might be if your family wasn't dead set on keeping things so traditional."

"You think I haven't had this conversation countless times?" He looked at me again. "Do you think I haven't tried to figure out ways to keep the Crown happy and the people happy? It's not as simple as you may think it is."

"You're right. I don't imagine it is."

"It's a lot of pressure. The king dying."

"Your father, you mean."

"My father, the king." His eyes searched mine. "I don't expect you see him as a father or a husband. Just as a strict ruler who wants the last say in everything and the reason a lot of people are suffering."

This time, I glanced away and looked back at the ocean. The turmoil in it matched his eyes, and I couldn't seem to find solace in it. He wasn't wrong. A lot of people were waiting for his father's demise. There were hungry people in the street. People losing their houses, their jobs, their families. It wasn't something the king could possibly understand and up until tonight, something I didn't think Prince Elias could understand either. Maybe I'd been wrong in my judgment. He seemed like a man who carried loss well, but felt the burden of it nonetheless. The sound of sand swishing behind us made us turn our heads as one of his security detail approached.

"The Princess of Austria is looking for you," he said.

Prince Elias sighed heavily, throwing his head back as if

to ask the universe for patience. It was yet another glimpse of the person he hid beneath his stoicism. He stood up slowly, the sand on his pants falling on the skirt of my dress with the movement. The security detail walked away and Prince Elias stood there for a long moment in silence, watching the ocean, with only the sound of the waves to disturb his thoughts.

"I'll see you another time, Miss Adeline," he said. "Thank you for indulging me and attending the party, as short-lived as it was."

"Thank you for inviting me as a guest." I smiled slightly, looking up at him. "For what it's worth, I'm sorry your father is dying."

His smile was small and pained just before he turned around and walked away.

CHAPTER TEN

I WENT TO THE SECOND FLOOR OF MY VILLA AND SAT OUT ON THE balcony with my coffee. The sun had risen an hour ago according to the weather forecast, and I was sad to have missed it. It was always the one thing that stood out about this place to me. The sunrise hadn't been like this anywhere else I'd been. As I sat there, I noticed someone walking out of the ocean. A man. I was close enough to the water that I could make out his toned torso and that damn V that disappeared into his board shorts. His hair was covering his face, but he suddenly reached down, wet his hand, and combed it back with his fingers. My heart skipped a beat. Elias. Fuck. Of course. He was so damn gorgeous. He tilted his head up and I could swear his eyes met mine. My heart stopped beating entirely. I held my breath. Would he walk this way or disappear into his villa? My answer came when a man walked out and said something to him. I made the decision for him and stood and went back inside my own villa. The last thing I needed was to look for trouble right now and Prince Elias, soon to be King, would definitely be trouble.

I placed the wicker basket by the front door and turned to walk away. There was no guard here, so I assumed they were inside with Prince Elias. Just as I turned to leave, the front door opened. I braced myself, as I turned around, for Prince Elias himself, but it was Pierre I saw. He smiled as he walked out of the villa and closed the door behind him.

"They're still picking up in there."

"I can imagine. It was quite the fete."

"You didn't stay long."

"I've been feeling a bit under the weather. I don't think Mrs. Meyers' chicken pot pie is agreeing with me."

"Oh. Well, they seem to be agreeing with me." He put a hand on his stomach and raised his eyebrows. I laughed.

"Hey, I meant to ask, what will you be doing on the eve of the big masquerade ball in Versailles?"

"You mean the night all of the aristocrats will show up with their daughters and try to hand them over to the prince?"

"Yeah." I managed to smile throughout, though inside, I felt weird. Maybe the pot pie had gotten to me after all.

"I won't be working that night. Do you want to reschedule our pub date till then?"

"Oh. No. Well, I sort of wondered if you'd like to go with me to the gala. I . . . my event business is putting it on and my mother said it would be good if I took someone and I thought of you."

"I was your first choice when thinking of a date?" he asked.

"It's kind of a work date. I don't want you to think—"

"Oh." He put up a hand. "I'm fine with it being a friendly non-date."

Just as I laughed at his response, the door opened behind him and Prince Elias appeared. The man had impeccable timing. He looked cranky tonight. Again. He hadn't been very cranky when we'd been alone on the beach.

"Planning another date together?" Prince Elias asked.

"Seems that way," I said. "Do you need the time and date so you can crash again?"

"Sure. When is it?" He cocked his head as he looked at me, amusement clear in his eyes.

"The night of your gala. I guess you'll be indisposed. Don't worry, we'll fill you in on all the details the next day." I smiled.

"You're assuming I won't leave the gala and come find you."

That gave me pause. I blinked and glanced at Pierre, whose eyebrows had reached a new height, and seemed to be taken aback by his words as well. I opened my mouth a couple of times to respond, but found nothing adequate to say.

"Don't worry, Miss Adeline. I'm joking. I won't intrude on your date," Prince Elias said after a moment, though he seemed to be enjoying seeing me at a loss for words. He reached down, grabbed the basket, and began disappearing inside. "Pierre. A word, please."

"Yes, sir." Pierre glanced at me. "We'll talk soon."

"Of course."

This time, I walked away.

Friday arrived quickly and I was soon on a plane to visit Versailles with my mother and Joss. When I arrived, I parked in the designated space, where the caterers and staff left their cars, and rode the bus to the main property. My mother and Joss were already there, both looking at their phones as they waited outside the main entrance while tourists side-stepped them on their way inside. Joss spotted me first, her smile brightening her entire face as I walked over. She threw her arms around me when I reached them.

"I miss you so much."

"I miss you too." I squeezed her back, then pulled away before hugging my mother with the same vigor. "I miss both of you."

"Just come back," Joss suggested.

"Nonsense. My brother-in-law would kill me if I pulled her away this quickly," Mother said. "Besides, some fresh air would be of great use to all of us." She kept her attention on me. "Have you not been eating? How is the villa? Was everything as we left it?"

"The town seems to be just as we left it," I said. "Though I haven't really interacted much with anyone there."

"Well, you were barely there when your father and I lived there, so I don't expect you to remember much."

"Prince Elias is there."

Both my mother and Joss froze, their jaws dropping.

"And?" Joss asked.

"Tell me you haven't spoken," my mother said at the same time.

"We have spoken," I said. "And he's a jerk."

Joss smiled.

"A jerk how?" Mom frowned. "He was always extremely charming."

"I didn't say he wasn't charming. I said he was a jerk."

"Why is he there?" Joss asked.

"He goes every summer," Mom said. "He takes his entire posse and rents out every available villa and has nonstop parties." She shook her head in disgust. "Drunk people everywhere. Naked people everywhere. Sex everywhere. They take advantage of the local women. It's disgusting."

"Sounds . . . just like them." Joss laughed under her breath.

"He invited me to a party the other day."

"Tell me you didn't go," Mom said.

"Of course I went." I stifled a smile as I looked over at Joss, who was enjoying this entirely too much. "You can't say no to the prince."

"Adeline." Mom exhaled, closing her eyes briefly. "The last thing you need is another scandal. We need you back on your feet, not on your back underneath a prince who won't remember your name in two weeks."

"Mother!"

"I'm just stating a fact," she said. "When we lived there, I watched as he and his brother seduced all of the women in that town. Most of them won't even talk about it and that alone speaks volumes." She shot me a look before turning and facing the palace. "Now, let's go. We have work to do."

Joss idled behind my mother and I idled behind her as the doors to the opulent palace opened and the grandeur inside was exposed to us. I'd been here before, once when I was a girl and again as a teenager. That time, I'd come by myself. It was only a two-hour drive from the beach, and my parents were sending me away to boarding school the next day, so I decided to run away for a while and come here. I'd started exploring with a tour guide, but halfway through, I somehow ended up completely lost. That was before social media and paparazzi started hounding under-aged socialites.

I got my first glimpse of the princes that day, though I didn't tell anyone about it. It wasn't like it had been an experience. They were walking the section of the palace that had been closed off to the rest of us and were headed into the back of a car. They never looked up or saw me, and even though I was inside the palace walls, I felt like an outsider. Even from that angle, they seemed untouchable. I assumed they were on their way to the beach that day, to the villas they rented out from my family each summer, when I was sent away and they got to stay. A part of me hated my parents for doing that. A part of me knew they did it to protect me, so that I wouldn't end up like all the other girls in that small town—vying for their attention and never achieving to sustain it longer than a few nights.

"The ball takes place in the GARDENS," my mother said, cutting into my thoughts. I blinked away from the beautiful mirrors and gave her my attention. "But we're set to meet Madame Rose, who manages everything that happens on the palace premises."

"Have you already contacted the dancers?" I asked Joss. "We'll need Madame Graciela's choreography. And acrobats. Call our contact in Montreal and see how many they can send over. We'll also need fire-breathers, the ones we hired for Tamara's wedding. The band and DJ . . . "

"The palace will provide flowers and food," my mother said, cutting me off. "I believe they also have a list of bands and DJs they'd like."

"That's helpful." I didn't enjoy dealing with caterers or florists.

Most of the time they already knew who I was setting up events for and overcharged me before I stepped foot in their office. We reached a door at the end of the hall and waited after Mom knocked a couple of times. It was opened by an older woman with beautiful white hair that was swept back and pulled into a classic low bun.

"Madame Perla," Madame Rose said, upon seeing my mother, then looked at us. "Mademoiselle Joslyn, Mademoiselle Adeline. Please, come inside." She stepped back and gave us enough room to walk into her office, which was breathtaking, like the rest of the palace.

"Thank you for seeing us," I said. "We're honored to play even the smallest role in such an important event."

"I'm glad you're aware that it is a very important event," Madame Rose said. "You come highly recommended by my daughter, who attended a wedding you planned. She raved so much and since she's already married and has no use for event planners, I'm hoping this will be the next best thing."

"Whose wedding did she attend?" I asked, smiling, grateful to know that my scandal hadn't made it all the way here, and if it had, it wasn't a big deal to them.

"Danika Smirnov."

"Oh." I smiled. "That was quite a big one."

"It perfectly showcased some of what we're capable of," my mother said.

"Well, if it were up to me, we'd have elephants and camels, but the Queen is much more demur than I am, so I'm curious to know what you have planned so far."

I was a bit surprised to hear that about the queen. I didn't know much about her, but from what I'd seen in magazines when they allowed photographs to be published, the parties had been dripping in extravagance. I explained to Madame Rose what I had in mind, with the dancers and band, DJs and acrobatic shows. She listened intently, writing things down every so often.

"I expect everything to go off without a hitch." She set her pen down and looked at the three of us. "I have a full staff at your disposal. You may use them for whatever you need. If you plan on bringing any staff of your own, they'll have to go through a background check and search when they arrive."

"We can use yours," I said quickly. "The three of us will be on hand and we have two other women I like to bring to make sure everything is seamless, but aside from that, I'm happy to use yours."

"Good." She smiled as she stood up and extended her hand toward me. "I cannot wait to see what you do."

"Thank you so much." I stood and shook it.

"If you have any questions, feel free to email or call."

"I will."

Joss and I walked out of the office with my mother and Madame Rose trailing behind us.

"We're going to do a quick tour of the grounds," I heard my mother say. "And draw up a plan for you. You'll have it by the middle of the week."

"Will that give you enough time to have everything ready?" Madame Rose asked.

"Plenty of time," I said, turning around.

"You have a lot of faith in your work," Madame Rose said.

"If I don't, who will?"

With that, I walked with my mother and Joss to the gardens and we started coming up with a plan. I found myself trying to ignore the fact that it was for Prince Elias and trying to put another face to the occasion, though I couldn't under-stand why. Thankfully, the gardens were so lavish and striking that roaming around freely allowed for me to put thoughts of him in the backburner. The lawn was so well manicured. Close to two-thousand acres of greenery. It felt endless and with as beautiful as they were, I couldn't imagine there being a time they weren't being tended to. I could barely keep a plant alive for three days, let alone be in charge of this. The party would take place in one area of the gardens, and that was the area we needed to focus on, with a large circular area that was perfect for a stage and dance floors to surround it. The circle around the area was elevated, like an amphitheater. It was absolute perfection for what I had in mind.

CHAPTER ELEVEN

THE BOOKSTORE LOOKED COMPLETELY DIFFERENT AFTER LENORA and Pedro were finished with it. It looked quaint, but beautiful on the outside, with bright green grass and a sleek, white storefront that made it look like a fancy boutique store. Upstairs, the café area was adorable, though it was still missing a lot of things, including an actual coffee maker and barista. I'd have to speak to my uncle about that when he got back. Instead of spending my time stocking books, I spent it drawing up ideas for the Versailles gala. I was on my fifteenth drawing when the door of the shop opened, making the bell above it ring and giving me pause. *A customer?* It shut and opened again. And again. And a fourth time. I set down my pencil, shut my iPad, and stood up, waiting for the customers to come into view. I saw the first man dressed in all black, followed by three others, and I already knew Prince Elias was due to follow. My heart slammed in my chest as I waited.

As usual, there was no use in bracing myself. Each time I saw him, I found myself surprised. Today, he wore khaki pants and a white short-sleeve button-down that gave me a full view of his muscular arms. The top two buttons were undone and I found myself licking my lips as I stared at his neck. He had an almost golden skin tone that I knew wasn't natural, but more so from being outdoors. The brown loafers he wore tapped atop the hardwood of the bookstore as he approached, and I forced myself to look into his dark eyes. He was staring right at me, yet there was no way for me to decipher what he was thinking.

"Hey," I said, my voice more excited than I intended. "Looking for a book?"

"Just here to browse." He walked to the first aisle, leaving a bookshelf between us, though I could still see the top of his head, and when he glanced up, his eyes. "You weren't here yesterday."

"No. I trust Mrs. Meyers delivered your basket nicely though."

"She did okay."

"Just okay?" I raised an eyebrow.

"Where were you?"

"Out of town."

"Will you be delivering it tonight?"

"The basket?" I frowned. "Yeah. I mean, I'm back. Why?"

"I like to know who's delivering my things."

"Okay. Your security knew. I informed Pierre that Mrs. Meyers would be delivering it." My confusion was clear in my voice. "Is there anything in particular that you're looking for?"

"What are you working on?" He ignored my question and walked around the bookshelf and over to me, eyeing the iPad in front of me.

"It's a work in progress. It's bad luck for you to see it in this stage."

"Bad luck for who?"

"In this case, both of us."

"Both of us?" He frowned.

"It's for an event I'm planning."

"What event?"

I picked up the digital pencil. "Your gala."

"You're planning the gala?" His eyebrows shot up. "How did that happen?"

"Madame Rose contacted my company and asked us to plan it."

"Did she now." His gaze dropped to the iPad again. "May I see?"

"I . . . I don't really like to show my sketches to anyone before they're ready."

"Even if it's an event for me?"

"They're extremely rough sketches." I pushed the button and entered my passcode quickly.

"The ball is in a week. I don't think you have time for extremely rough sketches." He watched me for a long moment. "I thought you had a date that night."

"I do."

"Will it be before or after the gala?"

"I'm actually taking him."

"A work date then."

"Sort of." I clicked on the iPad and swiped to the beginning of the sketches. "Maybe it would be unfair for me to take him there."

"I'd say." He shrugged a shoulder. "But I haven't been on many dates, so I don't know if I should be giving you advice on the matter."

"You haven't been on many dates?" I met his gaze.

"I haven't." His expression was completely serious, but his eyes twinkled as he looked at me. "Is that so hard to believe?"

"Yes."

"Have you been on many dates?"

"Define many."

"I've been on five," he said. "That's not very many."

"Five?" I balked, trying not to laugh. "You're so full of it."

"I'm being completely serious. Why don't you believe me?"

"Because you're Prince Elias, future king of France, most eligible bachelor in the world. People say you're handsome and charismatic and I just can't imagine you would have only been on five dates."

"People say?" His mouth twitched. "What do you say?"

"I definitely think you're handsome."

"Not charismatic?" He was fighting a smile.

"I mean . . . not to me." I bit my lip. "But maybe to others?"

"Not to you?" He frowned slowly, as if thinking about all of our past encounters. "I guess I haven't really been very kind to you lately."

"Not really, but it's okay."

"That should never be okay."

"Well, you said it, not me."

"I'm sorry." He sighed heavily. "I've had a lot on my mind."

"Thanks." I felt myself smile at his apology and positioned the iPad so that he could see it. "They're a very rough draft."

"This is nice." He turned his face to read the notes on the side. He raised an eyebrow. "Acrobatics? If this is a preview for a potential engagement, I can't even imagine what the wedding will be like."

"Me either." I laughed. "The theme is a seventeen-hundreds

masquerade, since you royals have a thing for masquerades and ballgowns."

"Us royals." He was fighting a smile. "I guess we do."

"I can't believe you've only been on five dates." I looked at him again. He was insanely gorgeous. Not that dates had anything to do with how many women he'd had sex with, but still. "How old are you?"

"Twenty-eight."

"You need to go on more dates, Prince Elias."

"Let me take you on one."

I blinked. "Me?"

"Why is that so hard to believe?" He chuckled.

"Why would you want to take me on a date?"

"Not for appearances."

"Of course not for appearances." I scoffed. I wasn't an aristocrat or a socialite or the Princess of Austria.

"Believe it or not, I mean that as a compliment."

"Okay." I glanced away, to the stack of books I was supposed to shelve by the end of the day. Why was I even entertaining this date idea? A date with a prince was definitely not the way to go unnoticed. I was just barely catching my footing.

"What do you like to do on a date?" he asked, beckoning my attention.

"I don't think we should go on a date."

"Why not?"

"A date with a prince is not on my schedule for this month," I said. "I came here to get away from the spotlight."

"Why were you in the spotlight?" He watched me closely.

"How does anyone end up in the spotlight?" I shrugged. "Poor decisions. They definitely weren't reporting on me feeding the hungry."

"Doesn't your father own the tabloids?"

"No." I diverted my eyes again. "He doesn't *own* the tabloids, he's just friends with some of the owners, but even he can't get me out of this predicament. They need things to report on and unfortunately, I was it this time."

"I can't stand them. If my father stands up and speaks in front of a crowd the only thing they report on is his insufferable tone. God forbid they talk about all the good things he's done."

I bit my tongue. The king did have an insufferable tone and a superiority complex that made the rest of us work hard not to cower at. I wasn't about to tell Prince Elias that, though. I looked at him again.

"When was the last time you went on a date?" he asked suddenly.

"It's been a while." I caught myself quickly. "Pierre aside, I mean. That was a real date until you interrupted us."

"Did that one end with a kiss?"

"No."

"Then it wasn't a real date."

"Says the man who's only gone on five and they've all been for pretenses."

"Says the man who's going to take you on one and make sure it's real."

"Oh." I swallowed as butterflies flapped deep in my belly. I shook my head. I shouldn't be entertaining this. "It doesn't change the fact that we shouldn't be seen together."

"Because your father hates me."

"No. Because I don't need more attention in my life right now. If I'm seen with you, it'll look bad for you as well. People will say you were trying to plot against your father or something."

He scoffed. "Who says I'm not?"

My eyes widened. "That's . . . "

"I know what it is. In the olden days, I would've been physically hanged. Nowadays we have death by tabloid rumors."

"And social media," I added. His eyes twinkled. It felt like a smile, though his lips didn't move. I felt mine pull up nonetheless and my curiosity got the best of me. "What kind of things do you want your father to do differently?"

"I'll tell you on our date," he said. "We can sit on my balcony, have dinner, and enjoy the view of the ocean."

"Okay," I said after a moment. "One date."

"Seven thirty?"

"That works for me."

A smile tugged at his lips. "I'll see you later, Adeline."

CHAPTER TWELVE

I WASN'T SURE HOW TO DRESS ON A DATE WITH A PRINCE AND LUCKY for me and the situation, I didn't have the closet of the Princess of Austria or personal shoppers at my disposal, so I opted for a black maxi dress and sandals with a gold leaf over each foot. There was a knock on my door at seven twenty-five, when I was just finishing my eyeliner. I set everything down, looked at myself once more to make sure I was presentable and once I decided I was, I made my way to the door. Surely, he hadn't sent Pierre to pick me up, right? That thought made me slow down as I walked over to open it. What if he had sent him? Would things be awkward?

It was one date.

One date with Elias and like he pointed out, my night with Pierre wasn't exactly a date. *Because the prince hadn't let it become one.* I shook the thought away and opened the door, blinking when I saw the prince standing before me looking handsome as ever, in jeans, a simple black T-shirt, and black loafers.

"You look beautiful," he said.

"Thank you." My breath caught.

He'd never called me that before, or said a compliment to me that felt like a compliment. Not since that night. I tried not to think about it. That was five years ago and this was now. This was one date. One date. I needed to make it clear to myself that nothing that happened tonight would happen again. The man was about to become engaged to someone and I'd never see him again.

"Are you ready?" he asked.

"I think so." I smiled, grabbing my keys and walking out behind him. I shut my door, locked it, and turned to him. "I'm surprised you didn't send someone to pick me up."

"That wouldn't be a date." His gaze slid to mine. "I'm trying to make a good first impression here."

"You made a good first impression." I bit my lip and looked away.

"Did I?" I could hear the smile in his voice, and even though I had no intention of confirming it, I really wanted to know if he remembered our night together or if he was talking about when I went over there with Etienne. When we reached his villa, he walked to the back and let me go ahead of him up the stairs. "Tell me about this scandal you're involved in."

"You looked me up." My face flamed.

"Of course I did."

When we reached the top floor balcony, I froze, taking it all in. There were little lights hanging from the back door to the columns of the balcony and a table with white linen and pink roses in the center. There were two place settings in front of two chairs sitting side by side that faced the ocean. Nearby, there was an ice bucket with champagne and a butler wearing white gloves, with a white napkin draped over his arm.

"Wow," I said.

"Come on." He chuckled beside me, grabbing my hand in his and walking me toward the table. He let go of my hand to pull a chair out for me, and I thanked him as I took a seat. He sat beside me.

"Do you get this creative for all of your dates?"

"Not once."

I smiled, looking at him. "I almost believe you."

"You should believe me. I'm not much of a liar." He tilted his head. "Well, most of the time, I'm not much of a liar."

"Good to know." I laughed. The butler came over and served us champagne in flutes and poured waters before disappearing into the house.

"Cheers to a good first date." Elias lifted a flute as I lifted mine and we clinked and drank.

"It's one date," I said, setting the flute down.

"You already cheered to it being a first date." He set his down as well. "Which means, there may be more."

"You do realize I'm planning your engagement gala, right?"

"It's just a gala like every other gala my mother has been putting on since I was born. They're all the same."

"Meaning there is always a herd of women who attend in hopes to catch your attention and be married off to you?"

"Exactly."

"Sounds . . . fun?"

"Not fun." He smiled. "I'd bet good money half of them would hate being married to me, but can't say otherwise."

"I'd bet otherwise."

"Even knowing I'm an asshole?" He raised his glass and an eyebrow.

"Even knowing that." I raised my own, with a shrug. "You're a prince. Everyone dreams of being a princess."

"Even you?"

"I used to." I took a gulp of the champagne. "Not so much anymore."

"Because of me?"

"Nah." I laughed lightly. "I think I just outgrew the fantasy."

"Hm."

"What about the Princess of Austria?" I asked suddenly.

"What about her?"

"You've never been on a date with her?"

"For appearances. Yes."

"For appearances?" My lips pursed. "How many dates have you been on that weren't for appearances?"

"One."

"One?" I repeated, my jaw dropping.

"It's why I like to come here in the summers. It's an escape from the appearances and the constant reminder that everything I do is for The Crown."

"So your one date that wasn't for pretenses was here?" Something akin to jealousy sprouted inside of me.

"That's right." His lips merely moved, but his eyes were laughing.

"Interesting." I took another sip of champagne and tore my gaze from his to look back at the ocean.

"Addie."

I met his gaze again.

"This is the date."

"The one date?"

He nodded.

"Oh." My heart skipped, though I still wasn't sure why it was important to me.

"Tell me about the scandal."

"There's not much to tell if you already looked it up and saw for yourself." I looked at the ocean again. It was dark, so it wasn't like I could actually see it, but I was thankful for its waves trying to drown out my shame. "Did you watch the video?"

"Why the fuck would I do that?"

That made me look at him quickly. "Curiosity. Everyone else does."

"I don't want to see you having sex with another man." His jaw was clenched as he spoke. "I'm going to make it go away."

"You can't." I smiled sadly. "Thank you for the offer though."

"I think you're underestimating my power."

"I think you're overestimating it and forgetting what year we're in."

"If you say so." He picked up his champagne again and got comfortable in his seat, leaning back a bit as he draped an arm over the side and stretching his legs out. He looked like a model without even trying.

"You know, saying things like that aren't going to get you points with me. I personally don't like the idea of one person having so much power." I picked up my own glass and sipped, shifting my body toward his as I crossed one leg over the other and got comfortable as well.

"Which is why you moved to London, where the mon-archs are just there for pretenses."

"They do a lot of good."

He shrugged, but the smile on his face told me he was biting his tongue. He looked sexy like that. When he looked away, to the ocean in front of us, I continued watching him.

"What's the best part of being a prince?" I asked after a moment.

"The best part or the part I like most?"

"Is there a difference?"

"I *like* helping people. I *like* being able to stand behind a cause and know that others will follow." He glanced at me, lowering his glass. "The best part is the power."

"But it's not the part you enjoy most."

"With power comes responsibility."

"Okay, Spider-Man."

"It's true though." He chuckled before getting serious again. "A lot of people, including your father, don't like how much power the Crown yields. They don't like how traditional my family is. They want us to become a commonwealth country. They want my father to relinquish his power and he won't, which means, I can't. By staying traditional and true to what the Crown means to our family, we're able to make a difference in the country, whether or not you see it. With that responsibility comes duty, one being that I must marry before or soon after I'm coronated king." He shrugged. "It's not something I agree with, but who am I to change thousands of years of history?"

"The future king." I waited a moment for him to respond. When he didn't, I added, "That's who you are. You can change everything once you become king."

"And risk losing all of my allies?"

"What do you need allies for? We're not at war."

"Not today, but what about tomorrow? We don't know

what the future holds. The reason people don't invade or try to take things from us isn't because they can't, but out of respect for the Crown."

"I disagree." I set my glass down.

Before he could respond, the butler came back with a helper carrying two trays they set in front of us and uncovered to show us a surf and turf dinner with fingerling potatoes on the side. They took the champagne bottle and set it in the ice and replaced our flutes with wine glasses, pouring red wine and setting it where the champagne had been. Everything was done efficiently, with a blink-and-you'll-miss-it swiftness. They were gone with a "bon appétit" as quickly as they arrived. I was still processing what had just happened when Elias spoke again.

"You disagree," he said, picking up his silverware and setting a napkin on his lap as soon as they closed the door. I did the same. "Explain."

"I don't think it's like the old days, where people used to invade and conquer land for the hell of it."

"It's been happening in the Middle East for a long time now."

"Well, yeah, but that's different. That wouldn't happen here."

"Why not?"

"It just wouldn't."

"Because we feel safe," he said. "Because the Crown has always been there. To dismantle that would cause chaos."

I thought about that for a moment as we ate in silence. Maybe it would. I hadn't considered that a lot of the problems going on in other countries may be because of the dismantling of organized government the way they once knew it. On the other hand, maybe the chaos had to happen in order for change to arise.

"Change is the only constant." I set my fork and knife down and wiped my mouth before taking a sip of the wine in front of me. "Maybe that's why people riot until governments are replaced and changed."

"And then riot more once they get what they wanted," he said. "We're never going to be satisfied."

"Maybe so, but that's not a bad thing. If you're satisfied with the way things are day in and day out, you might as well be dead. Isn't the point to work for more? To try to be better people?"

"The point of what? Life? Are we talking about life now? Because the topic of life and why we're here is different from whether or not the monarchy should stand."

"How is it different? You of all people should argue that it's the same thing. That your reason for existing is to be the king of France and rule over a nation that bows to your bidding."

"You've never bowed for me." He sipped his wine and leaned back in his seat again. "What am I to do with you?"

"Behead me." I shrugged. "I don't know. What do you do with people who don't bow to you?"

"It would be a shame to behead you." His gaze dragged over me lazily. "I'd find other ways to torture you."

"Like what?" My grip tightened on the stem of the glass. "I don't know that I'm cut out for torture."

"Torture can be delicious." He licked his lips after taking another sip of wine and when his eyes sparkled, I was sure he knew he was torturing me as he spoke.

"What are your marriage requirements?" I asked

suddenly, because I needed to remind myself I couldn't entertain this thing, whatever it was.

We both continued eating again, and when I set down my utensils this time, I was finished for good. He refilled our wine glasses before speaking.

"Marriage requirements," he said, as if remembering my question and the fact that he had an impending marriage. "I don't have any."

"You must have some. I mean, we all have requirements when it comes to a partner, and a life-long partner has to be even more daunting."

"What are your requirements?"

"He has to be kind, funny, smart, well-informed with current events, give me at least one compliment a day, good in bed, have a nice smile, treat people with respect—and by people, I mean waiters and anyone we encounter in the street—he can't be cheap, I'm okay with frugal or men who don't splurge all the time but I don't like cheap. I also have a thing for tall men with dark hair and a nice jawline, but that's just me being picky. At the end of the day, I just want to be valued and loved." I shrugged. "That's it."

"You've really thought this through." His brows rose. He watched me for a second before turning back to the ocean and sipping his wine. "Let's go down to the beach. Part two of the date," he said with a wink as he stood, picked up the bottle of wine, and waited for me to follow.

I was sure I'd scared him away, but it didn't matter. The prince wasn't mine to keep. Scaring him away wasn't a deal-breaker. Thinking of it that way, it felt kind of freeing, and a little sad, but I wouldn't focus on that. I couldn't have him, and that was final. The sooner I accepted that, the better it would be.

But then, he grabbed my hand and held it in his as we walked together down the stairs and onto the sand, and I couldn't help the butterflies that came alive in my stomach. A large covered area came into view and it took me a moment to understand what I was seeing. It was as if they'd covered a part of the sand with a king-sized blanket and placed candles all around it. Two of his security guards stood on either side of it.

"You really thought of everything."

"It's my first real date, remember?" He shot me a half-smile that made a warm sensation travel through me.

The security guys walked toward us as we reached the blanket. One of them was Pierre. I felt a twinge of panic, riddled with guilt, as our eyes met, but he seemed unfazed by the entire thing and smiled widely at me as if he knew this would happen. It made the guilt inside my chest expand. Elias said nothing. He simply nodded at them as we passed and let go of my hand once we kicked off our shoes and settled over the plush blanket. I wiggled my toes over it as I sat down. He sat beside me, close enough that our sides were touching, and poured us both another glass of wine. I'd had enough that I was feeling it for sure, my brain hazy, thoughts swaying, the warmth in my veins comforting. I felt great. Better than great.

"I guess you really haven't thought about it at all," I said, after a moment. "Marriage, I mean. Does that mean you're going to let your mother pick a bride for you?"

"If it comes to that." He glanced at me. His face was incredibly close to mine. "I don't expect you to understand. You have the freedom to do what you want. You choose who you go on dates with, who you're surrounded by, who you marry. I grew up with the world at my fingertips but no freedom to make my own choices. Everything from what I wore to who I became friends with was meticulously planned out for me. Even if I was interested in a woman, she had to be on the list of approval." He shot me a pointed look. "All of the women who surround me, with the exception of my sister, want me because I'm the future king, because they see power, and sure, maybe they find me attractive, but the power is what attracts them most."

"That's really sad," I whispered. "I've never really thought about it like that."

"Most people don't. They see us in our ivory castles and think we live wonderfully perfect lives."

"Would you give it up?"

"No." He scoffed, shaking his head and looking at the ocean. "I wouldn't know what to do if I gave it up. I was groomed for this role."

"What would you change?"

"This is starting to sound like an interview." He smiled as he met my gaze.

"A first date is an interview." I raised an eyebrow. "Not that I expect you to know that."

"Ah. In that case, I'll need to ask more questions."

"After you answer that one." I smiled. He chuckled. I pushed him softly with the side of my right arm. "Come on, you promised you would and a good king keeps his promises."

"A good king." He laughed again, taking another sip of wine. "Okay. I would work with the cabinet and take steps to create a Parliament and make this a commonwealth country."

My jaw dropped. "You would?"

"I want to."

"Your father would not be pleased with that."

"He'll be dead." He paused as if processing those words. "But no, he wouldn't like that."

"It goes against tradition."

"My siblings and I aren't much for tradition. My sister, Pilar, probably won't marry the suitor my parents picked out for her, despite the fact that they've technically been engaged for two years. She sees him like a brother. My brother, Aramis, does anything he can to act out. I think he thinks his actions will break the palace apart from the inside." He shrugged. "So, I need to be the one to make changes so that our children and their children won't grow to hate everything our ancestors worked so hard to build. I have the power to change history."

"You don't have to be a king to change history."

"No, I suppose not." He smiled. "You can be a queen."

"I meant, you can be a regular person." I pushed him playfully again with my shoulder. "My father is a commoner, and he's changed a lot already."

"He has. As much as I disagree with the way he's gone about it, I can't argue that."

"Have you met him?"

"Your father?" he asked. When I nodded, he lowered his wine glass and exhaled. "Once. He was nice enough." He glanced at me. "And then he went on national television and said I wasn't fit to be king because I was too much of a playboy."

"Oh, God. I'm sorry." I closed my eyes and turned my face toward the ocean, wishing the tide would rise and take me with it.

I couldn't even defend my father when it came to that. He was the kind of man who shook hands with a boyfriend of mine, came up with twenty reasons why he was no good for me, and said it to his face. I couldn't even imagine what he'd say about the prince if I ever took him home—not that I would. Not that I could.

"You're not responsible for your father's actions," Elias said beside me. My eyes popped open and I turned my face toward him again. He had a serious expression on his all-too-perfect face. "People judge me for everything my father says and does and that's fine, I can't convince them otherwise, but I've learned to accept that we're different people and I'm not responsible for any of those things."

"I have a feeling you're going to make a great king, Prince Elias."

"Does that mean you'll stick around to find out?" He inched closer, his wine-infused breath tickling over mine.

"I don't think I can." My heart skipped, at odds with the words I'd spoken.

"Why not?" He moved closer still, the tip of his nose brushing against mine.

"Because then I'd have to witness everything that comes along with you being king."

"Like what?"

"Like you courting women and marrying a princess and having children with her," I whispered.

"Are you supposed to show all your cards on the first date?" he asked, his tone soft, his mouth on the edge of my lips. He kissed me there.

"No." I shivered. "But it's our only date, so I figured I should say what's on my mind."

"You should." He kissed the other side of my mouth. "I like that you're honest with me."

"Are you going to kiss me now? Because I don't think my heart can take any more of this teasing."

He chuckled against my lips, but instead of making a retort to my statement, he pressed his lips against mine. My eyes slammed shut. My body acted on its own accord, my arms wrapping around his neck as his hands held me by the ribs, his thumbs just underneath my breasts. Breathing was a struggle. My brain wouldn't shut off, wouldn't stop conjuring things to do with him on the only night I had him, but I couldn't seem to do anything but kiss him back. Fire raced through my veins as our tongues met. His grip tightened. My nails dug into his shoulder blades as I lifted a leg over him and straddled him, deepening the kiss. It was unlike me, but I didn't care. I couldn't seem to get a grip and control everything that was happening inside of my body. I felt like I was floating, the butterflies in my stomach lifting me in weightless abandon. Elias groaned against my mouth, his chest heaving against mine as we both came up for air for just a moment, gazing at each other through hazy eyes before our mouths met again, wilder this time.

I didn't even hear anyone approach us, but the sound of a man clearing his throat made both Elias and I jump back and pull away. I stayed on his lap, frozen, as we both glanced up to see Pierre hovering over us.

"I'm sorry to interrupt," he said. "The Princess of Austria is here."

"She's here?" Elias sounded taken aback.

"We asked her to wait in the foyer so she wouldn't . . . interrupt," Pierre said.

"Thank you, Pierre. I'll be there shortly." Elias exhaled heavily, pressing his forehead against mine as Pierre walked away.

"I guess this is the end of our date."

"I don't want it to be." He pulled away slightly and met my eyes. "I didn't ask her to come."

"It's fine." I shook my head, hating the empty feeling in

the pit of my stomach as I lifted myself off his lap and stood, walking to the edge of the blanket and plucking my sandals off the sand. "I wasn't expecting this to last all night or anything."

"I swear I didn't know she'd just show up," he repeated, as if that would make it better.

"You don't owe me an explanation, Elias. It was one date and it ended with a kiss. That's a win-win in my book." I smiled for his benefit, though my lips barely moved. I began walking away, toward the stairs that led to my villa. "Thank you for the lovely evening. I'll see you around."

When I reached the bottom of the steps, I glanced over my shoulder and saw him still sitting on the blanket, with his head bowed over his bent knees. It was an image that didn't correspond to his persona, not the one he showed the public, anyway. One evening with him, and I already knew there was a lot more to the future king than met the eye, but I couldn't dwell on that. I had to keep tonight as a fond memory—that time I went on a date with the future king of France, before he got married, before he had children, before he ruled.

CHAPTER THIRTEEN

I'D SPENT MY ENTIRE WEEK FOCUSED ON THE GALA THAT WAS HAPPENING this upcoming weekend. After driving back and forth to Versailles on Monday and Tuesday, I decided to book a hotel and stay nearby for the week. There was no use going back to the villa when I was on the phone with all of the entertainment companies I had lined up, the costume company, the caterers, and Madame Rose. My mother and Joss were helping, but they also had a wedding in Paris to focus on, so I had to do the majority of the work. Because of this, I'd begged my uncle to let me hire a few teenagers for the bookstore and gave the basket task to Mrs. Meyers for the week. I hadn't heard from or seen Elias since our date on Saturday, not that I'd expected to. He didn't have my phone number and I hadn't really been in the villa long enough for him to contact me. It was for the best. I'd been so busy that I barely had time to think about him much, except at night when I lay in bed and replayed every single part of our date. At first, the memories made me smile. Then, I wound up getting upset at the Princess of Austria. I'd looked her up, of course. She was pretty. Blonde, blue eyes, warm smile.

I didn't like her.

As far as I was concerned, she was a cockblocker and a pest who arrived at the prince's villa unannounced and uninvited and ruined our date. Those were all things I should have been grateful for. If things had gone further, if I'd spent the night with him, I would have regretted it. I'd had one date with him and I already felt myself unraveling. I couldn't afford to be unraveled. I was in no state to fall in love with a prince, let alone one who would be king. No one ever was, but surely the Princess of Austria could bear it more than I could. At least she had a shot at being his, and planning this party was the only proof I needed of that. Every single detail was set to cater to the princesses and duchesses that were slated to be there on Saturday night. From the way they made their grand entrance, to the way they greeted the prince. They'd all be staying in the on-site cottages of the palace, which had been inhabited by those closest to the royal family back in the old days but had since been restored and kept for events like these. There were twenty-five cottages in total, counting the one I was currently staying in, which was right beside the one Prince Elias and his brother Aramis would be staying in this weekend. Princess Pilar, their sister, had her own cottage on the other side of theirs, which was where my assistant, Joss, had been invited to stay.

My phone rang as I was getting ready for bed, and I answered upon seeing Etienne's face on the screen.

"I assume you've been busy," he said by way of greeting.

"You have no idea." I sighed. "What's up?"

"What's up is that you have a certain monarch hunting you down."

"Who?" I perked up, my heart pounding in anticipation. Elias couldn't have asked about me, could he?

"I think you know who." I could tell Etienne wasn't smiling the way he normally would when he teased me about a man.

"What'd he say?"

"He wanted to know where you were and asked for your phone number. I told him that you're an extremely busy woman and I couldn't give him your phone number without asking permission first. I also told him it was a bad idea to call you."

"You told him that?" My voice was small. I sank into the couch bench at the foot of my bed. "What'd he say?"

"He hung up on me."

"Oh."

"It's not a good idea, Addie."

"I know."

"Did you sleep with him again?"

"No." I bit my lip. "We only went on one date and it ended early."

"You're planning his engagement party. You do know that, right?" Etienne asked firmly. "They will announce his engagement within the week and you'll be left for nothing. You had a scandal that flipped your world upside down and you ran for the hills. What do you think a scandal with a prince would do to you?"

"It would ruin me." My eyes slammed shut. "I like him. I know I shouldn't for a billion reasons, but I can't help that I really like him."

"You can like him all you want, but it doesn't change the reality of your situation. He'll never marry you. He's a traditionalist. And I know I sound like a total asshole right now, but you need to hear this."

"I know," I whispered. I opened my eyes. "Going on a date was stupid."

"Everyone who gets close to him even for a moment is enchanted. I've been friends with them for a long time and I understand the appeal. I also don't want my best friend to get hurt by one of them. Promise you'll stay away from him."

"I'm planning a gala in his name. I'm not sure I can stay away from him."

"You know what I mean. Keep things professional and as soon as this is all finished, move out of the villa and back home to London. You don't need this right now."

"Okay," I said, because I wanted to appease him.

I needed at least one more week in the villa to square away things for my uncle. I couldn't just whoosh in, make all those changes to his bookshop, and then leave him high and dry. I did need to get out of there soon though.

"Okay. I can't make the gala this weekend. I have to go home to visit Mom, but Mira will be there to keep an eye out for you. I know it will be fantastic and I can't wait to hear all about it."

"Thanks. We'll talk soon."

"Good night, Addie."

"Good night." I hung up and stood to set my phone to charge before climbing into bed.

I hated that Etienne was right about all of that. It seemed like everyone knew their reputation, especially in Normandy, where they vacationed every summer and spent their days frolicking and partying and bedding every willing local, but hearing it from Etienne was different. It turned gossip to truth.

CHAPTER FOURTEEN

"ARE YOU SURE THIS ISN'T GOING TO BE WEIRD FOR YOU?" I ASKED Pierre for the third time since he'd arrived.

I'd asked him to be my date to this, but thought for sure he wouldn't show after he witnessed my date with Elias.

"Why would it be weird?" Pierre smiled. "Because you went on a date with another man and I had to stand there and watch the entire thing?"

"Yes." I felt my entire body heat with embarrassment.

"Hey, I wasn't offended." He squeezed my arm lightly, still smiling that warm smile of his that reached his pale blue eyes. "You're allowed to date whomever you want, whenever you want."

"I feel like I should apologize."

"You shouldn't." Pierre dropped his arm and looked at me. "Don't apologize. We're friends and that's why I'm here tonight. I'll help with whatever you need."

"Thank you." I smiled for a second and gave him a once-over. He looked like he belonged in King Louis XIV's court. "All you're missing is a fluffy white wig."

"Thankfully they're not required." He laughed, shaking

the mask he was holding. "Otherwise, we wouldn't be able to put these on."

"You're totally right. In fact, I don't know how I'll manage to put this one on over this hairdo." I reached over the table and wiggled my own mask for him to see.

"I'm jealous that yours has feathers."

"We can swap if you'd like."

"I think I'd rather not." He smiled wide and looked at my entire outfit. "You look like you absolutely belong in the seventeen-hundreds."

"I don't know how those women managed to breathe."

I'd been wearing the dress for over an hour now, but it didn't feel any more comfortable than it had when the women who helped me dress tightened the laces of the bodice for me when I first put it on. I would have said it accentuated my small waist and full hips, but I couldn't imagine anyone putting this on and not automatically having an hourglass figure. As much as I thought I would love to always dress to the nines the way they did back in the old days, I was sure I would have never had the experience. Firstly, because I would have been some kind of housemaid back in those times and secondly, because I would have rebelled and dressed like a man just to get out of feeling like my insides were smooshed.

"I guess they believed in beauty over everything," Pierre said. "So, where do you need my help?"

"Are you sure you want to help? You can totally just join the party. I have enough hands on everything that I just have to idle around and make sure nothing crazy happens, but I should be free an hour before it ends."

"In that case, I guess I'll come back here and look for you at ten? Maybe we can grab a drink afterward?"

"Yes." I smiled. "In the meantime, enjoy yourself!"

As I watched him leave, I felt someone come up beside me and turned to see my mother standing there, wearing a similar dress to mine. We were all wearing similar dresses tonight. Mine was pale blue with ivory lace accents—the bodice, the sleeves, the skirt. Underneath the skirt, I had what looked and felt like a back pillow tied around myself and set on the small of my back to create an exaggerated bubble effect on my butt and make the skirt fuller.

"I can't breathe in this," my mother said beside me.

"Welcome to the club." I looked at her gold and ivory gown. "You look great though."

"Thank you, so do you." She looked around. "Where's Joslyn?"

"I thought she was with you."

"Nope."

"Hm." I glanced around the large tented area. "I'm going to make sure the stage is ready for the performers. I want them to start as the guests are arriving. Please make sure the flowers are correct and that the people are already pouring drinks through the ice sculptures."

I walked out of the tent and headed in the direction of the stage. The gardens were enormous. We had two tents set up with food and drinks in the four corners of the premises in hopes to discourage people from venturing off on their own. The pathway back to the cottages were lit up as well as the back of the palace. Even still, there were a few dark areas. I tried to block those dark crevices to keep people from falling into the fountains and keep them away from the woods that surrounded the gardens. Someone could easily get lost out here and I did not want to be responsible for anything going wrong tonight.

As it was, it was the first event in months that my company put together and I showed up to. We were far away from London gossip, but I wouldn't be the least surprised if Thomas Evans was in attendance tonight. Still, the thought of seeing my ex-boyfriend didn't compare to the nerves I felt at seeing Prince Elias again. I needed to keep my wits about me and remember what this party was for. It was a showcase of brides for him and after tonight, if everything went without a hitch, I'd be remembered as the person who planned the event where the future king and queen met. That was who I needed to be remembered for, despite the uneasy feeling inside my stomach every time I thought about it.

CHAPTER FIFTEEN

"**I** FEEL LIKE I'M GOING TO THROW UP."

My head whipped to the person beside me. She was wearing a mask, the way all of us were, but hers had purple feathers, which meant she must have been Princess Pilar: Prince Elias's youngest sibling. My mother, Joss, Madame Rose, and I agreed that the four of them—the Queen, Prince Elias, Prince Aramis, and Princess Pilar—would wear something purple on their masks to tell them apart from the rest of the crowd. Of course, their crowns and excessive jewels already did the trick in that regard, but it was an easy way for us to make the distinction in case anything happened and also for security, in case either of the princes or the princess decided to run off during the party without anyone in tow. I watched in horror as Princess Pilar placed a hand on her stomach and another over her mouth. We were standing directly over the food. If she threw up here . . . oh God. I grabbed her arm and yanked her away from the food and out of the tent, rushing over to the side of the hedges. Then, she bent over and started heaving. I reacted quickly, reaching out and holding her hair out of the way and making sure the small crown on her head didn't fall off. It was probably worth more than my life.

"Thank you," she whispered, yanking the mask over her head and holding it against the skirt of her dress. "I don't think I got dirty."

"Was it something you ate? Drank?" I asked. This was another reason I was glad we had nothing to do with the food or drinks.

"Drank." She coughed as she stood. I let go of her hair as she stepped closer to me. "I am so sorry."

"You don't have to apologize." I smiled. "It happens."

"My mother is going to kill me." She covered her face with one hand, bringing the mask back up and patted the crown on her head with the other. Even under the circumstances, she was beautiful. A beautiful Spanish princess, with long dark hair, dark almond-shaped eyes, and creamy white skin. She looked just like her mother. "Everyone told me to eat and I didn't listen and then I got here and the music was so good and the dancers and the acrobats and I just kept drinking and drinking." She groaned, lowering her hands. "I'm sorry."

"Stop apologizing. Let me get you to the toilets so you can clean up a bit." I started walking and she fell into step with me.

"My family is definitely not going to let me go on holiday with my friends after this," she said. "I never do anything and the one night I'm feeling rebellious and have three drinks this happens."

"You can't drink on an empty stomach. It's a lesson all of us have to learn." I waved at the security guarding the building with the closest restrooms and opened the door. When we got inside, I immediately looked for the basket I'd asked all of the toilets be stocked with—mints, gum, mouthwash, hair ties, brushes, aspirin, and oil towelettes.

"How'd you know this was in here?" Pilar asked beside me. I looked at her through the mirror in front of us and realized I was still wearing my mask. I pulled it from my face and set it aside, turning to face her.

"I planned the party."

"You're Adeline from Pirouette!"

"I'm Adeline." I smiled at the enthusiasm in her voice.

"Oh, this is even more embarrassing." She closed her eyes and threw her head back. "I love your events."

I laughed. "Trust me, it's not embarrassing. I haven't even stepped foot at one of my events in months."

"Because of the scandal?" She shot me a sympathetic look when I nodded. "All of my friends have had a scandal. My brothers are the kings of scandals. I don't think it's as big a deal as you think it is."

"Everyone says that, but it doesn't make it any easier." I shrugged and reached into the basket, picking up the mouthwash and handing it to her. She took it and opened it, reaching for a cup and rinsing her mouth.

"Is there anything in that basket that cures looking like absolute shit at the party of the year?"

"You look fine. Besides, we're wearing masks."

"Very true." She smiled as she straightened and put the mouthwash back into the basket. "You really thought of everything."

"I try."

"I went to Danika's wedding and by the end of the third song, I thought my feet were going to fall off, and then they announced that under the tables they'd provided flats. I wanted to make out with whoever came up with that idea. I heard it was you."

"It was. I hate it when my feet hurt at a party but I really hate taking my shoes off, so I figured, why not provide a solution?"

"It was brilliant. And then Erika Max's twenty-first birthday on the yacht? Oh my God. To die for," she boasted. "And Renee's engagement? Amazing. I can't even wait to see how the wedding will turn out."

"I'm sure it'll be beautiful." I smiled sadly. "They didn't ask me to do it."

"Not because of the scandal?" Pilar gasped.

"I lost a lot of clients." I shrugged. "It was my fault."

"I bet Thomas didn't lose anything," she said, frowning.

"It's a man's world."

"Don't I know it." Her frown deepened. "This entire party is proof of that. I'm so annoyed with it all. All of my friends are here, throwing themselves at my brothers as if they didn't grow up acting like they were like older brothers to them too. It's gross and incestuous."

"I'm sure there's some real incest somewhere in your bloodline."

"That's disturbing," she said, but laughed. "My mother actually says that to my father. It always gets a rise out of him."

"He wasn't able to come?"

"He made the trip, but not the party. He's exhausted." Her smile turned sad. "He's not doing well. I know people want me to lie and say he's fine, but he's not and I'm tired of lying."

"I won't tell anyone." I put the basket back where it was and set the mask on my face. "Tonight, you're just a girl who wants to have fun. I'm sure you have at least one friend who's not vying for your brothers' attention." We started walking outside. I looked at her. "What about Joss?"

"Joss." She laughed. "She's probably trying not to kill Aramis right now. She can't stand him and she's too stupid to see he's been in love with her for like ever."

"Aramis? In love? With Joss?" Each word that left my mouth sounded more incredulous than the last. "She's never talked to me about him."

"Because she truly doesn't like him." Pilar smiled. "She's a good friend."

If being a good friend meant not going after one of her brothers, I definitely wouldn't tell Pilar about Elias and me. Not that there was anything to tell. We reached the Ballroom Grove again and I was glad to see the DJ had taken center stage and everyone was dancing. It looked hilariously out of place—the DJ playing this music with everyone wearing these gowns. It was a complete mindfuck. If any of the past kings would have climbed out of their graves and stumbled upon this scene, they would have been highly confused.

"And to think, someone in this garden will marry my brother in a couple of months."

"A couple of months?" My voice was nearly a shrill, though I tried hard to play it cool.

Pilar nodded. "Father wants it to happen while he's still alive."

"That makes sense." My heart pounded harder, as if to state its complaint on the matter.

"Nothing in our lives makes sense, but we go along with

it anyway." She had her eyes trained on the party—the DJ, the costumed dancers on stage, the fire-breathers, the acrobats, the people moving on the dance floor.

I was proud of the way things were going. I had only seen a couple of the potential brides walk in through their designated area, but everything from the entrances to the shows seemed to be moving along.

"Where is your brother?" I asked. "I haven't seen him all night."

"Around." She waved a hand. "Eli hates parties."

"I find that so funny considering he's always hosting one."

"Like I said, nothing in our lives makes sense." She smiled, looking over at me. "Thanks for helping me out earlier. When it comes time to plan my engagement and wedding, I'm calling you."

"I'll be there." I smiled wide.

She walked away and disappeared into the sea of people in costume. I made my way back to one of the tents to make sure things were still running smoothly in there. I was surprised to find it pretty empty when I stepped inside, though there was a group of people congregating around the ice sculptures. I walked over to the food tables to make sure the trays were still filled. Once the caterers showed me they were, I walked back out of the tent and started making my way toward the other, checking the drinks next. As I walked out of that one, my foot caught on a rock, and I stumbled but kept myself upright. When I took a step again, I realized I'd lost one of my heels. I sighed heavily and closed my eyes to the sky. Of course I did. The cottages were nearby, close enough that I could change my shoes and come right back. I headed in that direction. My phone vibrated in the pocket of my skirt as soon as I stepped out of view from the party. I swore under my breath. It was as if my mother had a tracker on me. I answered the phone quickly.

"I'm changing my shoes and coming right back," I said upon answering.

"Oh, dear. What happened?" My mother's concern melted my annoyance away.

"Tripped over a rock. You know, the usual thing that happens when you're hoping the biggest event of your life goes off without a hitch."

Mom laughed lightly. "Well, Madame Rose is looking for you. She wants to introduce us to the queen, but I'll let her know you'll be back shortly."

"The queen?" I whisper-shouted. "Why?"

"I suppose she wants to thank us."

"Oh my God. I don't want to meet her."

"She's the queen, Adeline. Of course you want to meet her."

"I guess." I walked faster, hating the hop in my step each time I took one. "I'll look for you when I get back."

I slowed down as I reached the cottages. There was a couple going into one of the guest rooms. Not a couple. Prince Elias and a woman. It could have been his brother—they were both similar heights and builds, and wearing the same masks—but I knew it was him. Prince Elias was the man of the hour. His outfit was all gold, with gold stitching on the jacket and an ivory shirt underneath with frilly lace at the neck, that made it look even more lavish. He wasn't wearing a wig, so his dark hair was slicked back, and he looked more regal than any king I'd ever seen. My heart skipped a beat as he disappeared into the cottage with the woman. It wasn't his cottage. It wasn't his brother's either. It must have been hers.

I picked up the pace again and walked inside of my cottage quickly, taking off my shoes as I went over to the desk, to look at the layout again. It was where the Princess of Austria was staying. I wasn't sure why that bothered me so much. Why have this party at all if he'd already chosen his bride though? Why make us go through the hassle? I reminded myself that I was being paid a lot of money to plan this event, but that thought only silenced my annoyance for a second. I swiped the desk, letting the papers fall to the floor, and turned to the closet. The shoes I'd been wearing were very Victorian and matched the dress perfectly. Thankfully, I'd had it in mind to take silly pictures while here and packed what I liked to call my Mary Poppins shoes. I'd worn them for a costume party a couple of years ago, but they were sensible and cute, and I took them everywhere. I slipped them on, fixed my hair and makeup, and put the mask over my face again. If I was going to meet the queen, I needed to make sure I looked presentable. I walked back out of my cottage and was locking the door when the door to the cottage I'd seen Elias disappear into opened. The woman, who I assumed was the Princess of Austria, walked out first. She seemed to be fixing her hair and mask, as if she'd just had a quickie with the prince. My hate for her grew.

I stood quietly, waiting for them to leave. She walked away. He didn't. I waited. And waited. And finally, I decided I didn't care. I didn't care if he saw me or knew I'd seen him. We had one date. One date, and it hadn't been life-changing. He didn't even remember we'd had sex before and that had definitely changed me in a way, so no, he didn't deserve me obsessing over him or what he did. His face turned as I walked toward him. He nodded slightly, in greeting, and I continued walking. The beauty of the costume was that he had no way of knowing it was me.

I walked between the cottages to take a short cut, and felt someone grab my arm and pull me back. I yelped, turning around to face them. My eyes grew wide when I realized it was Elias. He didn't know it was me. Did he just grab at random women? My scowl deepened. He probably did. I yanked my arm from his grasp. He let me go. I could barely see his eyes in the darkness and his mask was covering half of his face anyway.

"I've been looking for you," he said.

"How do you know it's me?"

"I know your cottage." He leaned closer. I backed away and hit the side of the cottage beside me. "I know your hair and your walk. Your mouth. I've been trying to locate you since the night of our date."

"Stop." My words were shaky. "It was one date. Nothing more, nothing less."

"It wasn't nothing," he said, his face closer still. He brought a hand up to my neck, pressing it against the side as if to check my pulse. "Even in a room full of people, I can't seem to take my mind off you."

"You didn't seem to have me on your mind when you were in her room."

"Who says you weren't on my mind?" he ran his hand higher, to my jaw, his thumb just over my bottom lip. "Who says you weren't the reason I stopped anything from happening?"

"Did you?" I swallowed.

He licked his lips. "Would it matter to you?"

"Yes. No. I don't know," I whispered. "It shouldn't."

"Tell me, Adeline." He ran the tip of his nose along my cheek until he reached my ear. I forgot how to breathe. "Why do I want you this much? Why would I leave my own party and go into town just to find you? Why would one date with you, one we didn't even fuck in, make me think about you every waking moment of my life?"

"Is any of that true?"

"Would you kiss me if it was?" He pulled back and his eyes searched mine. "Would you let me touch you underneath that dress?"

"Maybe." I licked my lips, tilting my face higher, hoping he'd press his lips against mine.

"Maybe?" The side of his mouth pulled up. He brought his other hand over the valleys of my breasts and stroked with his long fingers, over the hump of my right, dipping in between them and pulling it out slowly, and over the hump of my left. "Would you let me pull down your bodice and put my mouth on you?"

"Are you going to do it or just stand here and talk about it?" I was panting, needy, as I pushed myself onto him.

"What good would it be?" He leaned back in, pressing his lips against my neck. "To start something we don't have time to finish?"

"Is that what you told the Princess of Austria when you went back to her cottage with her?" I pushed him away and ducked to the side. "We can't do this." I shook my head as I tried to catch the breath he stole from me. "We had our date. We can't do this again."

This time, when I turned around and walked away, he didn't follow.

CHAPTER SIXTEEN

BECAUSE OF EVERYTHING I'D HEARD ABOUT THIS ROYAL FAMILY, I always assumed the queen would be uptight. I hadn't expected her warm, radiant smile, or the way she shook my hand while holding my arm with the other as if to almost hug me as I stood from my curtsy.

"You've outdone yourself," she said. "This is exactly what I picture when I think of the Versailles in eighteenth-century France."

"Minus the toilet problem," I said.

"Minus the toilet problem." She laughed and glanced over at Joss, who was standing beside her. "Why haven't you brought her over for Sunday dinner?" She looked back at me. "You must come to Sunday dinner. It's friends and family and we love welcoming new faces."

"Yes! I agree with Mother." The excited voice was Princess Pilar's. She pranced over with a wide smile on her face, looking a lot better than she did when I left her. "You must come to Sunday dinner."

"Pilar." The queen said in a voice full of warning. "Pipe down."

"I'm fine, Mother." Her eye roll wasn't obvious on her face, but dripping all over her words. "So, you'll come this Sunday, Addie? May I call you Addie?"

"Pilar." The queen warned.

"You may definitely call me Addie." I smiled.

"So, it's settled. We'll see you Sunday," the queen said. "Will you join, Madame Perla?"

"Oh, I would, but I don't think it's appropriate, all things considered." My mother gave her a small smile.

"Nonsense," the queen said. "Leave the politics to the men. It's their shiny little annoyance to deal with."

"I really shouldn't," Mother said. "Neither should Adeline. It may look bad."

"No one will know," the queen said. "Do you know how many people come over that the press doesn't have a clue about?"

"She's been under a lot of scrutiny lately," my mother added. The shame of my past tainted my vision with unshed tears. I blinked them away and composed myself, but stood quietly as I waited. If the queen no longer wanted to invite me over because of my scandal, I would understand.

"All of us are under scrutiny," the queen said. "If I let the tabloids dictate who was allowed in my house, I would never have anyone over."

"I respect that," my mother said.

I smiled. "I'll see you soon."

"Oh! The dance. We have to make sure all of the ladies are lined up for Elias," the queen said.

"I'll get to it," Joss said, squeezing my arm as she walked by. Princess Pilar followed her, leaving my mother and me standing there.

"You shouldn't go."

"You heard the queen. I can't just not go if she invited me."

"Make something up. Go to London."

"I'm not going to turn down an invitation from the queen because my father doesn't know where to draw the line and back down," I whisper-shouted.

"Your father has worked his entire life for one cause. You already put his reputation in peril once. Do you really want to do that again?" she asked. "Remember who paid for your schooling. Remember who helped you get approved for loans when you decided to start this business. You'd be nothing without him." She turned to walk away. "Tomorrow, you'll leave before everyone else does, go back to the villa, and pack up and return to London. In their court, you're nothing but a jester, someone for them to befriend and then discard. Don't forget that."

I ran for the nearest restroom. I needed to be alone for a moment. The event was running smoothly without me anyway. Those were the perks of hiring trusted people to entertain. When I reached the bathroom, I went into a stall and locked it, letting out a breath as I leaned against the door. The main door opened and I listened as two women giggled and walked to the stalls beside me.

"Personally, I don't know why anyone would want to marry him," one of them said. "My friend Fergie had sex with him and he didn't even go down on her."

"I've heard that about him," the other replied. "Such a waste."

Both toilets flushed at the same time and the doors opened. They walked over to the sinks.

"He is good-looking though," one of them said.

"I prefer Aramis. He's so hot."

"Elias seems so angry all the time."

"Aramis seems like such a good time."

They both laughed at that and walked out of the bathroom. It was kind of refreshing to hear that not everyone here was in love with Elias. I thought about what they said and thought about my first time with him. He most certainly did go down on women. He'd done it to me and he didn't even know me, so they were wrong on that account. My eyes slammed shut as the memories flooded my brain. It had been so long, you'd think they'd be grainy at best, but the feel of his lips against my skin was as clear as if it were happening this instant. My heart pounded as I stood there. Earlier, he would have kissed me. He would have touched me, teased me. I had no doubt. The best thing I did was put an end to it. I opened my eyes and walked out of the stall, washing my hands and drying them before walking out.

By the time I made it back to the party, the dance was in full swing. Elias had one of the ladies in his arms as they danced across the makeshift ballroom floor we'd had set up. The music was soft and the lights were dimmed to a soft blue hue, just as Madame Rose had requested. It looked beautiful. Fit for a king. As I watched, I felt something akin to jealousy growing inside me. I'd never wished for much. I'd always been the kind of person who went along with whatever life threw at her. I tried my best to make life easier for my parents, the sex tape being the only slip ever despite it being a pretty destructive one. In that moment, I wished to be one of those women, because at least they had a shot in the dark at the prince. It was something I would never have. I felt someone stand beside me and smiled when I realized it was Pierre.

"Did you have fun?" I asked. He nodded once and looked at the scene ahead. "It's quite something, isn't it?"

"What?"

"This." I signaled at the dancers before us. "It's history in the making, really."

"I suppose."

"I should have never agreed to go on that date with him." I watched as he waltzed with another woman. "Everyone has had something negative to say about me even speaking to him, including my mother. And yet, I can't seem to help myself." I continued speaking, mostly because Pierre's silence was comforting and I had to tell someone what I was feeling before I blew up. "Having a connection with a man I could never have feels like an awful burden to carry, but it'll pass. I mean, it always does." I shrugged and smiled up at him. "I'm going to get changed so we can go grab that pint."

I walked away, leaving behind the dancing and the music. The only person I'd have to report back to was Joss. She'd have questions and I'd answer them as soon as I changed into comfortable clothes. Once inside the cottage, I took off my shoes, the mask on my face, ran my fingers through my hair to tear down the partial updo I had, and started going through my clothes to see what I had left to wear. The knock on my door startled me. I dropped the shirt in my hands and walked over, unlocking and opening it.

"Pierre." I frowned. "I thought we were going to meet—" I stopped talking when I sensed the seriousness as he took off the mask covering half his face. I blinked. "Elias? What the . . . what are you doing?"

He'd obviously changed outfits with Pierre at some point. Did that mean Pierre was the one out there dancing now? Pretending?

CHAPTER SEVENTEEN

"W HAT ARE YOU—"

"I don't think we should deny ourselves this."

"But . . . earlier . . . "

"I changed costumes with Pierre after our encounter."

"Why?"

"Because I didn't want to dance with any of those women." He stepped forward. "Because the only woman I can't stop thinking about refuses to see me again and I don't know what to do with that kind of rejection." He brought a hand up to cup my face. "Because I want to kiss you and taste you and do whatever else you'll let me do to you."

"It's not a good idea." I swallowed. "This won't end well for either of us. For me, especially."

"Are you going to let that stop you?"

"No, but we need boundaries. Rules."

"I'm no good with rules. Or boundaries."

"One night. Tonight and that's it."

"No."

"Yes." I searched his gaze, his eyes looking impossibly

dark. "I can't handle this being more than just a one-night stand. I won't survive it."

"I don't agree with that."

"You don't have to. It's a take-it-or-leave-it offer. I won't allow myself to fall in love with a man who's destined to marry another woman."

"Fine. One night."

"Okay."

He pressed his lips against mine as he stepped into the room and kicked the door closed behind him with his foot. My breath fled my lungs, but just for a moment before I pulled away. His eyes were wild on mine, hazy, unsure. It was the uncertainty that did me in.

"I have to tell you something."

"Now?"

"We slept together before."

"I know." His laugh was a bare wisp of air leaving his lips, but his eyes held a smile.

"You know?" I frowned. "I thought you didn't remember."

"Of course I remember." He leaned into me again, his lips on my jaw as he dragged them to my ear. My heart skipped as he whispered, "I could never forget you, Adeline."

"You don't have to say nice things. This is going to happen either way."

He pulled away. "Do I seem like a man who says things for the sake of saying them?"

"No." I watched him closely. I knew he didn't. That didn't mean he was immune to saying nice things under the circumstances.

"You're the only person I've ever taken to bed who had no idea who I was. You slept with me because you wanted to, not because of my name, not because of my status." He brought a hand up to cover my cheek, his thumb brushing my lower lip. "You wanted me as much as I wanted you, and despite reason, I want you even more now."

I wasn't sure it was his intention, but it was most likely the most romantic thing I'd ever been told. I reached up, wrapping my arms around his neck and pressed my lips to his, this time knowing I wouldn't stop. I couldn't. I was too deep into this and even though it was one night and I knew deep down it would kill me when it was over, I needed to feel his lips, his hands, all of him move against me.

"*Tu es sublime*, Adeline," he said, his voice low as he undressed me, tugging at the strings of the bodice of my dress until it was loose and falling away.

He took his time to look at me, put his mouth on my skin, with each item of clothing he removed. Between kisses, I started to work on his, tossing his tie, undoing his buttons. Soon we were both undressed and marveling at the sight of one another. I'd seen him in a swimsuit. I'd seen him naked, in the dark, but that was so many years ago. The man before me now was perfection. Not in a perfect six-pack model kind of way, but in a toned, powerful man kind of way. The kind who could overpower me easily, but still manage to be gentle. The kind who I had no doubt could be punishing with his tongue and fingers, but was looking at me like I was the most fragile thing in the world. Maybe it was the moment. It felt fragile. It felt like if we spoke too loudly or touched too quickly it would be over in an instant, and neither one of us could bear it.

He pushed me back onto the bed and began dragging his mouth down my body until he reached my thighs; there, he kissed and nipped, making me squirm. I gasped loudly as his tongue found my center, licking my clit slowly once, twice, and then ravishing me like a starving man. It was intense and I knew that even though he was trying to make the moment last, I wouldn't last long. His fingers joined his tongue and he began pumping them inside of me as he sucked on my clit. My legs started to shake.

"C'est encore mieux que je ne l'imaginais." He pulled away momentarily, his dark eyes meeting mine as I panted.

Something inside of me crumbled. I agreed with that because what I had imagined paled in comparison to the reality of having this man, this prince, this future king's head between my legs. His mouth pulled up slightly as if reading my thoughts and he went back to burying his head between my legs and I went back to panting and soon enough, shouting his name.

The cord inside of me that seemed to continue tightening suddenly popped as the orgasm hit me. My chest heaving as I came down from it when he began making his way up my body, his teeth leaving tiny tracks behind as he punctured fragments of my skin. He stopped at my breasts, licking and sucking each nipple into his mouth, groaning as he tugged and let them go free with a pop. I felt my heart pick up again to the point of hysteria, an orgasm that had no business building was gradually climbing and when he brought a hand between my legs, suddenly sliding his fingers inside of me as he continued to suck on my breasts, I knew I was a goner.

I sat up slightly as he finished rolling on a condom and positioned himself between my legs and he met my gaze, a question in them. I answered by holding onto his shoulder and lifting myself up so we were both sitting, and then wrapped my legs around him as he positioned me over him. My nails dug into his shoulder as I lowered myself onto him, holding my breath as his cock spread me inch by inch. He held my ass tightly as he fucked me, driving inside of me with long, hard strokes that were no longer gentle. His movements were punishing, searing, as if marking himself inside of me physically to match what he'd already done emotionally. We were at eye level like this and he pulled back to look at me. I bit my lip to contain my moans, which were growing with each time his cock was completely inside of me, with each time he squeezed my ass and pulled me onto him, hitting my throbbing, already sensitive clit with the movement.

"This can't be the only night, Adeline," he whispered, still fucking me relentlessly.

"It has to be." It was his intense gaze, the way he owned my body and made me feel that made me cry out in that moment, throwing my head back in ecstasy and saying his name when I felt him throbbing inside of me, growling out a curse in French in that low husky voice that made me come undone once more.

CHAPTER EIGHTEEN

I HEEDED MY MOTHER'S WARNING AND PACKED MY THINGS AS SOON as I got home. I wouldn't have, had last night not happened, but it did, and the feeling weighing in the pit of my stomach was worse with each passing second. I wasn't running from it though. I couldn't. I just needed to go back to London and check my flat and regroup all of my thoughts and feelings. I needed to find a box inside myself where I could store them all and shut the lid on the entire thing. Or burn it. Despite everything, I wanted Elias way more than I should and last night had made things worse for me. I would use the excuse of needing to check on my flat though. I'd been gone a while, and even though my neighbor, Mrs. Parsons, was making sure things were tidy and didn't get cobwebs, her services didn't extend to paying past due bills, which I was bound to have if I didn't go through my mail soon.

As I packed, I thought about Elias and wondered if I should say anything to him. I opted against it. He wasn't back from Versailles anyway. For all I knew, he was spending the day with one of the princesses he'd soon marry. Besides that, we'd agreed on one night and one night we had. One night that conjured memories of our first time and made me wish like hell I hadn't agreed to anything at all, but it was what it was. Even if we both wanted things to progress and see where this went, nothing could happen. Like my mother said, I was just a commoner to them. Like Etienne said, the future could hold nothing for us. I needed to do a better job at listening to those who loved me and wanted what was best for me. I'd regroup in London, come back and go to the queen's residence on Sunday for dinner, and by then I'd have put all of this behind me.

Nothing had changed in London. Not that I'd expected it to. As I took my keys out of my pocket and walked toward my flat, I looked at the park across the street and smiled at the sight of the elderly couple sharing the bench there, the way they often were. I lived in a vintage townhome, in a coveted street in Kensington, which I was renting courtesy of one of my father's good friends. Dad lived here for a short time when he was serving as an ambassador to France here in London. He'd kept the job for four years before moving back to Paris, but his contacts remained, and when I decided to move here, he was able to secure the very same townhouse I'd fallen in love with as a teenager. It was fancy and big, way too big for me, but Joss had moved into one of the bedrooms, so that helped. When I moved here after graduating college, I'd promised my father I'd pay the rent as soon as my business took off, and had since made good on my promise. Joss was still in France, so as I reached the door, I knew I'd find the place empty. I was turning to unlock the front door when I heard the door of the townhouse next door squeak open and saw Mrs. Parsons.

"You're back." She eyed me up and down. "You look rumpled."

"I slept on the train," I said, as if that would explain the state I was in.

Truth was, I did look rumpled. I'd barely slept, so I was sure there were bags under my eyes. My hair was a mess in a bun that I hadn't taken the time to fix. I hadn't ironed my linen coat and I was sure the buttons on my blouse were mismatched. I never looked rumpled. At least not in public, so Mrs. Parsons was right to be concerned.

"Come inside for tea," she said, her tone leaving no room for argument.

"I should set my bags down," I said, arguing anyway.

"I'll let you get settled then. Tea tomorrow at noon."

"Tomorrow at noon." I smiled and waited for her to disappear into her flat before going into mine.

Once inside, I began to shed my clothes, sliding off my shoes first before moving onto my scarf and jacket. I walked up to the pile of letters at the edge of my counter and leafed through them, sorting the bills from the trash, and setting aside invitations I'd received. Some of the letters were for Joss, so I set those in a separate pile altogether. Taking the bills and invitations with me, I walked over to each of the windows on this floor and pulled open the curtains, letting the midday sun wash over the space. I would go downstairs and upstairs later. For now, I wanted to pay my bills, do my laundry, and take a nap.

My phone woke me up. I reached for it blindly and answered it upon seeing Mrs. Meyers' number on the screen.

"Is everything okay?" I said as a greeting.

"No, everything is not okay. That man is insufferable and I will not deliver any more baskets."

"What?" I sat up in bed, looking outside. It was dark out. I must have slept all day. "What did he say?"

"He would not accept the basket. He said everything was wrong. I followed every single instruction you gave me." Her voice was a shrill. I cringed.

"I am so sorry."

"You don't have to apologize on his behalf. I just wanted to let you know that I'm passing the task along to Lucy Walters. Maybe she'll fare better with him. After all, they're well acquainted."

"Well acquainted?" I frowned. "Isn't Lucy the pub owner's daughter?"

"Well acquainted," Mrs. Meyers repeated. "Meaning, they've had relations."

"Oh." My heart dropped. "Oh."

"I will pass your number along to Lucy. She'll be in touch tomorrow." She hung up the phone before I could make a suggestion or argue that I did not want Lucy Walters anywhere near Elias if they'd had sex in the past. Fuck jealousy and the way it seemed to disregard all other senses.

I set my phone down and called Etienne. He didn't answer the call. I called Joss. She answered on the third ring.

"Missing me?"

"Always." I smiled slightly, but my jealousy would only let my mouth pull up a touch. "So, apparently Elias is being an asshole to Mrs. Meyers and she handed off the task to someone else."

"The basket?" she asked. "That task?"

"Yes."

"So what?"

"So, the person she handed it off to is Lucy Walters, who apparently had sex with Elias in the past."

"Okay. And?"

"And I don't want her delivering the basket to him."

Joss fell silent for a moment. "Because you like him?"

"Yes." I closed my eyes, wishing I could shut out all emotions toward him. It didn't work. All I could do was picture Lucy Walters and him in bed. My eyes popped open again. "I really like him. More than like him, if I'm being honest."

"That's not . . . " She sighed. "Addie. You realize he's not for you, right?"

"Everyone keeps saying that, yes." I closed my eyes again. "I know he's not. I'm not an idiot, but if he's not and he knows that, why does he continue to pursue me?"

"Because he's a man with little regard to others' emotions. Trust me, I know."

My eyes popped open again. "You two—"

"No. God no. I'm just saying, I've known Pilar long enough to know enough about the princes and their flings. To them, you're just another number. Another pair of tits."

"I don't think it's just that," I said. "He doesn't treat me like that."

"He can be very charming. He has a way about him. It's a façade."

I let that sink in. "I don't think I should come to dinner on Sunday."

"I think you should."

"But he'll be there and I don't think it's a good idea for me to see him right now."

"He'll be at his villa when you get back there too. He'll be on every paper and every magazine in a few months when he gets married and has his coronation. There is no escaping him."

"Seeing him in person will be worse than seeing him on a magazine cover."

"He's bringing a date."

"How do you know?"

"Pilar. Obv."

"Oh."

"Bring a date."

"I can't bring a date. The queen invited me, not me plus one. Besides, I wouldn't have a date to bring. I don't want to ask poor Pierre again and leave him high and dry."

"Bring Thomas."

"Evans?" I cried. "My ex-boyfriend?"

"Yeah, you know, the one you filmed a sex tape with. He owes you. You're still on good terms, and it will kill Elias to see you together."

"I don't want to play those kinds of mind games, Joss."

"Love is a game. You need to play to your heart's advantage."

"What kind of bullshit is that?"

"It's not bullshit, Addie. The royals like to play games." She lowered her voice. "While we're on the topic of royals, Pilar wants me to be her secretary."

"What?" I shrieked. "You have a job." I liked Pilar, but this was going too far. Using me was one thing, but trying to take my best friend and best employee I had was going a bit too far.

"I told her I'd think about it."

"Seriously?"

"I don't want to flat-out say no to the opportunity. She's as good a friend to me as you are and it would require travel and meeting people I'd never otherwise get to meet."

"I understand the glamour of the job, Joslyn. I just . . . I don't want to lose you too, you know?"

"I'd refer so many people to Pirouette Events, you'll have the longest list of parties to plan you've ever dreamed of."

I felt myself smile. "I still don't want to lose you."

"But you like that perk, huh?"

"Yes, I like that perk." I laughed. She laughed too.

"Take a date on Sunday."

"I'll think about it."

"Keep me posted."

I didn't like the idea at first, but the more I thought about Elias being there with a date, the more I liked the idea of taking one of my own. After all, showing up with a man was better than showing up alone and having to endure seeing Elias with a woman. I wondered if he'd chosen someone from the other night. I wondered if this would be the woman he'd announce his engagement to. I needed to armor up just in case. When I hung up with Joss, I texted Thomas. There was a lot to be said for staying on friendly terms with an ex, even when that ex was the reason you were hiding from the entire city.

CHAPTER NINETEEN

THOMAS HELD MY HAND AS WE WALKED INTO THE PARTY. I NEARLY jumped at the motion.

"If you want to make someone jealous, you have to play the part."

"I don't want to make anyone jealous," I said, but kept my hand in his nonetheless.

He snickered under his breath as the enormous double doors opened before us and my hand tightened in his. Even though I'd just planned a party in Château de Versailles and had been there as a tourist and stayed there the week of the festivities, I didn't consider it a real castle. It was a far cry from the truth, with as many kings and queens and courts as it had seen, but it still somehow seemed fake to me, like a fairy tale, whenever I walked its grounds.

Palace of Fontainebleau was different. Although lavish, it felt very real. Maybe it was because I knew this was the most used residence. It was where they took their Christmas and announcement photos. It was where the princes and princess grew up. I tried to picture a childhood here, surrounded by such grandeur, and failed. I couldn't imagine scattered toys or children running on these marble floors. It seemed untouchable. Just like them. I realized that this was what my mother and Etienne and Joss had warned me about.

As we walked the hall, I examined the portraits that lined the walls. With each step we took, kings and queens of the past seemed to have their eyes on us, looking at us beneath them, where we'd always belong. Their regard for tradition wasn't for naught. They truly lived it.

"This is crazy," I whispered.

"Wait till they announce us," Thomas whispered back.

"Announce—"

Before I could finish the question, the doors we were walking toward opened before us and a man stood on the other side with a paper in his hands. I looked forward and saw the room held at least thirty people and suddenly I wanted to retreat and bury myself in the sand. I was standing here with Thomas, of all people, who most of society had seen me naked with. Doing things with. My grip tightened in his. He tightened his own and brought his other hand to cover mine as well in a way that comforted me so much I thought I could cry. It empowered me to stand there, head held high, and not back down.

"Miss Adeline Sofia Isabella Bouchard and Sir Thomas Evans," the man said in a clear, loud voice.

"Sir?" I whispered.

"You don't know everything about me." Thomas chuckled.

The people gathered in the room, looked at us. My eyes jumped to each one of them, stopping on the queen before I saw Elias. His expression was completely unreadable, but his jaw was set and he looked pissed. *At me?* No. I'd given him no reason to be angry. Beside him stood a tall, slender, blonde woman with a warm smile and a small tiara on her head: the Princess of Austria. If I had to guess, I'd say she'd won the coveted position of future queen of France. Because I was uncomfortable with the attention, the thought didn't stab at me like it had before. She also didn't have a ring on her finger. *Yet.* Thomas pulled me along and introduced me to a couple of friends gathered there. I smiled and shook their hands, all the while, trying not to think about the fact that they'd all seen us having sex. They didn't have to outright say it. I could see it written all over their faces as they said hello. They weren't smug about it. If anything, it was awkward for all parties involved, and oddly enough, I was grateful for that. The doors opened again and the man beside it announced the next people to enter. "Miss Ambrosia Agnes and Mister Benjamin Drake."

"Holy shit," Thomas said beside me.

"Holy shit is right," I agreed. "I went to a party he was at recently, but I didn't get a chance to see him in all his glory."

Benjamin Drake was one of France's elite football players. Thomas and I were both huge fans of his. I had been following him since he'd started playing for our beloved Les Bleus and had two jerseys of his, one signed, which Thomas had gifted me for Christmas last year.

"Well, the good news is, you're free to flirt with Drake tonight and hopefully get together with him and invite me over for dinner," Thomas said.

I laughed, throwing my head back. When I straightened, my laughter caught in my throat as my gaze caught Elias's on the other side of the room. I knew coming here was a bad idea. I wasn't even anywhere near him and I felt like it was my back his hand was pressing against, not the woman he was here with. I wasn't sure what to do. Should I smile? Or wave? Or just look away? I couldn't seem to do any of those things. I wished I could hate him or find something wrong with him, but there was a longing in his eyes I hadn't expected, and it made it that much harder to find anything at all. Besides, my heart didn't seem to care about any of that. It was beating faster and unsteadily, making it nearly impossible for me to catch my breath.

"It's dinner time," Thomas said, reaching for my hand again.

I let him whisk me away to yet another set of double doors, but my mind was still on the prince. Always on the prince. There were name cards in front of each place setting. Thomas and I found ours and sat. I looked at the setting beside me and was glad to see Joslyn's name scribbled on it and Princess Pilar's on the one beside hers. I hadn't seen either of them yet. I focused on the water being poured by the butler followed by the wine he poured into the other glass. The china looked as expensive as everything else did. As Thomas spoke to the man beside him, I took in the rest of the room. The walls were red and gold, matching the chairs we were sitting on. It was lavish upon lavish and I couldn't for a second imagine living like this. I loved dressing up, but more than anything, I enjoyed lounging in sweat pants and maxi dresses and sandals and this palace made me feel like I wouldn't be able to leave my room unless I was dressed to the nines. It was an absolutely unattainable lifestyle. My mother's words came back to me and I reminded myself I was just here to serve as entertainment, as another mortal amongst gods, to remind them of their power.

"You made it," Joss whispered as she took her seat beside me.

"Hey." I smiled wide, relieved to see my friend. Pilar took

the seat beside hers, and I smiled at her as well. "Good to see you again."

"Thank you for coming. Sorry we kept you waiting," Pilar whispered. "My zipper got stuck so I had to change my outfit."

"You look beautiful, so I'd say this one works perfectly." I looked at her black dress.

It was short, but not too short, with a frilly tulle skirt and a form-fitting bodice with lace over her shoulders and chest. It was sophisticated and chic. Joss wore a dark purple slip dress that tied on the side to accentuate her waistline. I was grateful she'd chosen a short black slip dress and gold strappy heels for me. I would've probably worn a ball gown on principle that I was dining at the palace with the queen. Everyone looked very much like they were at a cocktail party. There were no obnoxious hats, though I really wanted to wear one myself, or over-the-top gowns. It occurred to me for a second that maybe my mother was wrong about the royal family. Maybe they were normal people with extraordinary circumstances. Maybe they invited people like us to dine with them, not because they wanted to remember their place, but because they longed to be in ours. It wasn't such a far-fetched idea. After all, the grass was always greener on the other side.

The rest of the table started filling in. The chairs across from us were still empty and my heart pounded a little harder at the possibility of Elias sitting there. I was starving, but I knew if he sat across from me, I wouldn't be able to eat my meal. My stomach was already in knots as it was. My attention turned to the door as Elias walked in talking to his brother. The Princess of Austria followed. And lastly, the queen. I kept my eyes on her. She glanced at me and smiled wide, waving a hand at me. Despite my shock, I felt myself wave back. She sat at the seat beside the head of the table, leaving that one empty. Prince Aramis sat in the seat directly across from Joss. Prince Elias sat in the one across from me. The Princess of Austria took the one across from Thomas. I looked down at my plate, which still had an ivory napkin folded over it.

"Did you see Benjamin Drake?" Joss whispered, leaning over.

"How could I not?" My eyes widened in excitement. "Did you meet him?"

"Not yet. Pilar is going to introduce us."

"I've only met him once," Pilar whispered, leaning over to us.

"You're the princess. Who cares?" Joss said.

"I care." She blushed. "I'm a fan of his as well, you know?"

"Thomas got me his jersey signed last year and I almost died," I said.

"I told my brothers to get me one when they went to watch Le Bleus play recently and neither of them remembered to," Pilar whispered.

"Bastards," I whispered back.

She and Joss laughed.

"He definitely has the greatest ass in football, doesn't he," Joss stated.

"I'd say." I nodded.

"For sure," Pilar added quickly.

"What are you gossiping about down there?" The queen asked. "I should have sat you nearby so I could join in on the fun."

The three of us straightened in our seats.

"Just talking about shorts," Pilar said, smiling wide.

Joss cough-laughed into her napkin. I bit my lip to keep from laughing, and then stopped when I caught Elias watching me with a small smile on his face. My heart stuttered. I tore my gaze away from him and looked at his brother, sitting beside him, who was talking to the man beside him. I'd never seen Prince Aramis in person, but he was gorgeous, with his golden skin and chiseled jaw. His eyes were green like Elias's, but his were a couple of shades lighter. They matched his easygoing smile. A smile that I was sure had unzipped many dresses and unhooked many bras. I smiled when he caught me looking at him. His mouth tilted in a lazy smile as he looked over at me.

"Adeline, correct?"

I nodded, still smiling like an idiot.

"Where do you live, Adeline?" He lifted his wine glass and took a sip, holding it with his hand turned up as if he was holding a chalet. Paired with that face and the filthy promises in his eyes, I could definitely see the appeal.

"London."

"London." He raised an eyebrow. "You came all this way for this dinner?"

"No. I mean, yes, but I'm staying nearby. My family owns a few villas in Marbella, so I'm technically not traveling too far today."

"You're a Bouchard."

"Yes."

"Louis Bouchard's daughter?"

"Yes." I licked my lips.

"Ah." He grinned. "Your father has some interesting thoughts. I would love to hear yours."

"Aramis." It was a warning from Elias. He was looking

at his brother as he leaned in and whispered something in his ear. I couldn't make out what he said, but Aramis's smile only grew wider and when he looked at me again, he chuckled.

"We'll continue this conversation later, Adeline," he said. "But rest assured, we will continue it."

"I look forward to it."

His smile stayed put. I had to look away and focus on my wine and not lift my gaze again. Nobody at this table felt safe. Thankfully, dinner was served—duck, quail, oysters, lobster. It was a meal fit for a king, literally. My eyes drifted toward the empty seat at the head of the table. I knew the king was too ill to attend public events, but dinner at his own house? Thomas and Joslyn caught up with London gossip as I sat between them and listened in. When she turned back to her food, he leaned in to speak into my ear.

"Did you know that the video disappeared?"

I turned my face to look him in the eye, which was a mistake. I hadn't realized just how close his face was to mine. We bumped foreheads.

"Ouch." I rubbed my forehead.

"Like we're in grade school." He chuckled under his breath.

"What do you mean disappeared?"

"Wiped. I asked a friend of mine at *The Sun*, you know, Darren, the only one who would take the video down from their website," he said. I nodded. "Well, he said they were under strict gag orders. He couldn't even tell me anything past the fact that everyone had been given a warning and took it down."

"What kind of warning would be responsible for that miracle?" I asked, frowning. "I mean, we got lawyers involved and they weren't able to do much."

"Well, they did what they could, Addie. They did take it down from some places."

"I guess."

"To answer the question though, I don't know. I mean, the only person I know with that kind of reach is . . . " He stopped dead in his tracks as he spoke, and then looked at me like he'd suddenly found the answer to a riddle. "The king."

CHAPTER TWENTY

THE KING.

It was impossible, of course. How could the bed-ridden king make all of that go away? More importantly, why? My gaze traveled back to Elias, who was sipping his tea without a care in the world. His eyes lifted to mine. Of course. He had told me he would do this, after all, hadn't he? I'd asked him not to meddle, and he did it anyway. I should've probably been more upset than I was, but it was hard when I felt such relief. The video had disappeared just as quickly as it had appeared. It was gone and no one was allowed to talk about it. Wasn't that the exact thing my father hated about the monarchy? Wasn't that the kind of thing he fought against? He hated their power to silence the press, to take away freedom of speech. Personally, I didn't agree with it either, but in this case it was definitely benefiting me. I was being a hypocrite. I knew I was, but I couldn't help it. I just wasn't sure how to deal with Elias. Should I thank him for it? Berate him for it? Leave it alone? He raised an eyebrow and I realized I was still staring. I blinked and looked away.

The queen stood and clinked her glass in a total movie moment move and the entire table quieted down and looked at her. She was smiling wide, but it didn't reach her eyes.

"As many of you know, we have a lot of things happening in our family, but I'm keeping this light and will be toasting to my son, Elias, who has chosen to marry Emily, the Princess of Austria. Cheers to them. May they have a blessed and happy marriage." She raised her glass higher. Everyone in the room lifted theirs in a series of gasps and cheers. "Long live the Crown."

"Long live the Crown," everyone, including myself, repeated.

I set down my glass without taking a sip of champagne. It was bad luck, I was sure, but I couldn't stomach it right now. It was something I should have been expecting, of course, but to hear it and have it celebrated was different from having Joss and Etienne and my mother tell me about it. Now, it was real. And when I finally chanced a glance in the prince's direction and caught the Princess of Austria smiling and holding her hand up to show off her ring, it was definitely real. It took everything in me to stay rooted in my seat. It took everything in me to meet Elias's eyes. He looked solemnly back at me, as if he too was heartbroken at the fact that he was engaged to another woman. Maybe he was. It didn't matter though. Despite everything he said, he had an opportunity to put a stop to all of this and he continued to play the role of puppet and go along with his family's wishes.

Shortly after, we all stood from the table, and Prince Elias excused himself for the night. He gave Emily, the Austrian princess, a kiss on the cheek and waved at the rest of us as he left the room. The chatter continued. Joss and Pilar were talking to a group of women, while Thomas and I spoke to a group of investors. I felt a light touch on my elbow and turned to find the queen.

"I wasn't able to say hello to you earlier," she said.

"Oh." I turned and curtsied softly, smiling when I straightened. "Thank you so much for inviting me."

"Thank you for accepting." She smiled. "Will you take a walk with me?"

"Of course." I looked back and excused myself from the group, turning to the queen once more as she led the way.

As we reached the door, the man standing before it, opened it and closed it behind us. I wondered when the last time any of them opened their own doors was, if ever. She stopped just outside of the doors and turned to me.

"I wanted to ask you if you'd do the honor of planning the wedding. It would take place next month, and I know it's extremely short notice, but I'm willing to pay anything and provide you with the necessary staff. I just need this done," she said.

Footsteps rang out somewhere in the hall, but I didn't bother to look knowing it would be just another door holder or employee here to check on their queen and her guests. She was still looking at me, waiting for me to answer, and I was still trying to process everything that had taken place this last hour. After she made her announcement, I did my best to bottle it up and ignore it and pretend it was a joke. Now that she was asking me to do this and saying she was willing to throw money at me, I wasn't sure what to say. Yes, obviously. If my mother was here she'd have pinched my arm. If Joss was out here and not inside chitchatting, she'd have agreed for me. Yes was the only answer.

"Mother. You need to go to Father's chambers." The voice was Elias's.

I whipped my head and looked at him as he closed to distance between us, then I looked away, back to his mother, who was still watching me. I wanted to cry. The emotion hit me seemingly out of nowhere, but that's the only thing I felt like doing right now. Finally, I nodded at her.

"You can count on us."

"Thank you so much, dear." She placed a hand over my arm. "It won't be romantic or magical, we just have to make it appear to be so." She offered me a small smile and I could swear she saw everything written all over my face as she squeezed my arm and let go. "Now, if you'll excuse me. Please enjoy yourself. Thank you again for coming."

I nodded, swallowing back tears, not really able to speak. When she walked away, it was just Elias and me left in the room and still, I couldn't bear to look at him.

"You agreed to plan my wedding?" he asked. His tone was clipped. I didn't have to face him to know he was upset.

"What was I supposed to say? No?" I wiped my face, grateful we weren't facing each other, though he must know I was crying, and I hated that.

"You could have made up an excuse. Said you had another event that day."

"She didn't even tell me the date." I wiped my face again, took a breath, and dared to face him. "Do you have a date?"

"It'll be in two weeks."

A laugh escaped me. "Two weeks. Of course."

"Please don't do this. Don't plan this, don't go."

"Why shouldn't I? To save myself the heartache? It's a little too late for that."

"I can't go through with it if you're there."

"You just went through an engagement just fine. You agreed to it around the time that we slept together. I'd say you'll be just fine. Anything for the Crown, right?" I turned around and pulled the door open to the room leaving him behind. I walked right up to Thomas and told him I was leaving. He shot me a confused but understanding look.

"I'll walk you out. I should probably leave too. I have a long day ahead of me tomorrow."

"So do I."

I'd have to call my mother and Joss and let them know we were now planning the prince's wedding.

CHAPTER TWENTY-ONE

"WELL, I CAN'T SAY THIS ISN'T A SURPRISE," TIO ANTONIO said. "I'm just not sure if it's a good one or a bad one yet."

He'd finally gotten back from his trip and was standing in front of the bookstore. I'd been wringing my hands together the entire ride over here and now I felt like I was going to be sick. It was fine because worse case I'd blame my mother. It wasn't like she was here to argue with him about it. I bit my lip as he looked at the structure that looked completely unrecognizable to how he'd left it.

"Do you like it?"

"I . . . I think it's growing on me." He glanced at me. "Can we go inside?"

"It's your bookstore." I laughed.

I linked my arm in his and started walking so he had no choice but to step forward. I let go of him and unlocked the door, waiting for him to walk in before me.

"Addie!" He gasped and turned to look at me. "How much did this cost you?"

"Don't worry about that. Do you like it or not?"

"You even cleared that out." He laughed and looked up at the small area on the second floor.

"I think you could put a tiny café up there. Or at least offer tea and coffee." I shrugged. "You'd have to hire someone, but there are a lot of people in this town I can think of who would totally do it."

"I need people to come in here first."

"You'll have people in here. You just have to be better about advertising the place." I walked over to the window, where I'd set up a few displays that included a mix of self-help, travel, romance, biographies, and literary fiction books. I picked up the first one. "And keep swapping these out every few weeks. We've already sold a ton of these to tourists looking for beach reads."

"Beach reads," Tio Antonio repeated. "What do people consider beach reads? Light books?"

"Not necessarily. Something they can read on the beach is a beach read. It can be anything, which is why you can't only have travel books up here. A lot of people are on vacation already and not everyone is like you, looking for their next vacation while they're on their current one."

"I hadn't taken a vacation in years." He shot me a look.

"And now you want to take one hundred."

"True." He chuckled. "I got bit by the travel bug."

"Good. Now you need to hire someone to do this job so you can go enjoy yourself."

"I think I will." He nodded, looking around. "I may just stay here all day though. It really does look great." He looked over at me with a smile. "Thank you, Addie."

"Any time." I smiled.

He shook his head, still smiling. "So, you're still delivering a basket today, right?"

"I'll deliver as many baskets as you want, but remember I'm leaving soon. I have to get back to reality."

"You sure it's safe for you to come out of hiding?"

"It'll have to be."

"Have you spoken to your father?"

"Nope." I bit my lip and looked away. Even though I'd never been close to my father, the fact that he hadn't even responded to my texts after our fallout hurt.

"He'll come around. We all make mistakes."

"Some more public than others."

"Well, yes." His lips pressed together. "But you've been hiding out long enough. He can't expect you to stay away, especially not with as well as your company is doing. Your mother told me you planned the Versailles ball for the prince."

"I did."

"That's massive."

"It was. It is."

He frowned. "What's wrong?"

"Nothing. It's . . . " I shook my head. "I have a lot on my mind."

"Well, know that I'm proud of you. Your father is too, even though he won't say it." Tio Antonio set a hand on my shoulder. "Sometimes parents don't want to celebrate their children's successes because they think somehow it'll help them work harder. My father told me that when he was on his deathbed and it always stuck with me. He regretted it." He shrugged. "Too late, obviously. By then your father and I were shaped. He's a lot like him. It's not a bad thing, but I can see how he'd make the same mistakes with you. He'll come around."

"Yeah, probably when he's on his own deathbed." I wiped a tear from my face. My father would never admit he was wrong. "It's fine. I don't need my father's approval."

"That's the biggest lie we tell ourselves." Uncle Antonio laughed. "And then we all end up in therapy."

"You're hilarious." I stuck my tongue out, even though I knew he wasn't kidding about therapy or anything he'd said. "Anyway, I'm glad you like the store. I was a little worried out there. I didn't make plans to open it back up because I figured you should probably take over from here on out."

"Since you're leaving."

"Re-entering society, remember?" I smiled.

"Maybe you can come back for the grand opening."

"Maybe." I started walking toward the door. "I'm going to set up that basket. Let me know if you have any questions about anything."

The front door to his villa opened even before I reached it. I paused, my heart dropping as I looked at him. I'd arrived earlier than usual because after yesterday's engagement announcement I'd hoped I could avoid seeing him. Maybe it was dumb because like Joss had pointed out, even when we were both far from this quaint little beach town, I'd see him everywhere—on the news, in the papers. His Crown might not extend all the way to London, but the gossip would. Even without news trailing behind me, he'd be inescapable no matter where I went because the time I spent with him would remain a part of me.

"Hey," he said, brushing a hand through his hair.

"Hey." I lifted the basket, hoping it would help calm my nerves, but my shaky hands gave them away nonetheless.

Elias must have noticed, but didn't comment. I watched his Adam's apple bob as he stepped away from the door and onto the porch, closing the distance between us. He put his hands just beside mine on the handle of the basket, his fingers brushing against mine as he did. My pulse leaped. I let go of the basket as if my hands caught fire and turned away from him, not giving in to the urge to run, but not wanting to stay another second in his presence.

"Addie, wait."

My feet froze. I shut my eyes and breathed out, swallowing as I opened my eyes again, but kept my back to him because I needed another second to regroup.

"I'm sorry."

"You know what I think?" I turned around and faced him. He held the basket to his chest and waited for me to speak. "From here on out, we should keep our conversations at a minimum."

"What? Why?"

"You know why." I shot him a look.

"So what do you want me to do? Stay inside?"

"It's not like you're ever outside any other time, but it doesn't matter. I won't be back tomorrow."

"What? Why not?" He stepped forward, the basket still between us. "Are you leaving?"

"Not yet, but my uncle is back. I'm sure he can handle this better than I can."

"You can't just . . . I'll only accept the basket from you."

I blinked. "You sound like a child."

"Yeah, well, I don't care."

"Sometimes I forget how spoiled you are." I rolled my eyes. "Either way, it's done. I can't keep doing this."

"Please, Adeline." His voice was low, his eyes searching mine as if begging. "Please. It's the one thing I look forward to every day."

"Can't you see how much this is hurting me?" I whispered. "As it is, I have to plan your wedding to someone else. This is all too much."

"So don't. I already told you. Don't plan the wedding. Let someone else do it."

"And miss out on the opportunity? It's not only me, it's my company, it's my dream event." My voice rose as I spoke. I quieted. "Besides, my mother would kill me."

"Your mother. You're going to plan my wedding and ignore everything we had because of your mother."

"Yes. I've already hurt my parents enough this past year. I won't let another man dictate the way I live my life."

"I'm not . . . " He took a deep breath, his grip tightening on the basket. "I'm not trying to dictate your life. I'm trying to save you some heartache."

"Yeah, well, it's a little too late for that, Elias." I swallowed back my emotion and turned around, unable to look him in the eye any longer. "Please don't follow me."

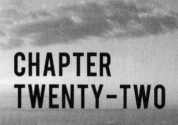

CHAPTER TWENTY-TWO

A NOISE WOKE ME FROM MY SLEEP. I OPENED MY EYES SLOWLY, looking around the dark room. My eyes landed on the clock on my nightstand that read two thirty-three. I rubbed my eyes upon hearing the noise again. It was the front door. My heart leaped into my throat. It could be my uncle, as he was back but, he wouldn't just come in here at this time. I stumbled over the sheet on my way out of bed and grabbed the stick beside the bedroom door. I didn't know what the stick was even for. Decoration maybe. Either way, it would have to do. I switched the living room lights on and the intruder brought his arm up to shield his face from the light.

"What the hell are you doing here?"

"I needed to see you."

"How'd you get in?"

"Key." He wiggled the key in his hand. I frowned, but then remembered he had never given back the key after the party.

"Are you drunk?" I blinked. I'd never seen Elias drunk.

"A little. Maybe. I don't know." He tossed the key onto the table beside him. It fell to the floor.

"You're obviously drunk."

"Maybe." He exhaled, rubbing a hand over his face. When it dropped at his side, he looked at me, eyes hazy and red. "My mother just called. I was . . . I was just with him, and he just . . . my father died."

"What?" I held my breath, my brain filing through all of the appropriate things to do in a moment like this, and the one thing that came to mind was that he was no longer Prince Elias, sought-after bachelor. He was now King Elias, if he kept that name. Nevertheless, I curtsied.

"Don't." His voice sounded shredded, as if he was trying hard to hold in tears. I looked up at him. "Please don't. Not you."

I felt my heart rip at the sight of him. Disheveled and sad. He looked like a lonely boy left to fend for himself, and in a sense he was. I pushed aside his title and walked forward, around the couch between us, my heart dropping with each step. When I reached him, I paused just in front of him. Close enough to touch, smart enough not to.

"I'm so terribly sorry, Eli," I whispered.

He nodded a few times, his head bobbing along with his Adam's apple. He licked his lips, in lieu of words, and continued to nod. He looked utterly broken and I hated seeing him like that. I felt my own sadness creep through and turn to tears, not for me, but for him, for his mother, for his siblings, for the country. He took a deep breath and let it out, bringing a hand to my face. I nearly jumped at the contact, but was left confused when I felt him wipe a tear.

"You feel so much, Addie. Too much. Even for men you detest," he whispered.

"I don't detest him. I didn't even know him." I swallowed. "I know you. I feel for you."

"God." He breathed out, stepping forward and crashing my head onto his chest. "You're too good to be true. Too good for anyone, definitely too good for me."

I let him hold me in his arms, breathing him in as he spoke those words about me. I wasn't too good to be true. I was just a girl trying to find my place in life. I thought I'd find happiness when I kicked off my company, or when I found a man who made me feel good, or when I finally started getting hired to do the big events I'd dreamed of. All of those things had made me happy for a while. As it turns out, finding happiness is an up-hill battle. Being good only accounted for so much. Being good would get me nowhere with Elias. I'd have to settle for bits and pieces of moments like these. After what felt like an eternity, I pulled away, but kept my hands on his arms.

"Have you gone to the palace? To pay your respects?"

"I came here." He blinked, shaking his head. "It was the only place I could think of to go."

"God, Elias. You say things like that—"

"It's the truth. I'm speaking the truth. After I spoke to my mother, my brother, my sister, you were the first person I wanted to see. The only person I wanted to see."

"When do you have to leave?"

"Tomorrow morning."

"Come. Get some rest." I pulled him by the hand and led him to my bedroom, turning the lights off as we went.

I wasn't sure why he'd come or why I'd been the first person he thought of. I wasn't sure if he wanted to sleep with me or just lay beside me. The only thing I knew for sure was that after today, his life would change drastically and the chances of us ever seeing each other again were slim. So slim that the mere thought of it made my heart ache more. As I closed the door behind us and led him to my bed, I tried not to think about it. He took his shoes off with ease and pulled the light sweatshirt he was wearing over his head, tossing it aside. I walked to my side of the bed and watched him walk to the other. I was wearing tiny pink silk shorts and a silk tank top to match. He left off, wearing gray cotton joggers and a black T-shirt that clung to his muscled torso. He got in bed dressed. I met him halfway and put my arm around him as he put his around me.

"Everything is going to be okay," I whispered as he brought his face to the crook of my neck.

"How do you know?" His breath tickled and I pulled away to look him in the eyes, even though it was too dark to see much.

"I don't, but I have the utmost trust in you."

"How could you? After everything."

"After what?" I brought a hand up and brushed his hair away from his forehead. "I knew what I was getting myself into. I chose you anyway."

"Adeline." He shut his eyes with a sigh. "What I would give for things to be different. To be a normal citizen and be able to have you."

"You have me now."

"I want you always." He opened his eyes again. "That's the problem. And I don't want to be a bastard and suggest something that others have done before me and I always promised I wouldn't do when I got married, but now I understand them. I understand their need to have a mistress. The one they loved, while married to the one they were obligated to."

I felt my heart stop. I'd heard the rumors about his father and all the kings before him. I'd heard rumors about so many of them, but had never heard the word *love*, and it was the thing I fixated on.

"King George IV got married in secret," he said, pushing his leg between mine so there wasn't a part of us not touching.

"And then he married another publicly. I know the story. It ended poorly for everyone involved."

"It's said he was buried with a locket that held a photo of her."

"Right. After a long life without her." I searched his eyes. He couldn't seriously be asking me to be his mistress.

"I need you, Addie."

"I couldn't do that, Eli," I whispered, blinking as fresh tears brewed. "I couldn't be your mistress, standing aside to watch you father children with another woman. Children I would want to share with you."

"Fuck." He shut his eyes, taking a deep breath. It smelled of whiskey when he exhaled. When he looked at me again, he looked terribly sad, and I wished I could agree to whatever he asked, but I knew deep down that I couldn't. "I'm sorry."

"Stop apologizing."

"I only feel free when I'm with you." He inched closer, his mouth merely inches from mine. "I only feel anything when I'm with you. I don't want to give this up. *Je ne veux jamais que cela s'arrête.*"

My heart broke with his admission. I never wanted it to end either. I didn't respond. Not with words. I wouldn't cave to his demands just because I felt sorry for him in the moment or because his words made me feel things I couldn't control. I'd been there and done that in the past and it left me running for the hills. Instead of saying anything, I leaned in and kissed him. It was a soft and tentative kiss that he matched. His hands moved underneath the tank top I wore and explored me as the kiss deepened. The gentleness of his touch would be my undoing. Without words, I showed him that I too only felt anything when I was with him, that everything inside of me matched everything inside of him. That knowing he had to marry another woman was killing me slowly. As we undressed and kissed and touched and explored each other's bodies slowly, I started to cry because I knew it would be the last time. This was the end for us and we both knew it. Elias took his time even in rolling on the condom. His eyes never left mine, his hands roamed over every inch of me, and when he finally positioned himself between my legs and started to fuck me, he was so gentle it left me breathless. Each thrust slower than the last. Each groan deeper. Each tug of my hair stronger. Each scratch deeper, matching the pain. I loved him. I had no doubt of that. And because I loved him, I had to let him go.

CHAPTER TWENTY-THREE

H<small>E WAS GONE WHEN</small> I <small>WOKE UP.</small> I'<small>D EXPECTED HIM TO BE, BUT IT</small> didn't diminish the pain in my heart. I turned the television on and watched as the news anchors covered the king's death. They were barely keeping it together as they spoke about it and it occurred to me how much people genuinely cared about the royals. Maybe it was the fact that I hadn't really grown up here or that my father was always at odds with everything the Crown did, but I always figured everyone was waiting for King Alexandre to pass away so they could take the country into their own hands. That wasn't the case, or at least not the one they portrayed on the screen. My phone rang beside me and I answered it upon seeing Etienne's name flash on the screen.

"Have you heard?"

"Yeah. I'm watching the news now," I said.

"I tried calling Aramis, but got no response. I assume Eli isn't in the villas."

"I don't think so." I looked toward the window, though I couldn't see anything from where I was sitting. "I haven't even looked outside today."

"I guess your basket duty is over."

"I guess so," I said absentmindedly. The news screen cut to a news anchor standing outside the wing of the palace where the cabinet met. My father was standing beside him. It shouldn't have been a shock to see him on there, but it was.

"Monsieur Bouchard is looking sharp," Etienne said.

"And old."

"He does look older. Have you spoken to him?"

"No."

"Seeing him on the telly must be weird."

"It was bound to happen."

"Addie." He sighed.

"It is what it is." I shrugged even though he couldn't see me.

Looking at my father right now I didn't feel the sadness I expected. I felt anger. This man was supposed to love me unconditionally and one slip up from me had him pretending he didn't even have a daughter. I knew he was busy, but that didn't excuse him of his fatherly duties.

"I'm going to have to go to the funeral," Etienne said after a moment. "Do you want to go with me?"

"Sure. I should pay my respects to the family if I can. I'm sure it'll be a madhouse."

"Probably so. I'll keep you posted when I know more."

We hung up the phone and I turned up the volume. My father was still being interviewed and I was curious as to what he was saying. Was he paying his respects or was he berating the Crown as he normally did?

"It's too soon to tell, of course," my father said in response to whatever they'd asked him. *"But we expect to meet with the king soon and see what he has in store for us."*

"*Do you think he'll want to involve the cabinet more than his father did?*"

"*I can't speak for the Crown. I have no idea what he has in mind, but I look forward to working with them to better the country.*" He waved at the camera. "*Thank you. We'll talk soon.*"

The camera stuck with him for a second before turning back to the main reporter. They continued talking about what this all meant for France. I wondered what it meant for Elias. He seemed so unsettled last night, so sad. I wished there was something I could do to help, but I knew I couldn't. Tomorrow I'd go back to London and leave everything that happened here behind. He wouldn't come back here. Not tomorrow, not next summer, or the one after that. His years of relaxing were over at least for the time being. It hit me that it was all he'd done since he'd arrived. He had one party and then barely left his villa. I'd called him lazy, boring, but in retrospect, that was exactly what he wanted to be.

CHAPTER
TWENTY-FOUR

THE FUNERAL WAS UNLIKE ANYTHING I'D SEEN BEFORE AND WE weren't even inside the Basilica of Saint-Denis yet. It made me wonder why the queen had asked me to plan the wedding at all when they obviously had a prepared in-house system. I turned to Etienne, beside me, and asked him that very thing. He shrugged as he looked at me.

"My guess is she wants the wedding to be more like the soirée you put on for the engagement and less like this." He nodded up at the church we were walking toward. "Less stuffy."

"Well, this is a funeral. It's supposed to be stuffy."

"Depends whose funeral it is."

"The same can be said for weddings."

"Exactly." Etienne smiled. "God forbid the planning was left to Elias. It would be as stuffy as you can get."

"He's not stuffy." I frowned. "Their parties are insane."

"Aramis's parties are insane. Elias is bored by them, remember?" He smirked.

I glanced back up as we reached the church doors and let go of Etienne's arm as he opened the door for us. No one looked back at the sound of our entrance, which was good since the priest had already started talking. We took the first empty seats we could find, right in the back, near the door, and listened as the priest spoke about life and death. I stared at the larger than life coffin. It had a red cape draped over it with a red and gold crown up top. It matched the outrageous flower arrangements that lined the long entrance to the chapel. I leaned out in hopes of catching a glimpse of Elias, but there was a sea of suits and dresses in front of us and I couldn't see him. Knowing I was in the same room as him would have to be enough for now. My heart sank. Was that how things would be from now on? I'd have to be glad to just be breathing the same air as him without being anywhere near him? It shouldn't matter. I didn't even live in this country. But it did. It did matter. My mother received a call from the queen's secretaries to tell her the wedding had been postponed, but they hadn't given an indication of a date and we didn't want to pry under the circumstances. Even Joss hadn't dared to ask Pilar, so we simply assumed they'd let us know when they were ready. Personally, I hoped it would be canceled altogether. And for what? So he could find another princess to marry in a couple of years? I needed to stop thinking about him as if he was just someone who was hard to get and come to terms with the fact that he was impossible to get.

The service seemed to go on forever. When it ended, everyone stood and watched as the casket was rolled forward, everyone turning toward it and bowing to pay their respects as it passed. I finally caught sight of Elias. My pulse instantly quickened. I hadn't seen him in a week and even though I did miss him, I hadn't realized how much until this very moment. All I wanted to do was break protocol and run up to him and hug him. He was walking on one side of the casket while Aramis walked on the other. They both looked stoic. A far cry from the Elias that showed up at my villa a week ago. As he walked by, his gaze cut to mine and held for a long moment. I could've sworn I saw relief or maybe gratitude in there somewhere, despite his expression merely changing. Maybe it was what I wanted to see. Nevertheless, I felt seen and that was enough.

"Where will they take him now?" I asked Etienne.

"He'll be buried here. I guess they'll take the casket to a waiting room and do that when it's family only. His heart will be buried elsewhere."

I blinked and looked at Etienne. "What?"

"His heart. His organs were . . . " He paused, frowning at me. "You didn't learn this in school?"

"I went to boarding school in Connecticut. I learned about the Revolutionary War and Rosa Parks."

"I know about the Revolutionary War and Rosa Parks." He rolled his eyes. "Leave it to America to only teach about American history."

"Will you just tell me about this heart thing?"

"All the kings have their organs taken out. Their hearts are buried wherever their wills state, but it's always in a place important to them. It's a way for them to make their political mark in the land."

"With their hearts?" I felt my brows pull. "Why couldn't they just have a sculpture made or something?"

"They do, but this is different."

"So all of them have done that?"

"Not all, but I know he chose to."

"How do you know?" I met Etienne's eyes again. He smiled and brought up his hand, waving something in it.

"Because it's in the pamphlet as well as everything else I recited." He cocked his head. "Do you really think I paid that much attention in history class?"

"Probably just enough to annoy people with tidbits of knowledge." I took the pamphlet from his hand.

Afterward, we went to the palace. I didn't want to go, but Etienne insisted, and I knew Joslyn would be there so that gave me the push I needed. I hadn't expected to see Emily, the Princess of Austria there, but there she was in all her pretty glory. She said hello to Etienne, and since I was beside him, to me as well. It was the first time we'd really spoken at all directly to each other. As she shook hands with Etienne, I stared at the ring on her finger and focused on not reacting.

"Everything has happened so fast, I don't think we got a chance to formally meet," she said to me. "I'm Emily."

"Adeline." I shook hands with her.

"I heard you'll be planning the wedding." She smiled. She said *the* wedding, not *our* wedding.

"Do you plan to be involved?" I asked.

"I'm not sure I can or should be. The queen knows what she's doing. I'm sure everything will be handled."

"But it's your wedding," Etienne said. "Surely you can't be the only woman on the planet who doesn't care much about a wedding."

"Well, I guess I am. I've never given it much thought." She shrugged, still smiling. "I figure it'll be grand and beautiful regardless of my input. I'll see you two around."

"Admit it, you think she's nice," Etienne said.

"She is nice, but I still don't like her. That's allowed, right?"

"Hey," Joss said as she came up to us.

"Where have you been?" I asked, giving her a tight sideways hug before she moved on to Etienne.

"Around. With Pilar. She's sad, poor thing."

"They all seem pretty put together," I said. "I haven't seen the queen."

"She's as stoic as the rest of them right now, but they're all sad."

"Maybe they should show it a little," I whispered. "Wouldn't that be good? For the people?"

"That's not like them, you know that. They show as much as they absolutely need to and that's not much at all." She shrugged, then brought a hand up to twirl one of the ends of my hair that had lost its curl already. "How are you doing? Things have been so crazy I haven't even run into you at home."

"You've been here most of the time," I reminded her.

"I was in our flat on Wednesday and you weren't there at all."

"I was running errands with my mother. Wednesday is only one day of the week you know."

"I've been sorting things with Pilar's current secretary."

"Right." My jaw clenched tightly. I didn't want to discuss the fact that I would be losing her to the Crown as well. Not now.

"Have you spoken to him?" Joss asked after a moment.

I looked up quickly, and the moment I did, my gaze landed on Elias and I found that he was looking right at me. I felt my cheeks warm as I forced myself to look away.

"I haven't. Not today. I should pay my respects though. To

all of them," I said, raising an eyebrow so they knew I didn't just mean him.

Etienne grabbed my hand and started leading me in that direction. I wasn't sure if he was trying to call my bluff or just walking over to pay his own respects, but I wanted to slap him for forcing me into this. I needed another hour or five years to get into the headspace of seeing Elias in public. Everything was fine when it was just him and me, but having people around us hadn't been our thing. For many reasons, starting with the fact that there was a photographer in our face as I reached him and Aramis. I shook Aramis's hand first and as I expressed my condolences, the only thing I heard was the snap, snap, snap of the camera. When I reached Elias, I did the same thing, shook his hand, but my insides became jelly and warmth spread through my entire body. I knew it would show on my face. Snap, snap, snap again. I ignored it though and kept my gaze on Elias as he leaned in. He brought his mouth to my ear.

"Thank you for being here."

"Of course."

"My coronation is set for three days from today. Will you be there as well?"

"If I'm invited. I wasn't planning on it."

He pulled back, but my hand was still in his and I didn't need anyone to tell me that this was definitely the longest handshake of the night or that I'd be on the news by tonight. My father would be livid, I wouldn't know how to explain it, and this would set my relationship with him back once again. Did I care? I wasn't sure. A part of me always would, but a bigger part of me just wanted Elias to never let go of my hand at all, tradition be damned.

"Have you thought about what we spoke about?" he asked. This time, I let go of his hand and smiled sadly.

"I can't. You know I can't."

I felt a hand at my back and nearly jumped before realizing it was just Etienne. He shot me a look and then turned to Elias and shook his hand.

"You two are taking entirely too long and there's a line," Etienne said under his breath.

"There's always a line," Elias said. "I'm trying to catch up with an old friend."

"An old friend that's going to end up in the headlines if you two don't stop flirting."

"We're not flirting," I whisper-shouted. We weren't.

"Well, half of the women are pregnant now just from the looks Elias has given you these last two minutes, so you're welcome."

My jaw dropped. Elias's mouth moved, just barely, and I knew he was trying to fight a smile, which made me bite the inside of my cheek to not smile at all. It was a disaster.

"I need to leave," I said.

"Yes. I'm taking you home after you say bye to Pilar and the queen," Etienne said.

Elias and I shared one more look, filled with sadness and so much longing I wasn't sure what to do with it, so I walked away.

CHAPTER TWENTY-FIVE

ELIAS

THE WORD *CHAOS* WOULDN'T SUFFICE IN DESCRIBING THE STATE OF my life at the moment and somehow, I hadn't stopped thinking about her. It could never happen. That was what I kept telling myself. I was set to marry Emily, and Adeline's event company was planning the entire thing. The wedding itself was a scheme, a distraction, a way to get the people to take their minds off my father's death and focus on a happily ever after. It was for that reason that Pierre wanted to schedule public events with Emily and me. It was because of Adeline that I continued canceling the events and setting others in their place.

Part of me felt like maybe if I could buy some time I could delay the wedding, delay everything and sneak off with Addie. But the date was looming and with it the burden I'd shoulder for the rest of my days. It was in times like these that I wished my father was alive, not only so that he could continue doing this job, but so he could give me advice on the matter. I didn't know who else to turn to, and I found myself turning to the most unlikely person I ever expected to receive relationship advice from—Aramis.

"Just spit it out already," Aramis said across from me. We were having scotch in the tea room of the palace. The expensive kind, meant to be savored with each sip. We'd been sipping for a long while. Long enough for me to gather the courage to admit this aloud.

"I think I'm in love with someone and it's not Emily."

"Not what I was expecting." His brow raised as he lowered his glass slowly. "Who is she?"

"Adeline."

"Bouchard?" He sat upright. "Are you insane?"

"I don't know. Maybe." I sighed, setting my glass down and bringing my hands to my face to shut my eyes behind.

Most days I wondered just that. Was I insane? I must have been to fall for a woman who not only could I not have because of traditional reasons, but could also be the one person people would blame for the demise of the Crown, should things go wrong if we made things public. It was the reason I didn't argue when she demanded our date be in private and was glad she didn't complain that we kept things behind closed doors.

"She could end you, you know?" Aramis waved a hand around. "End all of this."

"She wouldn't be to blame for that." I looked up at him. "It wouldn't come to that."

"Eli. I know you." He shot me a serious look. "If you're even admitting this to yourself, and to me, it's because you've reached the point where you can no longer hold this in and I'll be honest, being that you're the responsible one in this family, that terrifies me."

I took in a breath and exhaled heavily. "I'm not saying anything will come of this."

"You're also not saying it won't." He raised an eyebrow. He leaned back in his chair and picked up his glass again. "What does Maman say?"

"Maman knows nothing." My breath caught at the mere thought of my mother's disappointment. She'd given up everything in Spain to marry my father out of obligation. If she caught wind that her own son couldn't do the same, she'd have a lot to say and none of it would be good.

"So, where are you going with this?" Aramis asked after a moment. "Are you going to take a mistress? Is that what it'll come down to?"

"She won't accept that."

His eyes widened. "You asked her?"

"I had to know."

"You're a real asshole." He shook his head. "I wouldn't even ask that of someone."

"I know."

"And you love this woman?" He frowned. "I couldn't imagine asking a woman I love to be my side piece."

"You would if you had no other choice." My voice was a roar in the otherwise silent room.

"I'm just making a statement." He put his free hand up and took another sip of his scotch. The single ice in mine had all but disappeared into the amber liquid in my glass. I had barely touched it.

"Do you think I would ask that of her if I thought I could fix this?" I asked after a moment. "I don't want to lose her."

"Eli," he said, and it was the seriousness in his tone that made me meet his gaze again. "You already lost her."

"How could you possibly know that?"

"Your ascension already happened. Your coronation is currently underway. After that, it's done. You might as well forget about her."

I already knew that, of course, but his words still brought a sting with them. I picked up the scotch I'd been ignoring and drained the glass. What good was savoring something exquisite if you had no shot at keeping it?

CHAPTER TWENTY-SIX

"I TOLD YOU THAT YOU'D BE SEEING HIM EVERYWHERE," JOSLYN said.

I set the tabloid down and glanced at her. She was giving me a look I hoped to avoid—full of compassion, kindness, and a little bit of *I told you so*. She had told me so and the reality was far worse than I'd anticipated. Seeing Elias with another woman was the most painful thing I'd had to endure. Forget being the subject of a sex scandal and having my video leaked everywhere. Forget my father's dismissal of his disgraced daughter over it. This was, hands down, the most heart-wrenching thing. I guess you could say that the moment I realized that I was in love with Elias was the moment I saw him with another woman. Then suddenly everything became crystal clear. I wanted him to not go through with the coronation. I wanted him to say fuck tradition and run away with me instead. I wanted him to give up decades of history because he wanted me more than he wanted to rule. I focused on the items on the conveyer belt in front of me and paid the grocery bill when they were finished bagging them.

"At least you can move on now." Joss grabbed the handle of the grocery cart and started pushing it outside.

"I know you mean well, but I need you to shut the fuck up," I said as I put my wallet and receipt away, walking beside her. "I can't just move on. That's not how it works. I need to be mentally prepared for it and I'm not. I want him. End of story."

"I wish you didn't."

"You think I don't?"

"I think you're still waiting for a miracle to happen."

"Maybe I am." I shrugged a shoulder. "Just because he's out with Emily doesn't mean . . . " I stopped mid-sentence and frowned.

Was I really saying this? Did I really believe it? Joss waited as I struggled to finish my sentence, my thoughts. I pushed the button to open the trunk of the car and started loading the grocery bags. Joss took the cart and walked back as I was closing the trunk. When we both climbed into the car and snapped our seatbelts on, she turned to me.

"You know as well as anyone that once they choose to make something like this public, it's over," she said. "I'm sorry, but that's the way it is."

"I know. I just . . . " I closed my eyes as I shook my head. "I hate all of this."

"Hey, you fell for him." She set her hand over mine. "It's totally understandable."

"I wish I could take it all back." I opened my eyes and looked at her.

"In time, you will." She smiled sadly as she pulled her

hand back. "I feel bad leaving you for them. Especially now."

"Don't feel bad. We talked about this. It's a cool opportunity for you. Personal Secretary to the Princess of France. Who else can say that?" I smiled. "You'll have the cutest stationery."

She laughed. "If I was going to work for anyone else, I'd tell you that no one uses stationery anymore, but they definitely do."

"You'll have to write me a letter." My smile weakened and fully disappeared as the sadness of it all crept up on me. "I'm happy for you. I am. I'm just going to miss you so very much."

Tears began trickling down my face mid-sentence and continued as Joss leaned over and threw her arms around me and held me tight.

"You're going to be just fine, Addie. You've built an incredible company, you have all the contacts you need, and everyone wants to hire you. Besides, Seth isn't bad on the eyes," she said, referring to the man we'd hired to take on Joss's role once she fully stepped out, which was last week. I laughed through my tears as I pulled away and wiped them.

"He is handsome." I sniffled. And gay. And married. I didn't feel the need to tack any of those on since Joss already knew that. "He's bringing his husband by the office next week."

"You'll have to keep me posted on that." She smiled, straightening in her seat and setting her hands on the steering wheel. "Let's go put these groceries away and make some lunch."

As we drove, my mind stayed on all of the changes happening in my life. Joss would be moving out this weekend and heading to Paris, where Princess Pilar lived, to move in with her. I'd have to make a choice between getting another room-mate or trading in the flat for a smaller one. I had a wedding on Saturday that Seth would be working as we transitioned Joss out of the company entirely, though she did promise to help with the royal wedding. The thought alone made me want to cry, but I wouldn't. I needed to let him go.

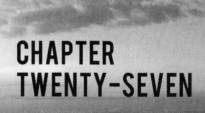

CHAPTER TWENTY-SEVEN

THE INVITATION IN MY HAND FELT HEAVY AS I READ IT A THIRD TIME. I set it down on the counter and looked at Joss.

"Maybe it was meant for you."

"I have my own." She lifted the ivory envelope in front of her. "They meant to invite you, which makes sense. You are planning the wedding, after all."

"I don't think I can stomach going to this." I looked at the invitation again. "Emily will be there with him."

"She was at Sunday dinner with him."

"They weren't this official yet then." I gnawed my bottom lip.

"It was their engagement announcement. They were official enough." Joss raised an eyebrow. "You've agreed to plan their wedding, Addie."

"I hate all of this." I sighed heavily and reached for my phone and began a text. "I wonder if Etienne will be there."

"I'm sure he's invited."

"How upset do you think the queen will be if I back out of planning the wedding?" I glanced up at Joss, whose eyebrows had reached a new altitude.

"Very, but not as upset as your mother will be."

"You're right." I shook my head. "I need to stop letting whatever this was dictate my professional career."

"I agree."

"And I'm going to the coronation. I'm going to prove to myself that I can do this."

"Good."

"And I will no longer be charmed by him. Especially not in public."

"Very well." Joss stood from the barstool across from me. "Let's go shopping. We have a coronation to attend."

CHAPTER TWENTY-EIGHT

ELIAS

"I**T FEELS STUFFY IN HERE.**" I PULLED AT THE COLLAR OF MY shirt.

"That's because you're in the room." Aramis smirked as he walked over to me.

"Hilarious."

"Are you nervous?"

"What do you think?" I shot him a look.

I would love to say I'd been preparing for this my entire life, but that would be a lie. While I'd been bred for this, my father always acted as if he never expected to die. As if all of us would be under his rule forever. And so, I was truly lost in this role. I knew what my responses would be during the coronation. I knew I'd have to finally face the members of the cabinet and had a speech prepared for that, but everything this entailed and everything that would be expected of me after today? No, I was not ready for it. I hadn't met a monarch thus far who said they'd been truly prepared for it.

"This will be the first coronation to be televised since . . ." Aramis whistled. "Well, since Queen Elizabeth II." He chuckled. "No pressure."

"You're a real jerk, you know that?" I exhaled as I continued to tug on my collar and looked at Pierre. "How many will be in attendance?"

"Several billion will be watching." He couldn't even hide his laughter. I wanted to kill them both. Pierre cleared his throat and added, "Inside of the palace walls, there will be two-thousand-four-hundred and thirty. Outside of the palace walls, probably all of France if I had to guess."

"Probably cheering for the demise of the throne," I said under my breath.

"Well, at least you know what to expect," Aramis quipped.

I shot him another glare. Everything about this was ridiculous. As I looked in the mirror, I saw my brother standing behind me and wondered how he'd fare as king. We looked so much alike, no one would bat an eye if he went up there today and accepted the crown. As if he sensed what I was thinking, he shook his head, a sad smile on his face.

"I would never want to be in that position. I'm sorry you have to be."

"Me too."

"Miss Adeline confirmed her attendance," Pierre said.

My brother held my gaze in our reflection. "You invited her?"

"Maman did. She's planning the wedding, you know."

"Adeline is?" Aramis's mouth unhinged. "This is so fucked."

"Extremely," Pierre agreed, clearing his throat when I

looked over at him. "Addie is kind, but she has a strong spirit. She can do whatever she sets her mind to."

"How very traditional of you to have the woman you're in love with attend the event that will either push her away completely or push her to take a place as your mistress," Aramis said.

"Fuck you. You know that's not my intention." I turned and faced him. "I don't even want her planning the wedding. I'd rather her not be here at all."

"Yet here she will be."

"Not because I wanted it."

"But you're the king now. Can't you say no to your own mother when she pushes your buttons?"

"Jesus. You're being a child." I shut my eyes and ran my fingers through my hair. "Do you like to see me upset on one of the most important days of my life?"

"I didn't realize this was that important to you."

"Billions will be watching." I pointed at the window. "All of France will be here."

"Something else you should know," Pierre said.

"Yes?"

"There's a women's march happening in the courtyard. It's contained and they're being escorted outside."

"A march? How did they get in here?" I blinked. "What are they complaining about?"

"A guard who got fired, and from what I gather, they're complaining about the inflation in the price of food."

"Fuck." I sighed heavily as I walked over to the desk, where I had all of my papers scattered from my meeting with the cabinet.

A cabinet consisting of five people, all of whom hated

me. To their dismay, they'd all been handpicked by my father, who believed in the keep-your-enemies-close theory. They weren't allowed to do much, as everything was ultimately the sovereign's decision, but their judgment rang through for sure. I located the economy folder and flipped through it. Everything was inflated because of our current deal with the Saudis. Unfortunately, petroleum was valued as gold and we had none of our own. I closed the folder with a thump. The people were right to riot, but my hands were tied. I'd have to get on a plane and go meet with the Crowned Prince myself in order to sort this out.

I glanced at my brother and Pierre. "I have to get on a carriage and parade around from here to the Basilica while the people riot? They already tried to kill me once. Who's to say it won't happen again?"

"We would never let that happen, Your Majesty." That was Pierre.

"Stop it with the Your Majesty bullshit when it's just the three of us." I turned around and faced the mirror again, undoing my tie quickly and tossing it aside.

"Do you want a different tie?" Pierre asked.

"I don't want a tie at all."

"You'll wear this to the coronation." Pierre pointed at the extravagant costume set over the bed. "And the tuxedo to the party afterward, so maybe you should change into the first outfit first and I'll get the collar taken care of."

"I fucking hate parties." I shrugged the tuxedo off, tossing it on the bed and walked over to the first costume.

It looked like something out of King Lear, but it would do. It was the same thing my father wore for his coronation, which was similar to what his father had worn, and the list went on. I couldn't be the first person to say no to this. I was supposed to hold this palace together. I was supposed to solidify that the sovereign wasn't going anywhere just because my father was no longer with us. Sure, I'd try to modernize things a bit, but today was not the time for that. Today, I'd fall in line like I was expected to. Tomorrow, during my meeting with the cabinet, I'd try to work with them more. Something my father was always criticized for not doing.

Riding in a chariot wasn't all it was worked up to be. I'd only done it once before, when I was a child. It was one of the things I was glad our family didn't do often. As traditional as we were, we opted for cars rather than horses and carriages when we had outings, but in this case, we held onto the tradition. We had to stop three times due to rambunctious crowds on our way from Versailles to the Basilica of Saint-Denis and all three times the horses took a massive dump that left the chariot smelling like shit. It was shit I was sure the crowds would have loved to pick up and throw at me. From what I could tell, my reception was cut in half. Fifty percent of them loved this and the other fifty percent were spitting on the ground as the gold-plated wheels passed them. There were people carrying signs that said *"Je t'aime, King Elias!" "Vive le Roi Elias!"* and those would have been fine, if they hadn't been followed by *"A bas la monarchie!"*

It was something I knew was coming, but hadn't expected it to be this blatant, this soon. They weren't just rioting over the economy. They wanted the throne to suffer. It was as if they weren't even giving me a chance to prove to them that I could be a better ruler than my father. They just assumed. Maybe they were right to. After all, I'd only met with the cabinet once and unlike my father, I did believe that the people were allowed to make demands when they felt things were unjust. The very last sign just before the carriage disappeared into the private, underground parking of the basilica read: "I hope you starve." It wasn't the words that hit me in the chest as much as it was the person holding it—a man with greasy long hair, tall and lanky, all bones. I couldn't even fathom when his last meal had been. As if that wasn't enough, there was a child standing beside him that mirrored him.

I turned to Pierre. "Find out who that man is and where his family lives."

"I'm on it." Pierre pushed the button on his earpiece and relayed the remark to the rest of the security. After he spoke, he turned to me. "Maybe we should find out where a handful of them live. You can pay them a visit with Emily. Let them see things will be different."

"That's what we'll do." I gave a nod. It seemed like a solid plan.

"Won't the people you so desperately want to impress see that as a publicity stunt?" Aramis slid his phone into his pocket and looked up at me from the other side of the chariot.

It was a valid question. One I didn't have an answer for. I looked at Pierre beside him. I was so far removed from it all that I had no idea how people saw me at all. I thought of Adeline. Adeline, who was sweet and kind but also fiery. Adeline, who made me question things because she questioned me without judging my responses. She pushed me in a way nobody else dared. Even my brother, who said whatever was on his mind all the time had a limit. Adeline didn't. She just was. Limitless.

"Earth to Eli." Aramis snapped his fingers. I blinked. "What the hell was that?"

"Just thinking about something."

"Someone," Pierre provided, his mouth turning with disapproval.

"What?"

"You're going to see her tonight and I'm afraid of what you'll do," Pierre provided. "Afraid of what I'll have to clean up tomorrow, and she doesn't deserve that—to be something I clean up. Don't bring her into this mess, Eli."

"I'm not." My frown deepened. "I'm not a monster."

"Monsters seldom think they are."

The words came from my brother's mouth and I found myself unable to contend them. The more time I spent around Adeline, the more I found myself wanting to twist things and do the wrong thing because in my head and heart she was the right one to do the wrong thing for.

CHAPTER TWENTY-NINE

ADELINE

THE AIR WAS CHARGED. IT HADN'T YET STARTED, BUT anticipation rolled through me nonetheless. The deceased king didn't allow anyone inside his coronation. I wasn't sure he even had one. The Queen Mother held hers behind closed doors. Elias was having his televised, had opened the door to the outside world when he invited people like me, a commoner, in here. It was so quiet, you could hear a pin drop, and I leaned in closer when the doors opened and they started playing a hymn. The archbishop walked in followed by a row of bishops behind him—one held a sword, another a large gold crown with stones, another a chalice, another a red coat, another a pillow with a ring on it. We all remained standing, as we had been since we walked in, worried we'd miss something. I hadn't seen the Queen Mother or Princess Pilar, or Prince Aramis, or Emily, the Princess of Austria, for that matter, but the moment I caught a glimpse of Elias walking behind the bishops, looking larger than life and handsome as ever in regal red and gold attire, I felt like the air was sucked out of the room.

A hand covered and squeezed mine on either side. I turned my attention to my right side, where Etienne was, and my left, where Joslyn was, and squeezed back, grateful for the comfort they provided. Then, my eyes were back on Elias. He didn't look at anyone, just forward, his march steady, his head held high. He didn't even look nervous, but I couldn't imagine he wouldn't be. Behind the long train of his red coat, his brother Aramis, and behind him, his sister and mother. Emily was still nowhere to be found. I was momentarily grateful for that. At least this wouldn't turn into a surprise royal wedding. For now.

Once they were out of view, we all sat down. The basilica was too big and we were too far to see them from where we were. We could barely make out what they were saying, but we followed along with the pamphlets provided to us.

When the archbishop asked, Sir, is Your Majesty willing to take the Oath?

We heard Elias respond, I am willing.

The archbishop spoke again, Will you solemnly promise and swear to govern the Peoples of France and the other Territories to any of them belonging or pertaining, according to their respective laws and customs?

Elias said, I solemnly promise so to do.

The archbishop followed up with, Will you to your power cause Law and Justice, in Mercy, to be executed in all your judgments?

Elias replied, I will.

Everything else was lost on me. The songs, the prayers, the hymns. He'd taken his oath. He'd chosen the Crown. I knew he would, but I hadn't expected to feel this void inside. When it was over, we were all escorted out of the basilica. As I walked outside, I glanced over my shoulder and saw Elias standing from the chair he'd been sitting in and following the bishops to the back of the basilica. I kept my eyes on them until they disappeared, and when his mother, sister, and brother stood, I noticed Emily was there after all and she too disappeared to the back. It wasn't a surprise wedding, but it might as well have been, with the way my heart felt like it was shattering inside of my chest.

The ride to Versailles was quiet. I was grateful for that. Etienne and Joss seemed to understand that I needed silence to process it all. It was an hour car ride though, and I knew the silence wouldn't last long. Joslyn's phone vibrated first. She met my gaze for a second before answering it and I knew instantly she was speaking to Pilar, who was obviously wondering where her personal secretary was. Once Joss assured her that she was on her way to Versailles, Pilar stopped asking questions and she hung up the phone with a heavy sigh.

"They're not far behind."

"Addie?" Etienne asked. I glanced up at him. He was sitting in the driver's seat and I was the lone person in the back. "You okay?"

"Yeah. Fine." I forced a placating smile. He frowned and shook his head, eyes back on the road.

"I think you should tell the queen you can't plan the wedding."

"I can't." I shut my eyes and pushed my head back into the seat. "My mother would kill me."

"Speaking of parents, did you see your father?" Joss asked.

"No." My eyes widened. "Did you?"

"I saw him when we walked in."

"Where was he sitting?" My heart pounded faster.

"A few rows behind us."

"I'm sure he'll be at the event," Etienne said. "The cabinet is always invited to everything."

"One more thing I don't need in my life right now," I mumbled.

"You have to speak to him sometime." That was Joss, in her encouraging voice with her hopeful, bright eyes.

I glared. "I'm not the reason we're not speaking."

"Well, technically," Etienne said. I leaned in and pinched his shoulder. "Ouch! What the hell, Adeline?"

"Keep your comments to yourself unless you're going to be supportive of me."

"I am supportive of you. You're the reason I'm driving an hour and a half away from my comfortable flat."

Joss scoffed. "Right, because you wouldn't be here otherwise."

"Maybe I wouldn't."

Joss and I started laughing. "You live for this stuff."

"Which reminds me, where's Mira?" Joss raised an eyebrow. "You haven't even mentioned her."

"We're on a break."

"On a break?" My mouth dropped. "We love Mira. What happened?"

"Life. Work is taking her to Spain for a month and then Rome and I'm tired of the distance." He shrugged a shoulder. "If it's meant to be, it'll be."

"Still. That's kind of a bummer." My lips pursed.

I thought for sure Etienne would be proposing to Mira this year, not breaking up with her. If they couldn't make it work,

I wasn't sure who could. I knew we were almost at the castle when I saw the row of cars in front of us slowing down as they made their way through security. To our left, there was a row of protestors. I wondered how Elias felt about them.

"He probably doesn't care," Etienne said.

"He has to care," Joss argued. "I'm going to ask Pilar about it."

"What do you think, Addie?" Etienne eyed me in the rearview. Joss looked at me over her shoulder.

"How am I supposed to know?" I frowned. "It's not like I talk to him."

"You don't?" Etienne raised an eyebrow.

"I don't. I told him to stop calling and he did."

"Hm."

"When?" Joss turned as much as her dress allowed. "Why? You didn't tell me this!"

"The other night. We discussed the coronation briefly and I asked him not to call anymore because I didn't think I could handle being his friend."

"I told you." Etienne shook his head. "Let me guess, he asked you to be his mistress?"

"No." I crossed my arms and glanced out the window. He hadn't. Not outright anyway. But technically, he had, hadn't he?

"He's a fucking asshole." Etienne slapped the steering wheel, making my body jerk.

"It doesn't matter. I would never agree to that and yes, he's an asshole, but he's also kind, so if I had to guess, this display of hate outside our windows on the way into the palace is breaking his heart."

"Well, I for one, hope he pays attention and makes some major changes," Etienne said.

"Yeah, because your family is starving." Joss rolled her eyes.

"Obviously not, but I know people who have families who are struggling. And for no good reason."

"Maybe you should bring that up to him since you're friends," I said.

"Maybe I will."

Thankfully for all parties involved, our discussion was cut short by our arrival at the gate. The guards checked our car, our identification, verified that we were invited, and finally, let us drive in. Flashbacks of the ball I'd planned here came rushing back to me as we drove in. Flashbacks of Elias and my first time together after six years. Flashbacks of his confession and my mother's warnings. I held the skirt of my dress tightly as the door was opened for me and I climbed out of Etienne's Land Rover. Tonight, I would lay low, stay on the other side of the room at all times, and not make eye contact with him. If Etienne and Joss were right about my father being in attendance, the last thing I wanted to do was give him more cause to run to my mother with poor gossip about me.

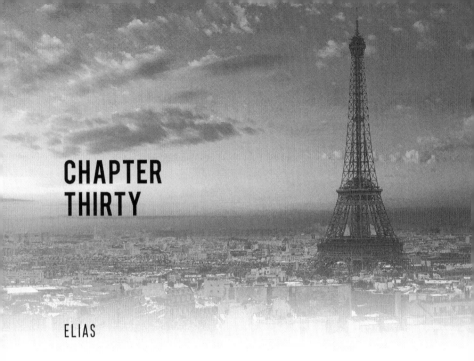

CHAPTER THIRTY

ELIAS

I T DIDN'T TAKE ME LONG TO COME UP WITH A PLAN. I DISCUSSED IT with Pierre and Aramis first and decided I'd bring my mother and Pilar in on it before the celebration ball began. I was in my chambers getting dressed in the tuxedo Pierre had picked out for me when I heard the knock. My mother didn't wait for me to respond before barging in, her heels stabbing at the marble floor with each step she took toward me. Behind her, Emily, her footsteps a little lighter. I wish I could have been the kind of man who felt bad in this situation, but Emily was just collateral. She'd move on to the next prince, maybe my brother, or the Grecian Prince Aros, who was also in need of a quick marriage. I'd known Emily most of my life and always wished her well, but whatever she decided to do didn't matter to me.

"What is this Pierre is talking about?" My mother stopped walking when she was just a few steps away from me. Emily stood beside her quietly. "You're going to break off your engagement with Emily to court a commoner?"

"It'll be good for our image." I continued buttoning my cuffs and looked over at Emily. "I'm sorry you had to find out this way. It was my intention to tell you as soon as I finished up here, but it appears my secretary decided to go ahead and do it for me."

As if on cue, Pierre walked into the room. "Your Majesty. Your mother overheard Aramis and I discussing."

"Just as well." My eyes stayed on Emily's. "You'll find a better fit for you."

"I wanted you." She frowned. "We'd be perfect together."

"For a while. For appearances," I agreed, "but not for long."

"Appearances are the only thing that matter," my mother said. "Appearance is everything."

"Not everything." I raised an eyebrow and went back to my tie.

"What is your plan then? Why this sudden . . . change?" Mother asked.

"I have to visit those people's houses tomorrow. Poor people. Starving people. How will it look if I show up there with another rich monarch?"

"What they say does not matter," Emily said. "They'll take this as a sign of weakness."

"They'll take it however we sell it to them."

"And where will you find this commoner?" my mother asked.

I stayed silent. The question wasn't where I would find her. The question was whether or not she'd still accept me. She didn't have to know about the ulterior motives. Hell, I didn't even care about the ulterior motives. As far as I was concerned, they were the icing on top. I was just glad I'd get to keep her.

"We already found her," Pierre said, speaking up on my behalf. "She's perfect. You have nothing to worry about, Your Majesty." He bowed to my mother, as if to dismiss her, and she knew it. Her eyes flared at him before turning to me.

"You better know what you're doing, Elias. The future of this monarchy is sitting on your shoulders." She reached for Emily's hand and dragged her out of the room as if she were a child.

When the doors slammed shut behind them, I let out a breath and looked at Pierre.

"That was a good save."

"Somebody had to say something." Pierre handed over my jacket. "What are you going to do?"

"I'll have to ask her tonight." I shrugged on the jacket. "And hope that she accepts."

"She'd have to uproot her entire life for you. That's what you'd be asking of her," Pierre said. "Her life is in London and unlike Emily, Adeline has a company to run. She'd be giving up a lot if she agrees to this."

"I know." I took a breath and exhaled it. It was a lot to ask of anyone. I wasn't blind to that.

"I'll start a list of names in case she says no." Pierre headed to the door.

"No." My voice rung out in the room.

"Just in case." He turned to look at me. "You need a backup plan."

"I don't want a list. If Addie won't do it, we'll figure out another way."

"Eli, you need to have a plan."

"Give me a couple of days. I'll have one."

He gave a nod and walked away, leaving me in the

chambers by myself. I'd never liked staying in Versailles and had never envisioned myself sleeping in the king's bedchambers. My father loved it. He said he felt closer to his roots, to the Sun God, and it served as a reminder of why he was here and what he was to accomplish. I felt haunted by those things, not inspired. I finished dressing and walked out of the lavish room. Pierre was waiting just outside the door with my crown and royal cape. I put them both on, looked in the mirror beside me, and saw all of the things haunting me inside my eyes. Having Adeline would ease a lot of it. I felt that deep in my core, and it was with the determination of getting her that I walked all the way to the Hall of Mirrors, where the celebration was taking place.

CHAPTER THIRTY-ONE

ADELINE

I WATCHED PRINCE ARAMIS WALKING IN MY DIRECTION, HIS GAZE ON mine. He looked so much like his older brother that it took a moment for my heart to settle.

"Adeline." He bowed his head slightly as he reached me.

"Prince Aramis." I bowed mine as well, unsure of whether or not I was to curtsy to him as well. His mouth lifted slightly, as if he was reading my mind.

"I'm not the king."

"Good to know." I smiled shakily. "I'm never sure what to do in these situations."

"That'll make all of this that much more interesting." He winked and walked away, stopping at the bar a few feet from where I was. I turned, a frown on my face, as I watched him. What did that even mean? Was he talking about my reaction to Elias and Emily? My stomach turned at the thought. Just when I was thinking about bailing on this entire thing, the soft jazz music the band was playing stopped and a trumpet rang out as the doors at the end of the hall opened.

"Elias Francis, crowned King of France," the man announced. "Long live the King!"

Everyone, including me, repeated the phrase, "Long live the King" as we watched Elias walk into the room. My heart skipped. I knew I missed him. I thought about him every waking second of the day since we'd been apart, but seeing him now, the longing was magnified. I tried hard to push it down, to cover it with the anger I was sure to feel in a few minutes when Emily, the Princess of Austria, joined him, but it didn't help. Longing mixed with anger only deepened how much I wanted him. All of the guests created a circle for him to go around and greet. I watched as one by one, each man bowed as he shook their hand and every woman curtsied as he kissed the back of theirs. I hated every single hand he touched because it was not mine. When he was just six or seven people from me, I retreated a foot with the intention of leaving, but hit someone standing behind me. I turned, confused, and saw Pierre smiling at me.

"You can't leave the room until he greets you," he whispered.

"Oh." My eyes widened. What would happen if I defied the rule?

The thought stuck with me as I turned around again, gathering all of my courage to stay put. When Elias greeted the third person from me, he glanced up and our eyes met. Even as he continued shaking hands and kissing the back of the women's, he stared at me. By the time he reached me, I was sure my heart wasn't my own and that it had taken place inside his chest somehow. He lifted my hand and I tore my gaze from his, looking at the ground as I curtsied. Instead of letting go of my hand, as he'd done for everyone else, he held on tightly to mine. I managed to bring my gaze back to his. My pulse quickened as he leaned in and brought his lips to my ear.

"We need to talk."

"I don't think you're supposed to speak to me while you're greeting everyone in court."

"I think the king is allowed to do whatever he wants."

"Eli," I whispered.

"I miss you."

"Please. Not here." My heart leaped into my ears.

He couldn't speak to me like that in public and expect me to keep a poised and stoic appearance. There were photographers everywhere, snapping photos of every single moment. There were journalists ready to rip him apart for any misstep. I pulled away and took a step back with a smile, for their sake, and let go of his hand. He looked at me for one more second before moving on to Pierre, now standing beside me. I let out a breath when he was far enough, but maintained my composure because I'd learned the way the media worked. I'd learned that their lens would stay on me long after I thought they looked away. When Elias was finished greeting and thanking everyone, the room applauded and erupted into cheers once more, and I finally managed to breathe out.

"They probably photographed him doing that," I said to Pierre in a voice as low as I could muster.

"They definitely photographed it." He glanced away from me and looked around momentarily, suddenly smiling wide. "They're photographing us right now. Smile. Or laugh."

"I'll be on page one tomorrow." I laughed. It sounded fake, but thankfully sound didn't translate in photographs. "What was he thinking?"

"Funny you should ask. I need you to come with me when this is over."

My smile faltered. "Where?"

"To the King's State Apartments."

"For what?" My pulse quickened.

I didn't know what state apartments were, but I assumed it was some kind of bedroom? Surely Elias didn't mean to seduce me on his coronation day, when Emily was present. I looked over at the dance floor, which was mostly empty, save for an elderly couple in the corner. Everyone else seemed to be mingling with their drinks. Emily caught my attention. She was standing in the corner speaking to Elias. Or arguing. It seemed like they were arguing. He didn't look very happy. I tore my gaze from them and looked at Pierre again.

"For what? Why does he need to see me in private? Can't we speak here?"

"I don't advise it."

"Since when do you advise me at all?" I crossed my arms and brought a hand to my lips, chewing on the tip of my fingernail.

"Don't show them you're nervous."

I let my hands fall at my sides again, blinking at him. "I already told him I wasn't willing to . . . you know."

"Be his mistress," Pierre provided with a serious nod. "I'm glad you declined the offer."

I stared at him for a moment. Was he glad I declined because he thought something could still happen between us? No. I liked to think I knew Pierre better than that. He was too loyal to Elias to try anything with me at this point. Maybe he was looking out for my best interest.

"So, what is it we need to discuss?" I asked again. I was too impatient to wait.

Pierre opened his mouth to answer, but his gaze shifted to something behind me and he shut it quickly and forced a smile. "I'll see you later, Adeline."

I opened my mouth to question him, when I heard the sound of my father's voice just behind me.

CHAPTER THIRTY-TWO

"I WASN'T EXPECTING TO SEE YOU HERE," HE SAID.

My heart stopped beating for a millisecond. I turned around and faced him. Being stoic in front of my father would prove to be far more complicated than doing it in front of Elias. This was the man who raised me. The first man I loved. Also, the one who banished me without a second thought the first time I fucked up. And yet, with him in front of me I couldn't seem to summon the anger I should be feeling. He had bags under his eyes and his black hair was thinning, leaving a crescent-shaped, nearly bald patch on the front of his head. It had been nearly eight months since I last saw him and, in that time, he looked like he'd aged a decade.

"Father," I said.

"Whose friend are you?" His gaze scrutinized me. "Pilar?"

"No. I mean, yes, we're friendly, but I don't think Pilar can invite people to this."

"Hm." His eyes narrowed slightly. It took everything in me not to cower. "The Queen Mother then. Your mother told me you planned a ball for them."

"Mother also planned the ball. She does own half of the company, you know."

"At least she's putting the money from the separation to good use." He scoffed, putting a hand in the pocket of his tuxedo and rocking slightly on his heels.

"Yup," I emphasized the *p* in the word and glanced away from his inspection.

"The Crown is a joke," he said.

"Then why are you here?" I blinked back at him.

"I was invited."

"Yeah, and you came for what? To cast judgment on a king who hasn't even yet had a chance to show what he's capable of?"

"If he's anything like his father we know exactly what he's capable of."

"Do you think he is? Like his father?"

"Too soon to tell." Father shrugged a shoulder. "He hasn't been tested."

"There are riots everywhere. People like you who would rather dismantle the thrown than give him a chance."

"You're one of those." He pursed his lips, shaking his head.

"One of what?"

"One of those women who think we should give him a chance because he's good-looking and charming."

"That is not true." I frowned.

"Speak of the devil." Dad scoffed again and looked up at someone walking up to us. I looked in that direction, surprised to see Elias closing the distance between us. I felt the sudden need to shield him from my father's judgment. "Apparently you have my daughter's approval. Not that it means much for your future."

"You'd be surprised at how much it means," Elias responded, not taking his eyes away from mine.

"So you two have met," my father said.

"We have, and now, counselor, if you don't mind, I'm going to ask Adeline to dance."

"To dance? Absolutely not."

"I don't think Adeline would leave her king hanging." Elias offered me his hand to take. I stared at it for a beat.

"Her king." Father scoffed again. "What are you playing at? Have you been keeping tabs on her all this time? Stalking her? Is this all a ploy to get back at me for not giving you her information all those years ago?"

My eyes widened. "What information? When?"

"A dance, Addie," Elias said, his voice stern. "I'll explain."

"Do not get close to this man, Adeline. I know a good one when I see one and he's not it."

"Oh?" I blinked. "Have you looked in the mirror lately? What do you see then?"

"I have my faults, but I am not a bad man. This one, this king"—Father pointed at Elias—"He's not good. I've heard more than enough rumors about him and his brother's escapades and the potential children they may have fathered and left behind."

My heart dropped. Of course I'd heard those rumors, but I couldn't imagine them to be true. Not after meeting Elias. Not after . . . everything.

"One dance, Adeline." Elias cleared his throat. I swallowed. I knew people were watching and I needed to give him an answer and this would be the perfect time to ask him questions.

"Well. Far be it from me to deny a king a dance." I curtsied as I set my hand in Elias's palm and looked at my father one more time. "Goodbye, Father. Take care of yourself. And clean those mirrors while you're at it."

Elias's hand tightened on mine as he led me to the dance floor. When we reached it, he turned me fully in his arms and placed one hand on my lower back while the other held my hand up. He pulled me close, so that my chest was against his and there was no choice for me but to move with him. His face lowered, his nose brushing against my cheek and back up to my ear.

"I miss you, Addie. I wasn't just saying that."

"People are going to talk about this," I responded through my teeth as I plastered a smile on my face. "This won't end well. The media will have a field day."

"I don't care. Do you?"

"Yes." I pulled back slightly and looked him in the eyes. "And you should as well."

"The only thing I care about is this moment, with you in my arms."

"Eli." I sighed, my body melting into his. I pressed my head on his chest and pulled back quickly, realizing how that would look. "We can't do this in public."

"I'm the king. I can do whatever I want."

"That's the kind of talk that's going to make people hate you. I'm serious."

"And you don't want them to hate me." He smiled softly, keeping the hand on my back in place as he let go of my hand and brought his to cup my face. "You have the most beautiful heart I've ever encountered."

"What was my father talking about when he said you asked for my information all those years ago?" I asked, needing to get back to neutral ground.

"It was nothing." He dropped his hand from my face and picked my hand up again as we waltzed around the dance floor.

"I want to know."

He sighed heavily. "It was a long time ago."

"I still want to know."

"You have to promise you won't get angry." He held my gaze steady.

"I don't know that I can do that." I felt my frown deepen. "Why would I get angry?"

"I . . . about six years ago I met a woman, a girl, really, and we had an incredible night together. Mind-blowing. Intense. Real."

"You're right. I don't want to hear about this." I tore my gaze from him and looked away, smile forgotten. I couldn't pretend to be okay listening to his night with another woman.

"You were the girl." He brought his hand to my face again and turned it to his. "You left before morning but you'd told me your villa was next door, so I went looking the minute I realized you were gone. You'd already left for the States. Etienne was driving you to the airport, but your father was home. He refused to give me your information. He said I was a disgrace and he couldn't believe his daughter would ever be with the likes of me."

"He said that?" I stopped dancing and lowered my hand from his shoulder.

"It was why I didn't tell you from the first moment I saw you again that I recognized you. That I looked for you."

"Why would he want to hide me from you?"

"I was a playboy." He shrugged. "It was what he saw when he saw me. Summer after summer."

"I don't want to think about that. What about the child?

Is it true you got a woman pregnant and didn't own up to it?"
I asked. It had always been just a rumor, but now I wasn't so
sure. When he didn't answer right away, I shimmied my body
until he dropped his arm from the small of my back and let me
pull away completely.

"Can we talk about this outside of this room?"

I froze and looked around for the first time and saw the
photographers, the people looking at us and whispering, magnified by all of the mirrors around us, and the panic I thought
I'd left behind when the sex video with my ex went away
started creeping in. I wasn't sure if Elias saw it or not, but he
grabbed my hand and escorted me out of the Hall of Mirrors
and into the room across the hall.

"Are you okay?" he asked once he'd closed the door behind
us, took off the floor-length red royal shawl around him, setting it down on the chair beside the door.

I watched as he removed the huge crown on his head and
set it down on the chair as well, wondering if he was supposed
to be doing that, but not caring enough to ask. I took a deep
breath and looked around. The room was huge, dripping opulence. Definitely not the place to take someone who doesn't
want to be overwhelmed. As I walked around, in awe of everything, I forgot why we were even in here and what had led us
to leave that room, but just as suddenly, I stopped walking and
remembered.

"No, I'm not okay." I turned around and faced him. "You
didn't answer my question."

"I didn't. I've always been careful with who I had sex with
and I never slept with any of the locals. Only you." He ran a
hand through his already brushed back hair. "I swear on everything, Addie. I've never fathered a child by anyone."

"So it's just a rumor?"

"Of course. What kind of man do you think I am not to claim my own child, regardless of the consequences?"

"I believe you." I exhaled heavily after a moment. "I'm sorry. I've just had quite the evening."

"I have more for you to process." Elias walked over to me slowly, closing the distance between us. "And I hope you don't walk away from me this time."

"What?" My heart pounded. Was it about the wedding? Was it about the mistress thing because having him this close after not having him at all would make it that much more difficult to say no to that.

"I broke off the engagement to Emily."

"What?"

"I won't be marrying her." He brought a hand out and held one of mine. "I want to be with you."

"But I'm not a royal." I frowned.

"I'm the king now, Addie. I make my own rules." His lips turned up slightly. "Will you do this with me?"

"I . . ."

"I'm not asking you to marry me. I'm asking you to just try this out. I know it's a lot to ask and there will be a lot for you to give up if you decide you're in it for the long run, so think of this as . . . me courting you. The way I should have this entire summer." His thumb ran along the back of my hand. "Please?"

"Who am I to deny my king?" I whispered, a small smile touching my lips.

Elias's eyes lit up as he laughed. "Really? You'll try?"

"I'll try." I couldn't help the way my smile widened. Seeing him this happy was everything.

"Thank you." He grinned, bringing his hands to my face, and pulled me into a kiss.

"So, is this where you're sleeping now?" I asked, pulling away and looking around again.

"No. I'm still in my apartment in Paris." He was still looking at me when I met his gaze.

"Hey, Eli." I grabbed the lapels of his jacket.

"Yes?" He raised an eyebrow.

"I think you should show me to your bedchambers."

His laughter rang out, echoing in the walls. I felt giddy and wondered how many kings had laughed in this room and actually meant it. I didn't have time to wonder long, though, because Elias grabbed my hand and walked quickly in the direction of what I assumed would be the bedchambers. The halls seemed endless, but I knew we'd made it there when he opened an impossibly large gold door and led me inside. I stopped just inside the door, letting go of his hand.

"You can just . . . you're allowed to touch things in here?"

"Of course." He looked perplexed as he faced me. "This is my bedroom now, should I choose to use it."

"Will you?"

"I don't know, Addie. You asked me to bring you here. Will I?"

"I mean for sleeping." I was smiling as I rolled my eyes. "Will you stay here tonight?"

"Will you?"

"I don't think so." I laughed. "Etienne and Joss are supposed to take me home."

"Let me take you home instead." He lifted my hand and kissed the back of it. *"Mon trésor."*

Butterflies flapped their wings deep in my belly. I could

have, should have, given into the moment, but I had questions and they wouldn't stop until I had answers.

"Do you think you'll live here now?"

"No." He lowered my hand, but threaded his fingers through mine and held it as he looked around. "It's kind of creepy, isn't it?"

"And rich."

"And rich." He chuckled, then quieted as he searched my eyes. "What do you want to do?"

"I kind of want you to fuck me in King Louis XIV's bed."

"You mean my bed." He licked his lips, his eyes darkening as he shrugged off his jacket and tossed it aside. Before I could respond, he lifted me into his arms, my legs wrapping around his hips automatically. He leaned in and bit my bottom lip, tugging it into his mouth. "Say it, Addie."

"Say what?" I was already finding it hard to breathe and we hadn't even started doing anything.

"You want to get fucked by your king. You want me to bury myself deep inside that wet little cunt."

"God." I moaned, throwing my head back. His mouth was on my neck, licking, sucking, as he drove his erection into me over our clothes. "Please."

"Say the words, Adeline." He bit the side of my neck. "Say it."

"I want to be fucked by my king, please." My voice was shaky, unsteady.

Elias walked me over to the bed and threw me down on it. It wasn't a comfortable bed in the least, but comfort was forgotten the moment Elias's lips met mine again. We kissed like starved teenagers, begging for more with each lash of our tongues, each clash of our teeth, biting, tugging.

"Please, Eli." I pulled away momentarily, holding his face in my hands. "Please. I can't take much more of this."

"How much did you miss me?" he breathed against me, his gaze serious on mine, as if his life depended on my response.

"More than you'll ever know."

"Good." He pulled away and unbuttoned his pants, pulling them down until he was exposed to me.

He wasted no time in pulling my dress up and ripping my panties off and discarding them quickly. I knew this wouldn't be a long, slow night, but a fast and satisfying one. We were both too frenzied, too desperate for each other, to drag it out.

"Tell me again, Addie." He positioned himself between my legs. "Tell me you missed me."

"I always miss you when I'm not with you." I reached for him and stroked him once, twice, relishing the way he threw his head back and groaned. "I want to be with you without . . . " I bit my lip and stopped talking midsentence when he brought his gaze back to mine and I saw the heat palpitating from it.

"Tell me." His voice was low, guttural. "Tell me what you want, Adeline."

"I want to be with you like this." I stoked him again. He bit his bottom lip hard.

"With no condom?"

I nodded. If he said no, I would be completely okay with it.

"I've never done that with a woman before." His lip tugged, his eyes half-mast as I moved my hand again. "Trust issues."

"It's okay if you don't—"

"I want to with you." He leaned in, placing his forehead

against mine, forcing my hand to drop as he brought his lips against mine. "I trust you."

"I'm clean," I whispered against his lips.

"I know." He kissed me then, mashing our lips together roughly and parting my lips with his tongue. He pulled away, digging his fingertips into my inner thighs and spreading them wider. "Tell me again how much you missed me."

"I missed you so much." I cried out when he dragged a hand up, scraping my inner thigh and stopping at my clit. "So much."

He looked into my eyes for a moment before closing them. As he breathed out, he pulled me against him and thrust inside of me in a long, deep stroke, filling me entirely. My hips arched in accordance, to beg for more, to demand more. He reached for the top of my dress, bringing it down to pluck my nipples as he continued to move inside me. With his other hand, he reached between us and began to rub circles over my clit.

"Fuck, that feels good." He threw his head back, biting his lower lip, his hands continuing to move as relentlessly as his strokes.

I was so close. So close. I could feel the orgasm building deep inside me, begging to be let out. He brought his gaze to mine, hazy, seductive, completely lustful, and let go of my nipple, bringing that hand to the nape of my neck and pulling me into a deep kiss, his tongue exploring my mouth wildly as he moved inside me, his fingers against my clit. It was all I needed to go over the edge, and he followed quickly behind. We were panting breaths and heaving chests against each other as we lay there, in the king's bedchambers, where so many before us had made love and history. It was exhilarating and daunting all at once.

CHAPTER THIRTY-THREE

ELIAS

"Have you seen this?" Pierre walked into my office and set a pile of newspapers in front of me.

I glanced at the first headline. *The Playboy King.* I set it aside and looked at the next: *King Size Womanizer. The Sinful Kings Continue. Is the Throne in Peril?* And the next: *King's First Mistress Makes an Appearance.* All of the photographs were of myself and Adeline at the party last night, and others of my father's funeral, where I was with Emily, but couldn't seem to stop looking at Addie. I set them all down and looked at Pierre as I stood up.

"Fuck."

"I'm assuming Adeline is still sleeping?"

"Yes." I sat back down with a heavy sigh.

Last night, we didn't go back to the party. Instead, we left through my private entrance and I had my driver bring us to my apartment in Paris. I'd have sex with Adeline anywhere she'd let me, but I wasn't sure I'd ever be comfortable sleeping in an almost four-hundred-year-old palace. The office doors opened and both Pierre and I turned in that direction to see Adeline, wearing a white cotton robe, her hair piled atop her head in a messy bun, storming in waving her phone at us. I stood up again.

"Did you see this?"

"Pierre just showed me." I walked around the desk and hugged her into my chest. "I'm sorry, Addie. We were just about to start discussing what we should do about it."

"I knew this was going to happen." She pulled away, bringing her hands to cover her face as she started pacing the room. "They're going to paint me as the bad guy. I'll be the one who ripped apart an engagement. Or your mistress if you continue making appearances with Emily."

"There will be no appearances with Emily." I walked over to her and stood in front of her, so she'd be forced to stop pacing and look at me. "Hey, you and I are a couple. A real couple. There is no me and Emily."

"Yeah, but the press thinks there is." There was a question in her eyes that she obviously didn't want to voice. I wasn't sure if it was because of me or Pierre, but either way I had no answer to it.

"We need to address the public." I faced Pierre. "I want a camera crew and trusted reporters in here to do a live press."

"With all due respect, we've never invited reporters or the outside world to a monarch's private residence," Pierre said. "We can do it in Versailles or one of the other palace grounds."

"I want it done here. I don't want a stuffy interview. I want them to feel comfortable with me. I want the public to feel comfortable with me." I looked between Pierre and Adeline. "I also want to visit some of the protestors' houses with Adeline."

"With me?"

"We're a team now, remember?"

She nodded slowly, gnawing on her bottom lip. The way her eyes clouded made me uneasy. Would she back out of this to shield herself from the media? I wouldn't blame her. They put her through enough in London once before.

"Will you excuse us, Pierre?" I said, still looking at Adeline. I waited until the door opened and closed before I moved into her space. "Talk to me."

"What will happen with my company? I have clients to meet in London next weekend." She searched my eyes. "Will I be able to meet with them?"

"Of course." I placed my hands on her shoulders to reassure her. "I'll do the interview today. We'll visit people tomorrow. I'm heading to London on Friday for a meeting myself, so we can go together."

"Okay."

"You'll stay here?" I ducked my head a little so we were at eye level. She still looked unsure, but nodded nonetheless. I let out a breath and kissed her lips softly. "I love having you here."

"I like being here. I can see why you like your apartment more than Versailles. It's a lot less opulent." She smiled. "Dare I say . . . normal?"

I laughed. "It is normal."

"I mean, except for the insane industrial kitchen." She bit her lip to keep from laughing at whatever reaction was on my face. The kitchen was not insane. "And the huge bathrooms that look like mini-apartments. And the fact that it's not an apartment, but a three-story penthouse in the most expensive residential building in Paris."

"Addie." I cocked my head, amused by all of this. Nobody

had ever pointed any of that out to me. "This is normal to me."

"Maybe your normal is everyone else's unattainable."

"You're my unattainable."

Her expression softened as she reached up and touched my face. "I'm here now."

"And I plan to make every second—" Just as I was lowering my face to kiss her and moving my hand to slide into her robe, the door opened. I pulled back with a loud exhale. What was it with people and not knocking?

"Well, then, I guess that answers my question," my mother said, looking between me and Adeline.

"What are you doing here, Maman?"

"I was going to ask you if there was any truth to any of this." She lifted the newspapers. "But I see it's true. You're completely disregarding tradition because of a commoner. Because of this girl who's probably using you because you're king and that excites her."

"Maybe you should come back when you're ready to talk and not point fingers and accuse innocent people of doing things they are not doing." I stepped forward, shielding Adeline from my mother. She put her hand on my back.

"It's okay," she whispered.

"No, it's not okay. My mother can come back when she learns some manners."

"I'm not going anywhere." My mother walked forward and took a seat on the loveseat in my office. She crossed her legs at the ankles and folded her hands over her knee. "Maybe you should both take a seat and enlighten me on what you're going to do about this mess."

I turned to Adeline, trying to gauge her reaction to this idea.

She shrugged nonchalantly and brushed past me, taking a seat on the sofa opposite my mother, mimicking her posture, as if she too was dressed in head to toe CHANEL and not a pair of my sister's tiny cotton pajama shorts, a white T-shirt, and a white fluffy robe. It was a striking image: two women who, if I had my way, would hold the same position, but were from completely different backgrounds. I followed and took a seat right beside Adeline, setting my hand over her exposed knee. I loved my mother dearly and respected her like crazy, but I wasn't afraid of her. I had a list of nannies I'd cower to, and for Adeline, I had a feeling I'd go to war with every single one of them. My mother took a long, deep breath and looked at Adeline.

"I'm sorry I lashed out on you. That wasn't fair. I would like to start over if you'll allow me to."

"Thank you for your apology. I'd very much like to start over," Adeline said, her voice stern but soft.

"You must really like my son," my mother said, rather than asked.

Adeline's body tensed underneath my hand. She took her attention from my mother and looked at me. "I do."

"And you were willing to plan his wedding to another woman?" My mother cleared her throat.

"My mother would have killed me if I turned that down. As it is, she's going to be furious with me with all of these new developments." Adeline gnawed on her bottom lip, glancing at me briefly. "I need to call her before you do that broadcast."

"Adeline never asked me not to marry Emily. I made suggestions to her that we should see each other in secret and she refused."

"How long has this been going on?" My mother blinked between us.

"A lifetime." I brought an arm around Addie's shoulders. "It feels like a lifetime."

"That needs to stop." Mother pointed at us. "Sometimes being in a position like ours means giving up small privileges and that includes touching." She paused. "You will be given a list of things that you positively cannot do as King. You will never bow to her. Your father never bowed to me and I was rightfully Queen. Imagine what people will say if you bowed to someone without royal blood. Showing public affection is also on that list."

"Why is that?" I asked. "Because it makes us seem human?"

"Because it makes you seem weak. People will soon be wondering if you make all of your decisions with your cock."

Harsh, but I understood it. Adeline took a deep breath and let it out with a nod.

"She's right. Those are the kinds of things my father will crucify you for whenever he gets in front of a microphone."

"Another valid point," my mother said. "Does your father know about this?"

"No."

She smiled slowly. "This may be good. Knock him on his ass a little bit. Imagine his face when he turns on the television and his daughter is sitting beside the man he hates and they're proclaiming their feelings for each other."

"Maman," I reprimanded.

Adeline laughed. My mother smiled.

"I think it's a brilliant idea," Adeline added. "But I don't think I should join Elias in the broadcast."

"This is the way, dear. It's all or nothing," my mother said.

"I'm trying to ease her into it. I don't want to scare her away."

"She's going to be scared either way, Elias. She needs to know what she's getting herself into and what she's giving up." My mother looked at Adeline. "What will you do with your company when you get married?"

"Married?" Addie sat straight up. "He hasn't . . . we haven't . . . " She blinked and looked over at me. "We haven't discussed marriage."

"This is not your regular relationship, Adeline, where you can wait until the last minute to discuss major life changes. From here on out, every thought, every decision, every single time you think you need to use the loo you'll have to discuss it with someone on the staff."

"I understand." Adeline nodded.

"I don't think you do, dear." Mother gave her a sympathetic smile. "I was bred for this and I still don't understand things. My son was raised to be king and he's obviously having a hard time with it and his reign has barely begun."

"We'll make our own way." I held Addie's hand in mine and squeezed it. "I'll be there through it all."

"God help you both." My mother stood up. "I will be in Luxembourg unless you need me to come back."

"We'll be fine on our end." I stood. "I'll walk you out."

"It was good seeing you," Adeline said, curtsying slightly to my mother. "Despite the circumstances and my attire."

"Keep your chin up, my dear." She winked and walked away.

"I'll be right back." I kissed Addie on the forehead.

CHAPTER THIRTY-FOUR

ADELINE

MY STOMACH WAS IN KNOTS AS THEY FINISHED SETTING UP THE cameras in Elias's home office and checked the sound. I was standing in the corner of the room beside Pierre and Aramis. Neither one of them provided me comfort. They seemed as nervous as I was—Pierre checking his phone every two seconds and Aramis bouncing on his heels. He was dressed for a workout, with a T-shirt cut off on the sides, exposing his muscular arms and ripped torso. The royals were definitely into their fitness.

"This is taking too long," Aramis said.

"You have somewhere more important to be?" Pierre slid his phone into the inner pocket of his suit.

"No, but this is making me anxious as fuck."

"Me too," I said.

"Well, yeah, you're the reason we're here." Aramis looked at me, raising an eyebrow.

"Don't remind me. I'm telling myself that this would have happened with or without me."

"Yeah, right." Aramis laughed. "My brother would have never dreamed any of this would happen. Trust me. His number one priority has always been the Crown."

"It still is." I felt myself frown. "Just because he's dating an outsider doesn't mean it's not his priority."

"Some will beg to differ," Aramis said. "I'm some."

"Well, I'm sorry you feel that way."

"No, you misunderstand." Aramis turned to me. "I like this. He's happy. He's never been happy before."

"Surely, that's not right." I scoffed.

"We're actors, Adeline. We pretend a lot for the public. We smile, we laugh, we prance around for cameras to make sure the people paying taxes to afford all of the things we have think there's no possible way that while they're struggling financially, we're struggling emotionally. People think rich people aren't allowed to be in pain because they have money. We're told this so often that at a certain point we begin to believe it." He shrugged nonchalantly. "We're human though."

I looked at him for a few beats, at this man who looked so much like his brother, and let his words sink in. All of the things he said made sense, of course. It was just unfathomable that he would be so open about all of it.

"I like you." I set my hand on his forearm.

"Good." He smiled wide. "I like you too."

We turned back to where Elias was sitting behind his desk. He was wearing a navy suit with a white dress shirt beneath it. He'd opted not to wear a tie and unbutton the collar. His dark hair was brushed back and there was a light five o'clock shadow on his face. He looked so fucking handsome and while his brother, Pierre, and I were balls of nerves, Elias looked completely at ease.

"Ready?" the cameraman asked. There were three reporters in the room standing behind the cameraman, all with notepads and pens in their hands, their expressions eager and in awe.

"Ready," Elias confirmed. He looked over at me and winked. I smiled, but wasn't sure if it was believable, as nervous as I was.

"Let's roll," the cameraman said.

The three of us seemed to hold our breaths as he started to speak.

"Good evening," Elias started, in French. "You may be wondering why I decided to do a broadcast today, with little notice, and I'll get to that in a minute. As you know, my father wasn't big on broadcasts, and I'm hoping that's one of the many things I'm able to change now that I'm king." He paused for a beat.

"I woke up this morning to a slew of tabloids speculating on my personal life. This isn't out of the norm. My personal life, as well as my brother's and sister's, have been up for judgment and question for as long as I can remember. It doesn't bother us because we're used to it. What bothers me is when an innocent is caught in the fire, and in this case, that innocent happens to be a woman I feel deeply for."

The reporters looked over at me and back at Elias, still seemingly confused as to where this was going.

"I broke off my engagement with Emily, the Princess of Austria, not because she wasn't the perfect fit for me, but because it wasn't fair to her, or myself, to have gone through with a marriage I wasn't fully committed to. You see, I've been seeing another woman for quite some time. She doesn't come from a long line of royal blood or a family of knights. She's a hard worker, some would say, a commoner, but there's nothing common about her, as I'm sure there's nothing common about you."

There were gasps from the three reporters, who looked over at me, back at Elias, and back at me before they started scribbling things on their notepads. My stomach coiled. Aramis squeezed my arm and Pierre walked to stand on the other side of me, in solidarity.

"She has opened my eyes to things I wouldn't have otherwise been exposed to. She pushes me to try to be a better person and points out my faults so that I can fix them. It is with her that I will be visiting the houses of those affected by the economic crisis we are currently facing, and it is with her that I hope to fix what is broken in our current system." He smiled slightly. "And while I will not be giving up my throne or turning in the crown, like some of you may be hoping for, I pray this helps me grow into the kind of king you are proud of."

He nodded once. "*Dieu te bénisse*. We'll talk again soon."

The cameraman did a countdown before saying, "Cut!" and switching off the camera. He was already walking out of the room with it when the three reporters stepped forward. Pierre left my side then, and walked over to them.

"You may ask your questions now," he told them, "but remember that the king is entitled to not answer whatever he does not want to answer."

"May we ask her questions?" the woman asked, pointing at me with the tip of her pen.

"She's off-limits," Elias said, looking over at me, "unless she says otherwise."

I thought about what his mother had told me, how this was an all-or-nothing kind of deal. I'd already called my mother and told her about this so it wouldn't catch her off guard, and after a lot of screaming and bad words, she seemed to be a little more accepting of it, though I wouldn't be surprised if she showed up on Elias's doorstep tomorrow. I took a deep breath. Was I ready for this? Truly?

"I'm not ready yet." I smiled at the reporters. "I will say this—I've been treated unfairly by the media in the past and I hope this is different."

They wrote that down. The woman spoke up, "Are you happy? Are you truly a commoner?"

"I don't like the word *commoner* being used as a way to speak down to someone, but I am a regular citizen." I smiled, looking at Elias, who was watching me with a serious expression, but I could see the smile in his eyes. "And I am so happy."

"What is your name?" one of the men asked.

"Adeline Bouchard."

"Is your father Louis Bouchard?" he followed. "From the king's cabinet?"

"Yes," I said.

"Was that how you met?" the other man asked.

"No. This has nothing to do with my father."

"How does he feel about you being with a man he's constantly criticizing?"

"I am not my father's keeper." I kept the smile on my face. "You'd have to ask him that question."

Another reporter started to direct a question toward me, and Pierre interrupted him.

"Please direct your questions to the king," Pierre said. "Adeline declined questions and she has answered plenty for you. You'll have to wait until she's ready to sit down with you formally."

After that, they left me alone and continued firing questions at Elias. Aramis started talking to me about his apartment, which was apparently in the same building. I wasn't sure if he was trying to distract me from my nerves or if he genuinely wanted to talk, but I appreciated it nonetheless. When the reporters left the room, Pierre informed me that a stylist would be bringing me dresses and casual wear for the events we had lined up the rest of the week.

CHAPTER THIRTY-FIVE

"**W**HAT'S WRONG WITH MY OWN CLOTHES?" I ASKED PIERRE.

The stylist brought beautiful evening dresses, and those I would definitely use if necessary, but I didn't want to wear fancy clothes to visit families that could barely afford food.

"Queens wear pencil skirts and conservative dresses," he said. "Not ripped jeans."

"I'm not a queen." I grinned.

"Yet." He raised an eyebrow.

My grin was wiped off and dominated by the uneasy feeling in the pit of my stomach. Yet? I wasn't sure how I felt about that. I loved Elias. Loved. But to give up my life for this life? What would I do? Sit around here like I'd been doing the last two days while he went off to meet with the cabinet and work? I'd done enough sitting around in the beach house and I'd been so bad at it that I'd remodeled my uncle's bookstore. I walked out of the room and headed to the kitchen, where the cook, Sheriff, was serving lunch.

"I don't think you understand that every pair of eyes will be on you. There will be reporters there," Pierre said. "You can't wear cheap jeans and a T-shirt."

"First of all." I stopped walking and faced him. "My jeans are designer. They just happen to have holes in them."

"You paid money for those holes?" He frowned. "Why?"

"You're an idiot." I laughed. "Seriously, let me do this my way. I'll change into jeans with no holes in them if you want."

"I don't know." He raised the clipboard in his hand. "I have a checklist and it specifies pencil skirts and dresses below the knee."

"Are you . . . let me see that checklist." I took the clipboard from his hands and looked at the list. "I have to put my hair in a bun? Why?"

"How the hell should I know? I've never helped a woman dress before."

"Are you hitting on my girlfriend again, Pierre?"

I smiled wide at the sound of Elias's voice and walked quickly to the hallway, watching as he folded the sleeves of his button-down up his forearms. He smiled when he saw me and kissed me as I walked up to him.

"Missed you."

"Missed you too." I kissed him again and again and again. When I pulled away, I pointed at Pierre. "This isn't going to work. You need to take him with you next time."

"I thought you'd like having a friend here." Elias chuckled. "What'd you do, Pierre?"

"You left me in charge of an impossible woman. I did nothing."

"Impossible?" I gasped. "He wants me to wear a dress or a pencil skirt to those people's houses today."

"She wants to wear what she's wearing now." Pierre shot a pointed look at Elias.

Elias gave me a once-over. "What's wrong with what she's wearing? She looks sexy as fuck."

"Of course you'd say that." Pierre shook his head. "And I'm

not saying she doesn't." He raised a hand and laughed. "And I'm not saying she does. Fucking hell, I can't say anything anymore."

"I said I'd change into jeans with no holes in them if that makes him more comfortable, but I don't think wearing a Saint Laurent dress is going to be welcome. I would hate me if I walked into their houses like that."

"She has a point." Elias kissed the top of my head. "Maybe we should both wear jeans."

"The checklist—" Pierre took the clipboard back from me and held it up.

"Oh my gosh, fuck the checklist," I said. "We'll wear jeans. Eli can wear the button-down he's wearing so it'll look semi-formal."

"That is not semi-formal," Pierre said. "The minute you put jeans on it becomes informal."

"Listen, Soldier," I said. "I promise you jeans are fine."

"Let's just do whatever Addie wants to do," Elias said.

"You better never say that in public." Pierre shook his head. "I swear love equates castration."

"Fuck you." Elias laughed loudly.

"At least you're in a good mood all the time these days," Pierre said as he walked away with his stupid clipboard.

"It's because I'm truly happy." Elias hugged me and turned to me. I smiled up at him, hugging his hips. "Are you sure you're ready for today?"

"I'm totally ready. Are you?"

"If you're with me I am. To tell you the truth, I'm nervous they'll hate me. They all had horrible signs about me the day of my coronation."

"Nobody who knows you can ever hate you." I kissed his chest and pulled away. "Let's go get ready."

CHAPTER THIRTY-SIX

ELIAS

ADELINE WAS RIGHT ABOUT THE JEANS. THE MOMENT OUR CAR reached the first house we had scheduled to visit, I knew it had been the right call. It was a normal neighborhood. The roofs weren't falling apart and as far as I knew, they had running water, but it was definitely not the kind of place I'd ever visited. Addie had been right to judge me on my fancy apartment.

"We can't hold hands," Addie whispered when I stopped walking and tried to reach for hers.

"Addie."

"I'm serious, Eli. I'm not even supposed to be walking beside you. I was getting schooled on all of this when you were gone," she said. "Walk ahead of me and I'll follow."

She wasn't wrong. It was tradition. If I was being honest with myself, I'd never even paid it much attention until this moment. It was just something that was expected. That didn't mean I didn't hate it right now. I turned and faced the door once more, walking behind my security team as Addie trailed behind me and Pierre closely behind her. The door opened shortly after the head of security knocked. He was invited inside to check things out and walked back out and gave a heads-up that everything was clear. We already had two security guards inside, but one could never be too sure. That was something I learned a few years ago when someone tried to kill me, not because they hated me, but because I was the Dauphin and the people were becoming desperate even then. The woman at the door, who was probably in her thirties, curtsied when she saw me.

"Please come in. Thank you for visiting."

"Thank you for allowing me to visit," I said.

Her face brightened instantly and it surprised me to know that something that simple could make a difference in my welcome. Her husband I recognized right away. I wouldn't soon forget the man, face all hollowed, holding up that hateful sign. He'd shaved his beard and was wearing a black T-shirt with a logo on it. I recognized it to be the logo of the Crown's mining company. So he worked for me. Technically. He bowed deeply and when he straightened, I offered him my hand, which he shook.

"I wasn't expecting to ever host a king," he said. He was missing a few teeth when he smiled. I smiled back.

"I wasn't expecting this either, but I'm glad I'm here."

"Please, take a seat," his wife said. She turned to the door and I knew the minute Addie stepped through because the woman's smile was wide and bright. "You're the commoner."

"I'm the commoner," Addie said, laughing lightly. "It's so nice to meet you, Madame Lefebre. You have a lovely home."

"Oh, please." Monsieur Lefebre waved away the compliment. "You stay in the palace now. This is no Versailles."

"It's not," Addie said. "This is much cozier. Much homier." She winked.

The Lefebres laughed. My heart grew. If I ever had any doubt that she was the perfect woman for me, this put me at ease. We all sat down in the living room, drank coffee, and spoke about their concerns. I'd brought them enough money for food that would last them a few months and they gratefully took it, but what they really wanted from me was a promise that I'd make it so that they could afford their own food once that ran out, and I gave it to them. After all, I'd finally come to a deal with the Crowned Prince, and was set to meet with him in London over the weekend to ensure that everything was as solid as he said over the phone. We visited four more houses, all with similar receptions and outcomes as the Lefebres, and I knew without a doubt that none of it would have been possible without Adeline by my side.

CHAPTER THIRTY-SEVEN

ADELINE

"WELL, AT LEAST THE TABLOIDS LOOK BETTER," JOSLYN SAID. She'd taken a break from her new role as Princess Pilar's secretary to come to London and help me pack up the apartment. I'd already secured a smaller place down the street, but I would miss this one terribly. There was no point in keeping such a big place to myself though. Not when I wasn't even sure where I'd be in the coming months. The doorbell rang once, twice, three times and Joss and I stopped what we were doing and looked at each other. I stood slowly and headed to the door. Elias's security team was with me while he was in meetings this weekend, so one of them opened the door for me.

"This is my daughter's flat and I expect to see her," my mother said from the other side of the door. I exhaled heavily.

"Mother, what are you even doing here?"

"You tell me what you're doing here," she said, waving a newspaper. I ducked slightly, afraid she'd hit me with it. She looked like she was capable of it right now. "I had to find out through a tabloid that you were in town."

"I just got in," I said. She looked around and shot me an angry glare. I cringed. "I got in last night but I was going to call you as soon as I was done packing. I have to go down to the office and sort things out anyway and I have a meeting with the Wesleys tomorrow."

"Save it, Adeline." Mother tossed the newspaper on my counter and stormed in. "Oh, and you're here too? No phone call, Joslyn?"

"I am so sorry. I was going to the office with Addie tomorrow, though, and hoped I'd see you there!"

"Bullshit. Both of you." Mother shook her head and paced the room, the way I did when I didn't know what to do with my emotions. I stayed quiet. Joss bit her lip and watched her. "So now you're dating the King of France."

"I told you that." I held a finger up. "Do not even, Mother. I called you first."

"You called me two hours before the broadcast aired, Adeline." She stopped pacing and turned to me. "How serious is it?"

"Serious enough."

"What do you make of this, Joslyn?" my mother asked. "Now that you're in with the royal family in a big way. What do you think of my daughter dating the king?" She shook her head. "It's weird for me to even say that."

"I was opposed to it in the beginning but I think he really does care for her. And she's happy." Joss shrugged. "So I ship it now."

"Ship what?" My mother frowned. "What are you talking about?"

"I like it," Joss said. "It's something . . . forget it. The point is, I like them together."

"He's staying here or is this security the new norm for you?"

"Both," I said. "The tabloids have taken an interest in me so we have to be careful, but he's staying here. Should be home any minute."

"Home." Mother laughed. "That's another thing, where will home be for you now? Will you be traveling back and forth, because look at how well that worked out for your father and I." She raised an eyebrow. "Or will you give up your company? What will happen with Pirouette Events now that you're to become queen?" She gasped, bringing a hand to her mouth. "Will you become queen?"

The security began speaking by the door and soon it opened and Elias walked through it and into the living room. He froze as he assessed the situation—Joss on the floor surrounded by boxes, my mother and I having a standoff.

"Hey," I said, smiling softly.

"Hey," he returned, still undoing his tie. He gave a nod to my mother. "Madame Bouchard."

"King Elias." She instantly curtsied to him.

It was something that traditionally I was supposed to do as well, but knew Elias hated when we did it behind closed doors, so I was constantly reminding myself not to do it unless we were in public and he walked into a room, which hadn't happened yet. He walked over to me, the discarded tie in one hand, and put his other around my shoulder as he kissed my lips softly.

"Missed you," he whispered.

I smiled up at him. "My mother was just trying to figure out our dynamic."

"No. Her mother was trying to figure out whether or not this was real and how bad her heart will be broken when it's all over."

"Well, I hope it'll never come to that," he said, his hand squeezing my shoulder. "I don't foresee this ever ending."

"So she will be queen?" My mother's eyes widened.

"I think it's a little soon to discuss that." I shot her a look that would hopefully shut her up.

I didn't want to talk about an engagement I hadn't even discussed with Elias. Did I want one? Yes. Spending the rest of my life with him would be a dream come true. Having a fairy-tale ending with him, even if he wasn't a royal would be incredible, but I didn't want to rush into it.

"That's something your daughter and I need to discuss," he said. I could hear the smile in his voice without even looking up at his face. I kept my attention on my mother.

"And what do you think about her leaving Pirouette Events behind?" she asked. "She would have to give that up, wouldn't she?"

"Unfortunately, yes," he said. "She could still help you whenever she wants and has time, but because of what I'm envisioning for France, she'd have her hands pretty full." He smiled over at me. "She won't be bored like she is now."

"I'm not bored." I pursed my lips.

"You re-arranged my closet, Adeline. I pay people to do that for me." He shot me a look.

"Okay, I'm a little bored."

He chuckled and looked at my mother. "So, any more questions?"

"Will I have a room for when I visit?"

"Mother!" I gasped.

"You will have plenty of rooms to choose from." Elias grinned.

"Fine. I'm going to try to accept this," she said. "But next time I hear you're in town via the media, we will have problems."

"It won't happen again."

She picked up her purse. "I have to go to the office for a meeting. Do you want me to handle tomorrow's so you don't have to go in?"

"I have to go anyway. I need to pack up a few things," I said, unable to hide the sadness in my voice, or blink back tears at the thought. Elias pulled me into his side and kissed my head, as if to remind me why I'm doing this. I was grateful for it.

"See you then." My mother walked over and kissed my cheek and stood in front of Elias, unsure of what to do. He let go of me and kissed her cheek. Mother blushed before going up to Joss and saying goodbye to her and walking out.

"I don't think I've ever seen her blush," I said.

"That was great," Joss said with a laugh before she quieted. "Was I supposed to bow to you when you walked in? If so, my leg was asleep and I couldn't get up, so you'll have to forgive my informality. Also, it's weird."

Elias laughed. "Just do it when others are in the room so they don't think I've gone soft."

"Have you gone soft?" I smiled, looking up at him.

"Around you? Never." He winked.

And then I was the one blushing.

CHAPTER THIRTY-EIGHT

ELIAS

"WHERE ARE WE GOING?" ADELINE LOOKED OUT THE window the way a child would on a long road trip. I'd never tire of looking at her, but it made me yearn for miniature Addies running around with that same expression on their faces.

"I want you to meet someone very important to me."

"Who?" She turned in her seat. "I'm not even dressed to meet someone important."

"Trust me, she won't mind."

"Are you sure? Because if we showed up at your mother's house like this she'd judge."

"She won't judge." I smiled, reaching for her hand as the car slowed down in front of the small cottage in the countryside. "We're here."

"Oh." Adeline frowned. "I was not expecting this."

We got out of the car, security escorting us to the front door. This time, I didn't let Addie stay behind me. I held her hand and had her walk beside me the entire way up the walkway. When the door opened and Nana appeared on the threshold, she smiled wide at us, and I knew bringing Addie was the right move, despite it being unannounced.

"Well, well," Nana said, holding the door open for us.

"Adeline, this is my Nana. Nana, this is my girlfriend, Adeline," I said, letting go of Adeline's hand so that I could hug Nana.

"A girlfriend," Nana said, throwing her arms around me. "I knew this day would come." She turned to Addie next and looked at her closely before hugging her. "I like you already."

We went inside and Nana made us tea and asked Addie a million questions.

"Nana, I didn't bring her here for you to interview her," I said.

"I don't mind." Addie smiled at me. "How long were you Eli's nanny?"

"From the time he was born until he turned seventeen." Nana raised an eyebrow. "He was a good kid most of the time. Aramis on the other hand . . . " She shook her head. "My heart goes out to Patty for having to deal with that one."

"I can see that," Addie said, laughing. "Do you still visit?"

"Not really. They come and visit me once in a while when they remember I exist." She winked.

"I always visit you." I frowned. "I just have more responsibilities now."

"I'm joking. I know. How is it going for you?"

"Good. I think good. I've met with the cabinet a few times. There are two members I trust implicitly and already ran my idea by. I'm hoping to tell the rest of them at the end of the month."

"What idea?" Addie asked.

"My Parliament idea."

"Oh." Her eyes widened. "Already?"

"I figure it'll take us a long time to perfect it, so we better start now."

"And people will vote for the people in Parliament?"

"Yes."

"So you do like the way the English do things." She grinned.

"Don't tell anyone." I poked her.

"Your secret is safe with me." She laughed.

"I'd still have enough of a say in things, of course, but it would be a lot more democratic than it is now."

"My father will be thrilled," she mumbled, looking less than thrilled.

"Maybe he'll think his daughter was the brains behind all of this."

"I don't care." She shrugged and looked at Nana. "My father stopped talking to me for a mistake I made in the past and this whole thing hasn't helped."

"Oh, I'm sorry, love. That must be difficult."

"You know, surprisingly, it's not," Addie said. "I feel kind of . . . free. That's horrible, isn't it?" Her shoulders dropped slightly.

"It's not horrible. It's human." I set my hand over her knee. She smiled at me.

"You two look beautiful together," Nana said. "Your children will be the most gorgeous little angels."

"Not so fast, Nan." I chuckled, unsure what reaction Addie would have, but when I looked at her, she was still smiling, and that made me a lot more comfortable.

We stayed the entire afternoon at Nana's, just talking, like normal people, like all the commoners my father had looked down upon all those years and taught me to do the same, and I felt . . . free.

CHAPTER THIRTY-NINE

ADELINE

I'D OFFICIALLY BEEN LIVING IN PARIS FOR A MONTH AND AS ELIAS promised, I hadn't been the least bit bored. I was still commuting to and from London, which as my mother warned, wasn't great. It was exhausting and would definitely get old soon, but I enjoyed helping Elias with things for the Crown and seeing him whenever I had a chance. He'd been so busy setting things up for Parliament and a more democratic government that he barely had time to sleep, let alone travel to London to see me. Joslyn and Pilar had been keeping me company when I was in town and he was holed up in his office or holding cabinet meetings in Versailles.

I'd gotten into town yesterday, went straight to a shelter for abused women, and had tea with them on behalf of the Crown. It was part of Elias's newly established outreach, where each one of us—Elias himself, Aramis, Pilar, and I would back causes and build foundations. He was definitely taking a playbook from the English, and I was here to root him on along the way. Today, I had to fly back to London for a meeting, and after that, I promised my uncle I'd go to Marbella to attend the grand opening of his bookstore. I'd be back in Paris on Tuesday, then back in London on Thursday, and back in Paris next Sunday. It was definitely a lot, but for Elias, I'd shoulder the burden for now.

When we were together, we discussed everything before getting lost in each other's arms. In the morning, we woke up and shared breakfast before going about our days. Today was no different. I'd just finished packing a small overnight bag for my trip; since I had everything I needed here and in London, I didn't really need much. Now all I had to do was wait for Elias to finish up the meeting he was holding in his office so that he could drop me off at the airport. For now, I'd be flying in a private jet owned by the Crown and used by them and their staff. I didn't want to, but I also didn't want to be followed by frenzied cameramen asking questions about an impending engagement. According to the tabloids and all of the news channels in France, everyone was rooting for us to be married and start a family.

I was walking by his office when I noticed the door slightly ajar and slowed down. Maybe he was done with his meeting. When I heard voices, I stopped walking and waited just outside the door.

"Well, I have to say, making her your girlfriend definitely helped you with the press," the man said.

"It was a leap of faith," Elias stated.

"All because of a commoner," the man said. I couldn't see him, but I could hear the awe in his voice. "You have to keep her around until after Parliament is complete."

"I will," Elias said. "She's also taking up some responsibility on behalf of the Crown."

"That will boost morale through the roof," the man said. "Incredible."

"It is incredible indeed."

"I wanted to understand what would lead you to break things off with my daughter, and I guess I understand. Your father was always a very traditional man, but he'd lost his touch."

"The people lost faith in him," Elias said. "Probably because he held tradition a little too closely."

"I understand," the man said. "The throne always comes first."

"It does."

"Any chance you'll go back to my daughter once everything works out? Maybe you'll need to add a little flair to this love story and keep the people on their toes. Take the spotlight away from Parliament for a second while you finalize that," the man said with a hearty laugh.

"Maybe." Elias laughed. "You never know what might happen."

My heart sank. I pressed my back to the wall behind me.

Maybe?

Had all of this been to better his public image? Using me, a commoner. As I stood there, letting that sink in, it all started to make sense. It wasn't possible. *Was it?* I thought about what Aramis had told me. *We're actors, Adeline. We pretend a lot for the public.* Had he been pretending when he said he broke things off with Emily? Was he still seeing her while I was away? I felt sick. Clutching my stomach, I ran to the guest bathroom nearby and locked myself in it, dropping my duffel bag and holding onto the sink. It had to be a mistake. All of this was obviously a misunderstanding. I heard footsteps and doors open and close and when I was ready, I took a nice deep breath and let it out. I grabbed my bag and walked back to the office. The doors were closed, so I pushed one of them open, but it was empty.

CHAPTER FORTY

"**A**DELINE." It was Pierre. I turned to face him. He handed me a folded piece of paper. "We were looking for you. Elias had to run down to Versailles to handle some things. He left you this note and said he tried calling you but couldn't reach you."

"Oh. My phone must still be off from last night." I shoved the note inside the side pocket of my bag and focused on not thinking about the conversation I'd overheard. "Are you taking me to the airport?"

"Yes."

"Let's go then. I don't want to be late." I brushed past him and walked out.

"Are you okay?" Pierre asked in the elevator. "You're shaking."

"Just . . . a lot on my mind." I glanced away from him.

Pierre got on a phone call as we stepped out of the elevator and continued to talk as we were on our way to the airport. I took my phone out and turned it back on and saw a text message from Elias, one from Etienne, and another from my mother. My mother. She'd have a ball with this if I told her, so I decided I wouldn't. I wasn't going to jump to conclusions until I spoke to Elias directly. When Pierre hung up the phone, he exhaled heavily. I didn't look up from my phone, but I felt his eyes on me.

"Do you think you'll be able to handle this forever?" he asked. I set my phone in my bag and met his gaze.

"The traveling back and forth?"

"Well, you'd have to stop traveling back and forth this often at some point."

"Maybe. Maybe not. He hasn't proposed or anything." I shrugged a shoulder. And according to his conversation with Emily's father, it wasn't his intention.

"He'd be an idiot not to."

"Why? Because things are going so well?"

"I've never seen him this happy."

"Do you think that's because of me or because he feels like a good king now?" I asked as the driver parked the car. My door was opened by one of the security detail, but I remained seated, looking at Pierre.

"I don't understand the question."

"You're his personal secretary, right? His confidant. The person he runs everything by." I grabbed the handle of my bag.

"Yes."

"Was the reason he broke things off with Emily and asked me to be his girlfriend because he knew it would help his reputation?"

"Adeline." Pierre looked shocked, and it was the only reaction I needed from him to confirm my worst fear.

"So it's true." I shook my head, trying to fight the tears I felt coming. "He used me."

"No. He loves you."

"Does he though?" I blinked, wiping a tear. "Who else knew about this?"

"There isn't anything to know, Addie."

"Who else knew, Pierre?"

"The queen. That's it."

"Of course." I laughed, getting out of the car. "God, I feel so stupid."

"Wait." Pierre ran after me. "Adeline, you can't just leave like this. He'll want to talk to you."

"For what?"

"To explain."

"Explain what?" I yelled.

"Wait." Pierre pushed a button on his phone. "Eli. Yes, I know, but there's been . . ." He paused. "I know." He paused again. "Adeline needs to speak to you." He paused again, then frowned as he looked at his phone. When he looked up, I knew Elias had hung up on him.

"Wow." I shook my head again.

"He's in a meeting with the Pope. He can't just—"

"He shouldn't have answered the call then," I said. "You said I needed to speak to him and he hung up."

"It's the Pope, Addie."

"Yeah, well, I hope the Pope has time to listen to Elias repent for his sins." I walked toward the plane. "And let it be known that the only reason I'm still taking this flight is because I refuse to pay for a ticket right now. Let the Crown pay for their newest employee."

Pierre didn't follow me on the plane, but there was a security detail waiting for me. A woman named Mayra. I'd met her previously. Today, I didn't even wave at her. I just walked to the last seat, sat, and started to cry.

CHAPTER FORTY-ONE

ELIAS

"How could you let her get on that flight?" I paced the Hall of Mirrors, pinching the bridge of my nose.

"What was I supposed to do?"

"I don't know. Stop her and bring her here where I could speak to her." I dropped my hand and looked at him as I paced in his direction. "What did she say? How did she look?"

"She was upset."

"Jesus." I sighed.

"Why didn't you just tell her from the beginning?" That was my brother, who was standing by a window looking out into the gardens. "It's not like you were using her. Not really anyway. You love her and wanted to be with her. This was a good way to deal with both."

He was right. I should have just have been honest with her. At least then, I could have explained the timing but reassured her that no matter what I would always choose her.

"I need to go to London." I leaned into the mirrored wall, placing my forehead against it and closing my eyes.

"You have back-to-back meetings this week. You're meeting with the cabinet in fifteen minutes," Pierre said. I straightened and turned so that my back was against the glass.

"Meaning, her father," Aramis stated.

"Yes, I'm well aware that I'm meeting with her fucking father, Aramis. Thanks for the update."

"Just call her," he suggested.

"I don't think a phone call will fix this," Pierre said.

I glared at him. He didn't cower and I didn't expect him to. I glared at him, screamed at him, used him as a literal punching bag at times, which I wasn't proud of, and the man never backed down. It was what I liked about him. It was what made him stand out and why he'd gone from being my security to being my personal secretary. None of those things made me not want to kill him right now. He should have known not to let her go. He should have known not to answer questions that would be misconstrued. I said that last thought aloud.

My brother laughed. "No offense, but how did she misconstrue the fact that you broke things off with Emily and started dating her because you needed to appeal to the people?"

I turned my glare in his direction. He also didn't cower. Much. He did, however, have enough sense to leave the room without another word.

"He's right, you know," Pierre said. "It would have been impossible for her to believe anything other than the fact that she was being used."

"Why would you say that? Why would she think that? She knows me. Really knows me. She has to know I would never do that to her."

"She's always had her reservations about you."

"About me?" I frowned. "I've never given her reason to have reservations about me."

"Her father hates what you stand for and her mother doesn't trust you. Her friends, who know your family, warned her against you. How could she not have reservations?"

"Her friends like me. Her mother likes me." My frown deepened. "And Adeline is her own person."

"Do you remember what you said on the broadcast? When you told the world you left Emily for another woman?"

"Yes, that I'd been in love with another woman for some time."

"You never used the word *love*. You said you'd been seeing another woman for some time."

"No I didn't."

"I have the entire speech written down." He waved the stupid clipboard he was always walking around with. "You said . . ." He flipped papers and read from the page. "I've been seeing another woman for quite some time. She doesn't come from a long line of royal blood or a family of knights. She's a hard worker, some would say, a commoner, but there's nothing common about her, as I'm sure there's nothing common about you."

"You wrote that down?" I walked over to him and yanked the clipboard from his hand, reading the paper.

"I figured it would be good to write your speeches down from now on if you're going to continue to do broadcasts. You know, so you won't repeat yourself often." Pierre stared at me. "What do you think?"

"I think your penmanship is shit." I was brooding. I knew I was. I couldn't help it. "So you're saying because I focused on describing her like this . . . she thought I was using her? She liked this speech. She told me that herself."

"What is she supposed to say, Your Majesty?"

"I hate you."

"I agree. She should have said that, but she's too in love with you to think that."

"No, I mean I hate you for pointing this shit out now." I shoved the clipboard on his chest. "I'm meeting with the cabinet and then I'm going to London. I don't care what else I have lined up."

Walking up to the King's Apartments and into the room, where the four members of my cabinet were sitting around the round table we had set up there, was testing. The last person I wanted to see was Adeline's father. I hadn't seen him since the night of the coronation celebration here and that hadn't ended well. It wasn't like I was hiding from him. If anything, it was the other way around. He hadn't attended our last two meetings. The rumor was that he was putting together more parades and riots. If that was the case, I meant to get to the bottom of it today. The time for rioting was over. It should have been over when Adeline and I visited some of the families who took the biggest impact from the failed economy. The last thing I had time for was a bratty man and I fully intended to put him in his place if he stepped out of line. So far, they'd only seen the compliant king. Today, they'd see a ruthless one.

As I stepped inside, the four of them stood and bowed. I walked over to my seat at the head of the table.

"Gentlemen." I sat down. They followed suit.

"This is new." Monsieur Gaston tapped the wooden table twice. He was one of the two members I got along with best. One of the loyalists, if you may.

"I was tired of sitting down and being looked down upon when the four of you spoke," I said.

"It served a better purpose," Monsieur Bouchard said.

"Funny you should bring that up, because I'm finding it incredibly difficult to find what purpose you serve on this cabinet," I said. The four of them sat up straighter, their eyes widening. Good. "Do you have a reason for missing our last two meetings?"

"I'm in the middle of a divorce," he said. "I figured you'd know that being that you're my daughter's supposed boyfriend, though I will say, I like the new tabloid stories. The ones calling the entire relationship a sham."

"Similar to the rumors of you planning riots all over the city."

"Those aren't rumors." He smiled, a cynical smile. "The people do not like that they have no say in their government."

"The people have never had a say in their government before so this . . . anarchy you're aiming for will be disastrous if, God forbid, it came to that." I stood quickly, the legs of the chair I was sitting on scraping the oak wood floors beneath me. "Furthermore, if you'd been here the last two meetings, you'd have been informed about the Parliament we're hoping to form and incorporate, which will be voted on by the people."

"Parliament?" he asked. "Voted on by the people?"

"I just said that."

"Did my daughter put you up to this?"

"What if she did? What will you say then? That I've had my cock cut off and that an uninformed woman will now be ruling France?" I yelled.

He shook his head, seemingly still wrapping his head around the idea.

"I think Parliament is an excellent idea," Monsieur Gaston said.

"I agree," Monsieur Caron added.

"It gets my vote," Monsieur Berger said.

Monsieur Bouchard was still silent.

"I do have one question," Monsieur Gaston said. "What will become of us? Will we also be part of Parliament, voted on by the people?"

"That's one of the things we need to discuss. I'll need to keep a small cabinet of advisors," I said. "As for the first Parliament, we'll have to form a group that will go door to door and inform the people about this so that they can start campaigning. We should have a few representatives from each town. Men and women. We don't want anyone to feel like they're not being represented."

"Would you keep this cabinet?" Monsieur Bouchard asked. "I don't blame you if you want to get rid of us . . . of me, specifically."

"You know what I don't understand?" I sat back down, pulling my chair in again. "If you hate us so much, if you absolutely detest the idea of a monarchy of any kind, if you'd rather see us be attacked by every single person in our town, why be part of this cabinet at all? You could have easily walked away from my father's cabinet. You could have easily quit when I claimed the throne. You could quit right now and go back to a life in journalism. Yet you stay. Why?"

He took a long moment to think about it. "I never liked your father as a leader. I never liked the violence or the attack-now-and-ask-questions-later mentality. I didn't like the fact that he ignored the pleas that rang through the city and swept in here." He paused for a beat. "He spoke about you and the way he was training you to think just like him and well, I guess I didn't think to give you a chance. I didn't think you'd want to change the way things were. I definitely didn't expect talks of a Constitutional Monarchy."

"Yet here we are." I lifted the glass of water in front of me and took a sip.

"Yet here we are," Monsieur Bouchard said, a small smile on his lips. "I never thought I'd see the day."

"When will you know?" Monsieur Gaston asked. "About us being part of your board of advisors?"

"When will we know?" Monsieur Caron followed.

"All of you are in. If you accept." I stood up, this time calmly, though I really had to get out and go to London as soon as possible. "We'll have two meetings next week. Bring your best ideas."

I walked out of the room. Pierre handed me my cellphone as soon as I stepped out. I looked at it. Still no calls or texts from Adeline. My stomach knotted. Had I really fucked up that badly? The door opened behind me and Pierre instantly moved between me and the person.

"Your Majesty." Monsieur Bouchard bowed as I turned around. "I just want to apologize. I should not have made assumptions. Please know that I will do everything I can to support you and the Crown from here on out."

"I appreciate that, Monsieur." I gave him a nod and walked away. I only had one Bouchard to deal with right now and something told me she would be much less apologetic than her father.

CHAPTER FORTY-TWO

S HE WAS ALREADY GONE WHEN I SHOWED UP ON HER DOORSTEP. The nosey neighbor told Pierre she'd left in a hurry. While Pierre called Mayra to ask where they were, I asked the driver to take us to the Pirouette offices. On the way there, I checked the internet. The paparazzi had a way of knowing where everyone was before anyone else and this couldn't be much different. The last photo taken of her had been when she arrived yesterday. I'd missed her then because after I finished the cabinet meeting I had a slew of uninvited guests show up and delay me hours. The first moment I had to catch my breath was today, which was why I insisted we leave first thing this morning. As it was, the hour-long plane ride didn't help my anxiety. I kept mulling over all of the things I wanted— no—needed to say to her, but every time I thought I had it, I came up short.

"She was with Etienne last night," Pierre said. "So at least she was safe."

"What do you mean at least?" I grabbed his phone and looked at the screen. It was a gossip magazine with a photograph of Adeline and Etienne on the front page. It looked like they were walking out of a restaurant. The headline: *Future Queen or Queen No Longer? Adeline Bouchard Spotted with Childhood Friend, Investor, Etienne Bellerose out on the Town. Is She Back for Good or Just Packing Her Things?*

I handed the phone back to Pierre and sighed. He was right. At least she was safe. In the photo, she wasn't even smiling. Wasn't even pretending to be happy. I wondered what Etienne thought about me now. He'd already had his reservations about me dating his friend and none of this would help that cause. It didn't matter. At the end of the day, the only thing that mattered was what she thought of me and right now, I had a bad feeling about it.

CHAPTER FORTY-THREE

ADELINE

O NE GOOD THING ABOUT HAVING MAYRA AS MY SECURITY WAS that even though she was definitely reporting our every move to His Majesty, she was doing it hours after we left places and giving me the freedom to do whatever the hell I wanted—like get drunk on wine in a pub in Marbella. I'd driven straight to the meeting in London and flown right back out to Marbella on a commercial flight. As it turned out, there were no paparazzi following us there or here. I'd made it right on time for my uncle's bookstore opening and now I was just drinking. With my bodyguard. Because that wasn't the loneliest thing in the world.

"I'll tell you what. Men absolutely have no brains." I set down my wine. "I mean, they do, but they have no common sense."

"Not where women are concerned," Mayra said. She was drinking water, despite me pouring her two glasses of wine, which I'd drunk, because I wasn't going to let it go to waste.

"Especially not where women are concerned." I took another sip. "I just . . . I thought it would be different, you know? I was ready to give up everything. Everything. My life in London, my company, my friends."

Mayra handed me a napkin. I looked at it in confusion, until I realized I was crying. Then, I wiped my face and cried harder.

"He's an idiot."

"He is," she agreed.

"I can't believe he used me."

"Maybe we don't have all of the facts straight."

"We have all of the facts straight." I slapped the napkin down on the table. "I asked Pierre and he confirmed it."

"Right, but it's clear the king has feelings for you."

"Sure. Lustful ones." I took a deep breath and hiccupped. "Ugh. I hate hiccups."

"I think that's a sign that you drank too much. Or too fast."

"Well, you know what takes away the hiccups." I lifted the wine glass and downed it. Then I hiccupped. "That's supposed to help." I frowned looking at the empty glass. "It's not like I ever thought I'd be queen or anything. I mean, for a second I did imagine it but not in a legitimate, I'm going to be Queen of France kind of way, with people bowing at me and stuff."

Mayra stood up suddenly and curtsied deeply. I laughed at the sight. "Sit down, you weirdo. I'm not queen."

"Yet."

I gasped, sitting up straight and looking over my shoulder at Elias. But it couldn't be Elias. Except, Pierre was standing behind him and I knew I wouldn't imagine him in my fantasy. I looked around the bar and witnessed everyone bowing and curtsying at him and it occurred to me that he was really here.

I stood from my barstool, swaying a bit. Elias caught my arm and held it. I curtsied in front of him. Not as deeply as Mayra. Not as prettily. But as well as I could manage in my drunken state. When I straightened he pulled me into his arms.

"You don't curtsy to me," he said into my ear.

"Are you not my King?"

"Are you not my world?"

I pulled away slightly and met his gaze. The conversation I overheard between him and Emily's father replaying in my head. I wasn't sure whether to slap him or walk away. Setting aside the fact that I was completely shocked to find him here, that is, because even if he did know where I was I hadn't expected him to chase after me. Send Pierre after me? Maybe. Call me incessantly the way he had been? Maybe. But not actually show up. He was a King, for God's sake. Traditionally, the King didn't leave his throne unless he had important matters to take care of, and even then, the important matters went to him, not the other way around. The pub was so quiet you could hear the dripping of the not fully shut faucet nearby. Elias was still staring at me, waiting, assessing, the way a true King would. I let the silence drag on because I was enjoying his minimal discomfort, which no one else could see but I knew him well enough to take note. Finally, I licked my lips and spoke up.

"You don't need to sweet-talk me. If you need me to pretend to be your girlfriend, you can just ask me. I would have done you the favor."

"I don't want any favors from you, Adeline. And I want you to be with me because you want to be, so I fully understand if you want to walk away from me, but you can't expect me not to fight for what's mine."

"Maybe that's the problem. Maybe I'm not yours."

His eyes flashed. "Don't say that. Say anything but that."

"I'm not a prize, Elias."

"To me, you are, Addie." He stepped closer still. "The ultimate prize. One I don't deserve, but will work an eternity to earn."

"Elias." I shook my head, swallowing back tears. He was impossible.

"Tu me manques, Adeline." He exhaled lightly, his breath tickling me. He was so close. I could lean in an inch and kiss him, but I wouldn't, not yet. "You are missing from me when you're not with me and I don't want to live in a world where we make this a habit. I want you to be mine. With or without the press. With or without the title. With or without the throne. I want you, Adeline Sofia Isabella Bouchard, to be my Queen."

"What about Emily?" I asked finally, my voice hoarse as I blinked new tears. "What about going back to her if this doesn't work out?"

"That's what this is about?" He frowned, then sighed as he brought his forehead against mine. "Adeline. Adeline. Adeline. You overheard my conversation with her father?"

I nodded against his forehead, tears still streaming. I wiped them quickly.

"That was careless. I was trying to appease him because he owes me some things. I never . . . " He pulled away and brought his hand to my face. "I never meant for you to hear that and I definitely didn't mean to hurt you. I am so sorry."

"Thank you for saying that," I whispered.

"I'm not just saying that." He brought his other hand to my face and used both thumbs to wipe my tears. "I love you. I'm in love with you. There is no after you."

My heart stopped beating. "You love me?"

"Yes, silly girl. Do you think I'd risk the throne over a woman I wasn't completely head over heels in love with?"

"I thought I was helping your image." I felt myself smile. He loved me.

"Well, it could have gone either way." He tilted his head. "They could have hated me and said I was throwing away tradition."

"You love me." It was the one thing I was still stuck on. "A commoner."

"There's nothing common about you, Adeline." He brought his lips to mine and kissed me.

"Sir, public display of affection," Pierre said beside us. "People are snapping photos."

"Fuck tradition," Elias said, bringing his lips to mine again. I threw my arms around his neck and kissed him back with every ounce of devotion I had for him.

My head was pounding. I groaned as I sat up and realized I was in the underwear and bra I had on last night. Where was I? I looked at the wall in front of me, covered in an enormous television. It was a gray room and it smelled like . . . oh God.

"Feeling like shit, I bet," Elias said from somewhere in the room.

"Oh, my God." I gasped, bringing a hand to my chest. "You scared me."

"Don't tell me you don't remember last night."

I sat up in bed and looked over at where he was, putting a shirt over his head. I wish he'd be taking it off instead. He walked over to me, raking a hand through his wet hair, and sat in front of me, the bed sinking with his weight.

"I remember everything except the part where we left the bar and came home."

"Oh, that was the fun part though." He chuckled. "As soon as we got here, you started undressing and demanded sex."

"What?" I squeaked. "In front of Pierre and Mayra?"

"And the four new security personnel we brought along, yes."

"Oh, my God." I threw myself onto the pillows behind me and covered my face with my arm. "So embarrassing."

"They've seen worse."

"Meaning what?" I uncovered my face and narrowed my eyes at him.

"I mean they've seen worse behavior." He chuckled. "I can't imagine they've seen a better body on a more gorgeous woman."

"Shut up." I groaned. "I can't believe I did that."

"I'll let you shower and get dressed. We have a lot to discuss." He stood up, leaned over and gave me a kiss on the forehead, and left the room.

I did as instructed, and when I was dressed in the clothing that was on top of the bed—a nice, conservative floral dress with tags on it, that hadn't previously been in my wardrobe—I walked out of the room. I looked presentable and that was the important part. Only the security personnel were hanging out in the living room. Mayra pointed at the French doors that led to the balcony, so I headed there and found Elias sitting at the same table we'd had our first date. Pierre was standing by the edge of the balcony, looking at the ocean. It was a beautiful day to lay out in the sun.

"Let me guess, Pierre chose this." I pointed to my dress.

"I figured after last night you might want to cover up a bit." Pierre turned to look at me. My jaw dropped. I felt my cheeks heat. He laughed and added, "I'm just kidding."

"He's not kidding." Elias, who was reading a newspaper, glanced up, mischief in his eyes.

"We need to replace your personal secretary," I said, taking a seat beside Elias.

Pierre laughed louder. "I'll be back with champagne and orange juice."

"Oh God. Champagne?" I made a face.

"Not all of us drank our weight in wine last night." Elias looked at me over the paper.

"Not all of us were moping and mourning the loss of a fake boyfriend." I raised an eyebrow.

"Real boyfriend." He folded the paper and set it down, reaching for my hand. "Nothing about this has ever been fake."

"So, what did you want to talk about?" I asked after a moment of staring into his deep green eyes.

"Our future." He let go of my hand. "I need to know if you're genuinely okay with leaving your life in London and your company behind for this. For me."

I thought about it for a moment. I'd been willing to leave it behind before, and now that I'd been without him for a just couple of days and felt how that was, even more so. He looked nervous. I nodded.

"I'm ready."

"Good." He stood up, the chair scraping slightly on the pavement. Without warning, he took a knee beside me and pulled out a little black box from his pocket, opening it to show me the most beautiful engagement ring I'd ever seen. My heart pounded against my chest. I gasped, bringing a hand up to my mouth. "This stone has been in my family for centuries. Pieces of the original stone are on the crown of each King of France before me, and my own, and I thought it was time it was also in a queen's possession." He smiled.

"The first night I met you, right on this very balcony, you had no idea who I was. You just knew you liked me. You gave me a gift that evening when you went to bed with me. You showed me that I was more than my title. That I was more than what anyone said I was. You looked at me and you saw me. You knew me. Finding you again has been the best thing that's happened since that night. At the end of my reign—because all of them must come to an end—I will still believe that keeping you has been the greatest achievement I will have accomplished." He took a breath.

"I don't want to die like King George IV. I don't want to die with just a regretful memory of you and a locket with your picture on it. You make me a better man every single day. Your heart makes mine beat faster. Please accept me, Adeline. Rule with me, by my side."

I cried throughout his entire proposal, and my voice shook with tears as I tried to say yes, so I nodded, and nodded, and nodded furiously.

"Yes?" he chuckled, standing up. I stood with him, throwing my arms around him. He carried my feet off the ground and swung me around. "Yes?"

"Yes. Yes. Yes a million times," I said. When he set me down, I wiped my face and kissed him hard. "I love you, King Elias, even if you are a major pain in the neck."

"I love you, Queen Adeline, even if you do drive me crazy

most days." He grinned. "Probably because you drive me crazy most days."

I laughed as he took my hand and slid the ring on my finger. I marveled at it sitting there. The stone was large and navy blue and the band was encrusted in tiny diamonds around it.

"It fits perfectly." I wiggled my fingers.

"As it should." He kissed my forehead, and then fell into a fit of infectious laughter. "We're getting married!"

"We're getting married." I grinned so wide, my face hurt.

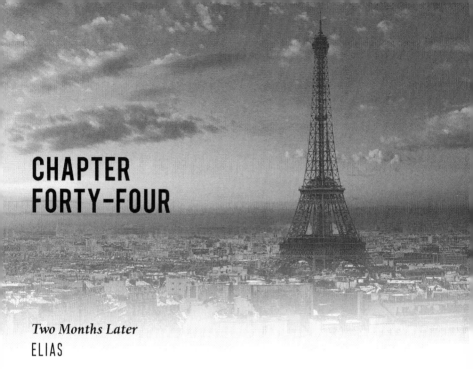

CHAPTER FORTY-FOUR

Two Months Later

ELIAS

I SAT DOWN IN FRONT OF THE CAMERA WITH A GRIN I COULDN'T seem to wipe off my face, but as soon as the countdown began, I managed to bring my expression to a more neutral position.

"Hello again. It brings me great honor to inform you that our efforts to make France a Commonwealth Monarchy is underway. With an outstanding show of support and great effort from the candidates from all regions, we hope to have it up and running before the year is over. My hope, as King, is to create a structural government in which every single one of you will become constituents and have your voices heard. I want you to bring forth your concerns without fear, in a peaceful way. I hope this will end the riots and disturbances that have become common. I hope this brings peace to us all.

"Now"—I paused and took a breath, my lips turning into a smile—"for the news that I'm sure you all tuned in for.

I have another announcement to make. I have asked Adeline Bouchard to marry me and she has accepted my proposal." I paused again, laughing when the seven reporters in the room erupted in cheers. "I asked a couple of months ago, but we wanted to keep it to ourselves for a little while before letting the world in on it. I hope you'll respect that. That's the only news I have for now. I'm going to let the reporters here ask questions while we're live on television, which has never been done before. Please bear with me if this doesn't go as expected." I grinned at the camera before turning my attention to the first reporter. My mother was going to have my head for this, but I spoke about this with Pierre and Adeline, who agreed this was a good way to earn the people's trust. Adeline, her mother, my mother, my brother, Pilar, Joslyn, Etienne, and Pierre were all in the room as I made the broadcast. Adeline had yet to come around to accepting her father back in her life, but she was working her way there slowly. He'd been apologizing to her the last couple of months and coming around more often, not solely on business.

"May we ask Adeline questions?" the reporter asked, catching me off guard.

"This is why doing this live may not be such a good idea." I chuckled. "Adeline is off-limits, unless she says otherwise."

"I'll answer a few questions," Adeline responded.

My head whipped in her direction. She was wearing a navy-blue knee-length dress that matched her ring perfectly and her hair was up in a low bun. She looked beautiful, but I couldn't wait to mess up that hair and rip off that dress. As she walked over to me, Pierre grabbed a chair and placed it beside me. She took a seat and smiled at me before turning her attention to them.

"I must warn you that I have not been advised on how to do this, so I may not be a very good interviewee," Adeline said to the reporter. "But I'll try."

All of the reporters laughed lightly.

"We'll go easy on you," one of the women in the back said.

"Go for it." She straightened her posture. "I'm ready."

"When did you meet the King?"

"That's quite a story, actually." Adeline blushed. "We met at a party right before I went off to college in the States. We hit it off right away, but didn't see each other again until last summer."

"Was it love at first sight?" another reporter asked.

"For me it was." I set my hand on Adeline's knee while I answered.

"He's just saying that because he spilled juice on my favorite blouse earlier," Adeline quipped with a wink.

The room laughed.

"Will you live here in Versailles?"

"Heavens, no," Adeline said. "All of this opulence and open space will give anyone nightmares."

"Not to mention the history," a reporter added.

"Right. I'm not quite sure I want the ghosts of past kings to watch me while I'm in the bath," Adeline said.

They laughed again.

"I know they're ghosts, but I may have to kill them anyway."

They laughed louder.

The entire interview went off without a hitch. When we'd answered enough questions, Pierre interrupted and told the reporters to wrap it up.

"Will Adeline be joining you on your broadcasts?" one reporter asked, hopeful.

"Maybe." I glanced over at Addie and smiled. "She's easy to fall in love with, isn't she?"

"As are you," Addie said, smiling back at me.

Just as the cameraman was counting down to cut the broadcast, I leaned over and kissed her lips. I could swear I heard my mother's gasp from across the room, but I didn't care. To hell with tradition.

Epilogue

"This is history in the making. This will be the first queen to have gone to college. The first queen who has no aristocratic blood. Today, we will get a glimpse of—"

I switched the television off and let the remote control fall on the couch beside me. My nerves were shot without the journalists reminding me of what I was and what I wasn't. Despite the media being kind to me, for the most part, I wasn't sure what to expect from the people. My stomach growled again. The seamstress making last-minute adjustments to my gown looked up at me.

"Are you sure you don't want anything to eat, Your Majesty?"

"I'm sure."

I didn't bother to correct the title she gave me. I'm not Her Majesty *yet*, though in a few short hours that would change. It was something I wasn't sure I'd ever get used to. The Queen Mother assured me I would, but she'd always been referred to as such. Pilar told me it'd grow on me. Aramis said he didn't know who he'd be without the title. I was unlike any of them. Without a title, I was still me. I'd spoken to Elias at length about the weight of the burden having such a title carried and he also couldn't relate to my stance on the matter. He couldn't seem to comprehend how I hadn't wrapped my head around the whole thing, despite my being in full-on queen training for the last eight months.

It wasn't the appearances or the work I was doing on behalf of the Crown that was awkward for me. It was people treating me like I was more important than them—like we weren't equals—that I wasn't sure I could get used to. I had the Queen Mother in one ear, reminding me not to hug people, not to kneel on the floor when I saw children I wanted to greet. In the other ear, I had my own mother, reminding me that I was a human being just like the rest of them. I looked in the mirror and let my gaze fall on the ivory gown I wore, with intricate lace details on the sleeves and bust. My hair was swept up in the front and held in place with a small tiara and a veil that would trail twenty feet behind me. My makeup was very natural. The makeup artist said it was too natural, but I didn't care. I felt like myself. Even though my dress and tiara were not unlike the queens before me, my smile was genuine, because unlike them, I was truly marrying the love of my life, the man of my dreams, and it wasn't for theatrics or out of duty.

When the door swung open behind me and the Queen Mother walked in with Pilar and my mother trailing behind them, the seamstress let go of my veil and let me turn around for them.

"You look beautiful." My mother's eyes brimmed with tears.

"Like an angel," Pilar whispered.

"Like a queen." The Queen Mother smiled.

"You're going to make me cry." I pressed a hand to my chest, blinking rapidly.

They all rushed over and fluffed me up just as the photographer picked up the camera and began snapping shots of us. Soon, we were ushered out. Every single aspect of this day was timed, even my bathroom breaks. We'd gone over everything for two weeks—dress rehearsals, photography rehearsals with stand-ins from the palace, food rehearsals, breaks. Every single thing that was to happen today would happen only if it fit into the schedule. Because it was being televised, we had no choice but to follow the timeline. Outside the palace, my father was waiting for me beside the carriage we were to take. To say it had been a long eight months would be an understatement. I had no intention of forgiving my father for shunning me and turning away from me in my time of need, but every day he kept showing up—for me, for Elias. He stopped speaking poorly of the Crown and what it stood for. Instead, he rallied behind Elias and when he didn't agree with his choices, he spoke to him in private.

He'd stopped taking my mother to court over the divorce settlements and paid her what they initially agreed upon. He took her to lunch and dinner and cheered her on when Pirouette was recognized as one of the best event-planning businesses in London and now France. I smiled as he walked toward me.

"You look stunning," he said, his eyes gleaming with tears.

"Thank you for doing this." I smiled.

"If it's important to you, it's important to me." He kissed my hand and helped me get into the carriage.

As we rode toward the gates, I focused on taking deep breaths. Soon, we'd be exposed for all to see, and from what we'd heard thanks to Dad's contacts in news, they were estimating more than two million people to take the streets and watch as I rode to the cathedral. I reached for my father's hand and squeezed it.

"You're perfect. You will be great." He smiled. "On the other hand, they may throw things at us when they see me riding in here with you."

"Oh, my God. I knew I shouldn't have asked you to do this."

"I hope you're joking."

"I'm not sure that I am." I laughed. He shook his head, grinning.

When the iron gates opened and the horses began riding out, I held my breath. But then people cheered. It was an uproar of whistles and clapping. I let go of my father's hand and started to wave. By the time we reached Notre Dame, my shoulder hurt from all the waving I'd done.

"Maybe this is why they don't hold their arms all the way up when they wave," I said to my father. "It's exhausting."

"Who doesn't hold their arms up?"

"The princesses and queens. You know, when they're in public, they kind of hold their elbow to their side as they wave." I frowned. "I think."

"I take it you're nervous."

"What? No. Why would you say that?"

"You've been talking nonstop for the last twenty-five minutes, which is fine, but waving? Really, Adeline?" He laughed. "You have no reason to be nervous. They love you."

"What if I'm not cut out for this job?"

"You've been making appearances for the last year. You're more than cut out for it. You're the reason people stopped protesting. You're the reason I stopped protesting." He raised an eyebrow. "And that's a tough thing for a lifelong complainer to give up."

I laughed and nodded. He was right. Even if I wasn't cut out for it, I'd make it work. For Elias. With Elias. I held my father's hand as I got out of the carriage and waved at the people standing behind the makeshift fences they'd put up around the cathedral. Butterflies swarmed my stomach as I walked to the door, and even more so as they opened them for us. I heard *Michel-Richard Delalande Sinfonies, Hugo Reyne 1* playing loudly and took one last deep breath before the set of doors opened up in front of me and the music switched to a hymn played on the harp. Everyone stood as I walked, but my gaze stayed on Elias who seemed to be millions of miles away. He was wearing a large gold crown on his head and a deep red shawl over his suit. Today, I'd walk out of here with a Queen's crown on my own head, one the archbishop would place atop my head once Elias and I said our I do's.

My heels tapped on the checkered marble floor as I smiled at some of the guests—Etienne and his parents, Joss and her parents, Aramis, some of my parents' friends. Pilar, who was standing beside Benjamin Drake. I did a double-take when I saw them. When we finally reached the front, my father handed my hand over to Elias and whispered something in his ear as he patted his shoulder. Elias took my hand in his and grinned at me; it was the happiest I'd ever seen him, and the look alone was enough to wash away all of my reservations and nerves. I forgot there were millions, maybe billions watching us, and focused solely on him and this moment.

"You look beautiful," Elias whispered in my ear just as the priest began to speak.

We weren't allowed personal vows. Everything had to be by the book and we settled for the fact that we'd made our own vows to each other every single day, we didn't need to say them aloud, especially not in public. This may not be a traditional marriage in many ways, but some things were better left alone. Besides, who was I to argue when I had this man to have and to hold every day? When it was time for us to kiss, we turned to each other and smiled so wide. Elias brought his hand to my face as he brought his closer and whispered, "I love you so much" just as our lips met.

After the ceremony, the media was asked to step outside during my coronation. Elias's coronation had been the first to be televised. Our wedding had been the first to be televised. My coronation, like the Queen Mother's before me, would remain behind closed doors, for only the clergy and guests invited to the wedding to witness. The queens before us were crowned with their respective kings, or alone, behind closed doors in Sainte-Chapelle or Abbey of Saint-Denis. Elias made it so that I would be crowned during our wedding ceremony.

Unlike his coronation, mine was to last a few minutes. They'd go through the necessary steps, give me communion again, and replace my tiara with a crown. My palms were sweating as I answered their pledge to remain faithful to my King and the country of France. It was an antiquated system, no doubt, but in the name of tradition, it served its purpose. The archbishop lifted my tiara from my head along with the veil attached to it. The crown I was to wear was brought out and I couldn't help my soft gasp. The crown Elias wore today was gold and large, with diamonds and emeralds surrounding it and a cross sitting at the top of it. The one they were holding out to me was similar, but had golden birds and diamond leaves. It was smaller than my husband's, but seemed to carry even more jewels than his. It had a small cross sitting on top of a big diamond-encrusted ball. I lowered my head slightly as they placed it over my head, and brought my gaze back to the archbishop as he blessed me.

"*Vive la reine.*" The archbishop smiled.

I smiled back, tears trickling down my face. I wiped them

away quickly and stood when I was supposed to, this time facing my husband. He took my hand in his and led me out of the cathedral as our guests cheered for us. As the doors opened for us and security scrambled to their places, Elias led me outside, still holding my hand tightly. He put an arm up and waved, and I put my free hand up and waved, laughing as people cheered. We'd rehearsed this, but this was different. The cameras were rolling and the people were surrounding us. I could no longer pretend that this was just between my husband and me. It really was for the world to see. Elias let go of my hand and turned to me. I turned to him, still smiling but confused. This, we hadn't rehearsed. He was supposed to kiss me and we were supposed to walk to the carriage that awaited. Instead, standing in front of millions, billions of people including those watching from across the globe, King Elias bowed to me, and loud enough for everyone to hear, he said, *"Vive la reine."*

I tried to swallow back tears, tried to remind myself that this was tradition and traditionally monarchs showed no emotion, but it was no use, emotion won and the tears trickled down my face. Elias grinned widely, straightening and bringing his hands to my face, his thumbs wiping my tears.

"Long live the Queen. May she always be by my side, not one step behind," he said against my lips.

"Long live the King," I replied just as his lips met mine and he kissed me for all of the world to see.

ClaireContrerasbooks.com

Twitter: @ClariCon

Insta: ClaireContreras

Facebook: www.facebook.com/groups/ClaireContrerasBooks

OTHER BOOKS

The Trouble With Love

Fake Love

The Consequence of Falling

Because You're Mine

Half Truths

SECOND CHANCE DUET

Then There Was You

My Way Back to You

The Wilde One

The Player

THE HEART SERIES

Kaleidoscope Hearts

Torn Hearts

Paper Hearts

Elastic Hearts

DARKNESS SERIES

There is No Light in Darkness

Darkness Before Dawn

Made in United States
Orlando, FL
05 May 2023

32836863R00169